STAR CITY STORIES

SPACE OPERA NOIR
FEATURING FRANK SLADEK, P.I.

BY GREG FOWLKES

Includes previews from the book

The Blood Red Sands of Mars:
Book One from the Murder on Mars Series

STAR CITY STORIES

© 2015 The Fictional Press
www.TheFictionalPress.com

The Fictional Press is a small, independent press specializing in the publication of fictional works by emerging authors. If you are interested in bringing your fictional works to life in print as well as electronically, contact us! We can help!

www.TheFictionalPress.com

ISBN 13: 978-1-937022-90-7

Printed in the United States of America

BOOKS BY GREG FOWLKES

TABLE OF CONTENTS

SPECIAL PREVIEW:

PROLOGUE

Star City – A Geography Lesson

I know that geography isn't the right term. It does, after all, refer to the mapping of Earth, and Star City is about as far from Earth as one can get, if not when measured in light years, at least in what passes for the life of its residents. I just don't know of a more appropriate term than geography. Perhaps it hasn't been invented yet.

It was roughly two hundred years ago that some unnamed genius drew some lines between the various star systems that make up that irregular blob which is so often inaccurately termed the "human sphere of influence." I'm sure others had done the same thing during the thousand years or so since man first left the atmosphere of the home planet, it was just that this guy was the first to realize the significance of a curious fact. A whole lot of these lines happened to intersect at a particular point in space, and because of that fact, that place would make an ideal "transit point," that is a place where starships could meet to exchange passengers and cargo, thus making interstellar transport more efficient, and more importantly, more profitable. The only problem was that this place happened to be basically in the middle of nowhere.

It turned out this wasn't quite true, for there just happened to be located almost exactly at this imaginary point, by which one means within a tenth of a parsec, a brown dwarf. Now a brown dwarf is a failed star—that is, a star lacking the mass to ignite the fusion reactions that drive real stars. Instead, what energy they emit is due to gravitational collapse, the energy released as the dwarf tries to make itself ever more compact. The result is that the brown dwarf shines with a dim ruddy glow mostly concentrated in the near infrared.

Still, there was something there rather than nothing. And this proved to be fairly important. For circling this failed star were a number of even smaller bodies. Not planets, really, but asteroids, planetoids, or whatever, and that meant that the transit station could be created from local materials rather than having to bring everything in from someplace else.

In due time, a scout ship was sent to survey the environs of this failed star, and based on the results of this survey, one particular planetoid was chosen. The selection criteria had mostly to do with the stability of its orbit, but there were other factors, as well, such as size, angular momentum, and mineral composition. Using this information, plans were made, grand plans, perhaps the most ambitious plans ever made by human beings, plans for a gigantic space station.

At this point, politics reared its ugly head over the question of who would control this station, for it was obvious that whoever controlled the transit point would control interstellar commerce. The contentiousness of the issue threatened to scuttle the whole project before it began. Surprisingly, wiser heads prevailed. Or perhaps, those who stood to profit most from the station decided to bypass the politicians. It was determined that the transit station would be constructed and run by an independent corporation funded by private investors from Earth, Crockett and most of the other human planets, and that the station itself would be considered a sovereign entity independent of the jurisdiction of any other government. This, of course, was to have consequences later on, but it did allow for the project to proceed.

The planetoid selected for the project was an irregular piece of rock described as being shaped like a potato, which as I understand it, is a sort of food stuff that grows underground back on ancestral earth. Roughly twenty kilometers long at the major axis and five kilometers in cross section, it occupied an almost circular orbit some fifty million kilometers from the brown dwarf. Its composition was mostly silicate minerals, but it also had a high percentage of iron and aluminum as well, both of which would be important for the construction process.

The actual construction would take nearly twenty-five earth years. During this time, the center of the planetoid was hollowed out. Some of the removed material was processed into refined products such as steel and aluminum, some was used to fuel the mass converters that powered the project, and the remainder was pushed around to make the planetoid a much more uniform cylindrical shape.

As part of the process, the original tumbling motion of the planetoid was stopped, to be replaced by a spin along the major axis. This was done to provide a sort of surrogate gravity from centrifugal motion. It had been determined early on, that this would be much more economical than the artificial gravity used on starships. Once spun up, the station would need only minor inputs of energy to correct any imbalances that might occur over time, rather than the significant amounts of energy required to maintain a gravitational field. The body was large enough that the rate of revolution would be low enough not to cause physiological difficulties for any inhabitants.

When construction was finished, the planetoid had been converted into a fairly uniform cylinder. The excavated space in the interior formed a cylindrical cavity three kilometers in diameter and fifteen kilometers long which provided almost 150 square kilometers of surface area. Down the center of this cavity a giant truss was created. Mounted to this truss were the gigantic systems of glow tubes that provided illumination to the surface below. An engineer once described to me how these work. I didn't understand a word of the explanation.

Two large docking rings protruded from either end, one for passenger liners, the other for freight. These docking rings were capable of handling a hundred ships at a time between them. Given the nature of the traffic, the passenger end of the station came to be dominated by hotels and entertainment complexes to house, feed, and amuse passengers awaiting connections. The other end is occupied by warehouses, service facilities and light manufacturing operations. The space in between is given over to housing the mass of people needed to make everything work.

Currently this amounts to about two million humans and some hundred thousand non-humans of various types.

One curious feature is that it is possible for one of these residents to go their entire life without ever having a view of the surrounding space. With the exception of a walkway off the passenger docking ring reserved for passengers in transit, the only views offered are from utilitarian ports on the docking rings and exterior surface facilities. It turns out that this lack is no big loss. Without a visible sun and no planets, there really isn't much to see.

Somewhere along the way, the transit station was given a name, "Star City." Perhaps not the most imaginative name, but short and serviceable.

As mentioned earlier, Star City is run by an independent corporation. As such, it is only interested in maximizing profits. This is fine with the various star lines that use its facilities as long as things function smoothly and fees are reasonable. As many of the investors in the corporation are also major shareholders in the star lines, this has never been a problem.

It has resulted, however, in a rather laissez-faire attitude toward the internal operations of Star City. As long as passengers in transit are not adversely affected, almost anything goes. Gambling is legal and virtually unregulated as are other forms of personal entertainment. And while most of the permanent residents of Star City are hardworking individuals interested only in making sure the great starships arrive and depart smoothly, the station has attracted a certain lower class of con-artists, grifters, and petty criminals who prey on the occasional unsuspecting passenger, but mostly prey on each other.

And it is with these individuals, that this volume is concerned . . .

Ray-Guns
on
Star City

Ray-Guns on Star City

The Blue Moon was different than other bars on Star City. It was dark and cool. But mostly it was quiet. There wasn't any sound projector blaring the latest jive samba. There weren't any holocasters spewing pitches for products no one needed. There wasn't even a televisor showing sporting events except for during the Worlds Series. That was one of the reasons I liked the place.

Mostly though, I go there because it's across the street from where I live, a not too crummy apartment building on the fringes of New Minglewood. New Minglewood is the district of Star City where the grifters, whores and all the other low-lifes with no regular employment live. They live there because the rent is cheap. Also it's the only place that will have them.

Star City was built on a hunk of rock that failed as a planet. Once a fortnight it orbits around a star that never made it to the big time, but is doomed to spend eternity as a brown dwarf stuck in the middle of nowhere. There's no reason at all for Star City to exist except that it happens to be at the place where a half dozen space routes intersect making it a convenient place for transshipments and for making connections. When they discovered it, they hollowed it out, spun it up to give it the semblance of the gravity it could never generate on its own, and built a pair of docking rings at each end. They can handle a hundred ships at a time, and there are always a dozen more parked in orbit awaiting a berth.

Half the commerce of human space passes through Star City, and with it comes half the population, or at least so it seems. Star City has grown up catering to the needs and whims of those travelers making a layover whether they are moguls or deck hands. You can buy any sort of food or beverage known. You can find entertainment to pass the time until your ship leaves. You can gamble a fortune away at a dozen casinos; or bet your last dollar.

Me, I was nursing a whiskey and soda in the middle of the afternoon. I knew it was whiskey because it was brown and ninety proof. If it had been clear it would have been gin or vodka. In either case, it had never been within a light year of Scotland or Tennessee or any other place on any respectable planet circling a real sun. I was drinking in the middle of the afternoon because I didn't have anything better to do.

I was alone in the place except for the bartender and one other customer who sat at the far end with a stack of Crockett dollars piled up on the bar in front of him. Every fifteen minutes the barkeep would bring him a shot of something blue and remove two dollar coins from the pile. He never seemed to take the empty glasses away. There looked to be about a dozen.

The guy was nondescript looking, about middle age, middle height, middle weight. He looked like he might be a travelling salesman. There was something that looked like it might be a sample case resting on the floor next to his barstool. He was leaning on the bar staring into space. In that position it was hard to tell if he was drunk or just weary of the world. He'd looked up for a minute when I had walked in, but after giving me the once-over returned to contemplating the blue liquid in the shot glass in front of him.

The bartender knew me well enough to know that I wasn't interested in conversation. The salesman wasn't talking, either. That suited the bartender just fine as it gave him plenty of time to polish glasses with the dirty rag he kept tucked in his belt.

It was almost with annoyance that he looked up when the door opened to accept a new denizen of the bar. This guy was anything but ordinary. Just shy of two meters tall he was wearing a flash suit that looked as if it cost what the average Joe made in a month. He had what is euphemistically called a "spacer tan." Of course, real spacers never see the light of a sun and are normally pale as ghosts. I was thinking he was in the wrong bar in the wrong part of Star City.

He walked up to the bar and motioned for the bartender. Like he needed to attract attention when there were only two other customers in the place.

"I'm looking for a woman. Tall, good-looking, red hair. She's wearing a black dress cinched at the waist and black, high-heeled boots. Has she been in here?"

"Sorry mister," the bartender said. "There ain't been no woman looking like that in here all day, and my shift started at eight." Truth was there hadn't been any woman in there all day, and certainly not one like he had described.

"You sure? She said she'd meet me here."

"Nope. No one like that in here today. You want a drink while you wait?"

"No, I'll pass. Are there any other bars named the Blue Moon on Star City?"

"Not that I know of. There is a Red Planet Saloon down by the spacedocks, but I wouldn't go there. It's a dive from what I hear." I knew the place. The bartender was right. The Red Planet was definitely not a place to go looking for a good-looking red head. Or for anything else unless it was trouble.

"Thanks. If she comes in here, tell her I was here."

"Who shall I say?"

"She'll know who."

He turned and headed for the door. The guy at the other end of the bar stood up, his hand reaching inside his jacket. For a wonder he didn't fall down. He called out, "Yano!"

The guy at the door turned to face him, a look of concern on his face. There were what sounded like three soft sneezes and suddenly three red spots appeared on his chest just where his heart would be. He looked for a moment stunned and then he slumped to the floor.

I looked towards the guy at the end of the bar. He was holding a needle gun in his right hand. It was an assassin's weapon, small and quiet, firing tiny darts at hypersonic speeds. I knew then that he was no salesman.

I raised my hands to show I was unarmed. Frankly, I didn't think there was a chance in hell of my getting out of there alive, but even if I had been packing heat I knew I couldn't beat him. Not if he could place three darts within a circle smaller than a fist at ten meters in a dimly lit bar. The barkeep took his clue from me and raised his hands as well, the look of fear on his face.

The salesman/assassin scooped up the pile of Crockett dollars from the bar leaving two as a tip. That gave me some hope unless he had a twisted sense of humor. He stuffed the coins in his jacket pocket, then picked up his case with the same hand. All this time he was holding the needle gun in his right pointed nowhere in particular. He strode nonchalantly towards the door, stepping around the body. As he reached the door the needle gun disappeared into his jacket. Then he was gone.

"Holy Shiva! Mathew, Mark, George, and Ringo! What do we do now?"

The barkeep's theology might be confused, but I shared his sentiment.

"I suggest we wait ten minutes, and then you call the cops," I said, trying to sound calm and like I knew what I was doing. I wasn't either.

"You going to be here then?" he asked.

"No reason not to. I still got some of my drink left."

I waited five and then poked my nose out the door, looking both ways up and down the street. There was no sign of an assassin with a sample case. No red head in a black dress either. I ducked back into the bar.

"You might as well call the cops, now," I said, resuming my place at the bar.

The cops showed up in ten, a couple of plain-clothes men. I knew one of them slightly, a big, beefy detective sergeant named Latimer. He knew me, too. Star City cops aren't particularly bright or honest, but they make up for it with attitude.

"Well if it ain't Frank Sladek, the private dick. Did you have to off one of your clients?"

"Not me, Latimer. I was just in here having a quiet drink." I gave him a brief synopsis of the events. He looked skeptical. I couldn't blame him.

"You packing, Sladek?"

"Not me. You know I hate to carry a weapon if I don't have to. Those things are hazardous to your health."

"Always the funny guy, Sladek. Well, if you ain't packing, you won't mind if Rossetti here pats you down."

"I've got no objection as long as he doesn't get fresh."

Rossetti gave me a dirty look. The pat down was efficient and more thorough than it needed to be. "He's clean."

"So what were you doing here, Sladek? And don't give me a line about you just came in for a drink."

"It's true. I live in the apartments just across the street. Business has been slow.   I felt the need for human companionship."

"In a bar empty of customers?" Latimer asked.

"I just wanted a quiet drink."

"Well you got it, didn't you?" he remarked sardonically.

"It was quiet most of the time."

"So you want me to believe that this guy walks in and asks for a red-headed broad, this other guy shouts out 'Yano', pops three needles into his chest and walks out leaving you and the barkeep still breathing?"

"That's about the size of it, sergeant. No one is more surprised than me that I'm still standing."

"That's Detective Sergeant. And your story stinks, Sladek," Latimer responded.

"I can't help it. Ask the bartender."

Latimer went over the same ground with the bartender and got the same story. That seemed to annoy him. The fact that he was beginning to think it was the truth didn't help matters any. Meanwhile, Rossetti had been poking his nose into all the corners coming up with nothing.

The doctor from the Medical Examiner's office came while Latimer was still questioning the bartender. He was a blueskin from Asimov III. The high oxygen content of his home world had resulted in an adaptation which gave a pale blue cast to his skin in the relatively lower oxygen ratio of Star City which was roughly that of Earth. I noticed the small oxygen bottle clipped to his waist that allowed him to breathe a shot whenever he felt hypoxia setting in. I wondered what he had done to get himself exiled to Star City.

He did his thing, taking holograms of the body, measuring body temperature, taking a blood sample, doing a scan of the wound.

"Well, doc?"

"He's dead, Latimer."

"I know that. What was the cause of death?"

"Three flechettes from a needle gun to the heart."

"Poisoned?"

"Not that I can tell. No toxins in his blood at least. All three darts penetrated the heart causing massive blood loss. He died almost immediately."

"Awful good shooting, wasn't it?" Latimer commented.

"Yes it was," the doc agreed.

"Can you tell me how far the shooter was from the victim?"

"Not exactly. It wasn't close range. More like five to ten meters. Like you said, good shooting. Well, if you've no further need for the body, I'll take it off your hands."

"Cart him away, doc. I ain't got no use for it."

The doctor wheeled the body out to the meat wagon that was waiting outside in the street.

"You done with me, Latimer?" I asked.

"Your current residence on file?"

"Yeah. Right across the street. Number 44."

"OK. You can go. But don't leave town." We both got a chuckle out of that.

Dealing with Latimer had left a bad taste in my mouth. I tried to eliminate it by ordering a meat sandwich from the diner on the corner. The menu didn't specify the type of meat, but as it all came from the same tanks it didn't really matter. Only three star eateries at the uptown end of Star City had meat that came from real animals. It did the trick, though. All I could sense in my mouth was the aftertaste of "meat."

I didn't have anything else to do, and as my favorite watering hole was still overrun with cops, I headed home to my apartment on the fourth floor of the Aldeberon Arms. I don't know if the misspelling was intentional or not. The building certainly had nothing to do with the star of the almost same name. At one time, probably before I was born, it had been a halfway swank place, but located as it was on the borders of New Minglewood, it had been left to run down ever since. That was all right by me. My apartment was spacious but cheap. It even had a balcony of sorts. On nights when the haze was low and the glow tubes that ran down the center of Star City were turned off you could make out the lights on the far side of the inner cylinder that was the city. It was kind of pretty.

It was still too light out and the air too hazy to make out anything on the far side when I walked out onto the balcony. At the Blue Moon across the street the cops were still at it. There was an evidence wagon parked out in front and a uniform was standing guard at the door. I went back inside.

The place had come semi-furnished, probably because it would have cost more to have the stuff hauled away. But there were some decent pieces once I had cleaned up fifty years of grime and sweat. The building super let me pick through things that were being tossed out when tenants moved. It might not be in the height of style, but it was comfortable. I thought of it as home.

I had parked myself in my favorite lounge chair. It was done in the "space pilot" style of thirty years ago and covered in upholstery a hideous chartreuse in color, but it was the most comfortable chair I had. Unfortunately, I didn't have time to get settled in before the door buzzer sounded. I tried to ignore it, but whoever it was was insistent.

Getting up I gave the voice command for the door camera to turn on. When I saw what it showed I was glad I had, though in retrospect it would have been better if I'd never gotten up. Standing in the hall looking nervous was a good looking dame, about thirty. She had shoulder length red hair brushed back over her ears that looked natural with brilliant green eyes that weren't. A black dress cinched in at the waist by a black leather belt wrapped tightly around the curves of her body. She must have stood close to one-eighty-five centimeters in her high heeled boots.

"Mr. Sladek, can I speak to you for a moment," came a breathy contralto through the doorcam's sound projector. I didn't bother to wonder how she knew my name; there was a tag with it printed on the directory board at the entry. I also didn't wonder how she had gotten into the building. Security at the Aldeberon Arms had been a bit lax for the last two decades.

If I had been thinking, I would have pretended I wasn't home. She could probably hear me through the thin door, but I could have at least pretended. But I didn't. Maybe it was the green eyes. Maybe it was the black boots. I'm a sucker for women in boots. Whatever the case, I opened the door.

"What can I do for you Miss—?" I asked.

She pushed past me into the apartment on the eight centimeter spikes of her boots without answering my question. I closed the door behind her.

"I understand that you were a witness to what happened across the street, Mr. Sladek?"

"I was there." I didn't see any reason to deny it, though I wondered how she had found out so quickly. Latimer, for all his faults, wasn't one to let info slip.

"Would you mind telling me what happened?" she asked in a husky contralto.

"Not much to tell," I answered.

"Please?" Her voice was more pleading this time.

"Like I said, there's not much to tell. This guy comes in—says he's looking for a red headed woman in a black dress and boots. Sort of like what you're wearing I'd say. She wasn't there. He turned to leave and this other guy at the bar called out 'Yano' and popped three rounds from a needle gun into his heart. He then picked up his case, the shooter I mean, the other guy was dead, and walked out. The barkeep called the cops. That's all I know, lady."

"They say you're a private detective, Mr. Sladek. Were you there on business?"

I wasn't surprised that she knew I was a detective. I'm listed on the info net. Besides I had stuck one of my business cards in the directory at the entry. "I was just there having a quiet drink."

"In the middle of the afternoon?" she asked.

"You might not believe this, but the middle of the afternoon isn't usually one of the busy times in my line of work." I was beginning to get tired of her attitude, boots or no boots.

"Do you expect me to believe that, Mr. Sladek? You've got something of a reputation."

"I don't care what you believe, sister. And I've got some questions of my own. Like who the dead guy was? And who, or what, is 'Yano'?"

"I don't know who the murdered man was."

"Now it's my turn to find that hard to believe. He seemed to have your description down pat."

"He had asked to meet me in connection with—, with a certain item. I gave him my description so he would know it was me. I picked the Blue Moon at random. He was early. I, unfortunately, was detained and arrived late. The police were already there."

"Ok. Fair enough. It might even be true. Who's 'Yano'?"

She never got a chance to answer. There was a buzz at the door. The camera was still on and I could see Latimer and Rossetti in the hall.

"Open up, Sladek. I got a few questions," he called through the door not bothering with the pickup and projector.

The green eyes were pleading. I pointed to the door of my bedroom. She took the hint.

I waited until she had shut the door behind her and then opened the entry to let Latimer and Rossetti in.

"You took your time, dick."

"I was in the bathroom, flat-foot."

"Don't get wise with me, Sladek."

"And here I thought we were on a first insult basis. My apologies, Detective Sergeant Latimer."

"Where's the dame?"

"Dame? What dame?" I replied in my best innocent manner.

"The red-head in the black dress and boots. The uniform guarding the door across the street saw her go into this building."

"Maybe she knows someone else. There are a hundred apartments in the building, you know."

"Yeah, but you were the only one across the street this afternoon."

"I'm telling you, there's no red-head here."

"You don't mind if we check it out then?" Latimer asked.

"You got a warrant?"

"A warrant? Are you kidding? This is Star City, and New Minglewood to boot. I don't need a warrant."

"This side of the street isn't in New Minglewood, Latimer."

I was going to tell him he needed a warrant, too, even though we both knew that was a joke, but the red-head chose that moment to come out of the bedroom. Only she wasn't a red-head anymore, but a short haired blond. She wasn't wearing the black dress or the boots anymore either. What she was wearing was one of my white dress shirts and not much else. I thought Rossetti's eyes were going to drop out of his face.

"Who are your friends, Frankie?" she asked. The voice wasn't a contralto anymore, either but a somewhat annoying soprano.

"Nobody, sugar. They were just going."

To Latimer I said, "Now you still think I've got a red-head in here?"

"Guess not, Sladek. But you could have saved us both some aggravation if you'd just told us you had company."

"You didn't really give me time. Any word on who the dead guy across the street was?"

"Naw," Latimer said. For some reason he seemed to be in a better mood. Maybe it was the fact that the woman was still standing there in my shirt which came down only just as far as it had to. "He didn't have any ID on him. His prints and face aren't in the info banks, either."

The latter was strange to say the least. All of the permanent residents of Star City were on file, and everyone landing had to go through security and be ID'd as well.

"Look, Latimer. I'm sorry we got off on the wrong foot. If you have any other questions, you know where to find me."

Surprisingly, he took the hint and left dragging Rossetti behind him.

When they had gone and the door was shut behind them I turned and looked at the red-head.

"Don't look so shocked. It's a wig. I had one in my bag. A girl never knows when the mood to go blonde will hit her."

I hadn't even noticed that she had had a bag, though thinking back I remembered that she had one of those big shoulder purses women seem to carry. Now I know what they keep in them.

"I don't suppose you have another dress in there, as well?"

"As a matter of fact, I do. Would you like to see it?"

"I'm in no hurry," I responded. Without the boots, I could see the whole length of her legs from where the thighs peeked out from under my shirt to the tips of her nicely shaped toes.

"You can be cute when you're embarrassed, Sladek," she said. "I'll be right back."

She was true to her word. This time she was wearing a very skimpy sleeveless dress that wasn't much longer than my shirt. The boots had been replaced with pink tights and low heeled slippers of the same color. The shoulder bag was gone, exchanged for a tiny clutch purse. She'd changed her makeup as well to look paler and a couple of years younger. She looked nothing like the red-head that had showed up at my door.

"I'd like to stay, Sladek, but I don't think that would be wise right now. I'll be in touch. I left my things in the back of your closet."

Before I could think of anything to say she had let herself out.

Out of curiosity I checked the closet. On the floor towards the back was a black dress with a pair of black high-heeled boots and a red wig laying on top of it. None of the items had any labels on them, or even any indication of the planet of origin. I checked the bag, too. Except for a small stun gun it was empty. No cosmetics or communicator. No papers, no ID, no money. Not even a tissue. For such a big bag she was travelling light.

The stun gun was a cheap, local model like the ones some of the hookers carry. Non-lethal, not a serious weapon, but effective at what it could do. I guessed it wouldn't fit in the little purse she had carried with her when she left.

I didn't want to leave the stuff laying around in case Latimer came back so I took it and stuffed it in a travel bag that I had, zipped it up and sealed it with my thumb print. I put it on the top shelf of the closet behind a tennis racket that I hadn't used in years. It wouldn't remain secret if someone decided to toss the place, but it would probably be safe from casual prying eyes.

The police were gone from the Blue Moon by the next afternoon. You'd never know that a man had died there violently less than twenty four hours earlier, but then the same could be said of too many places on Star City, particularly in and around New Minglewood.

I was in the bar for a mid-afternoon drink for want of anything better to do. Unlike the day before, there was a small crowd, mostly gawkers, only a few of whom had recognizable faces. The snatches of conversation that I could overhear were all speculations on the shooting, most of which were wildly inaccurate. The incident was already passing into legend.

"I understand that you were in here when it happened," a voice next to me said out of the buzz of random conversation.

I looked at the man. I didn't know him. He was obviously not a resident of Star City. The style of his suit was subtly different, the tailoring a bit too good, at least for the fringes of New Minglewood. He was medium height, neither skinny nor fat, and somewhere in middle age. His skin had a tan that could only come from a planet circling a star with a high amount of UV. I couldn't quite place the accent.

"Where'd you hear that?" I asked.

"It's true, though, isn't it, Mr. Sladek?" I noted that he hadn't answered my question. As far as I knew, only the cops and the barkeep knew I had been there, and I was pretty sure the barkeep didn't know my name. As for the cops, well, they tell or don't tell what they feel like.

"You're not a cop. Are you a reporter?" I asked innocently.

"Oh, nothing like that, I assure you, Mr. Sladek." If he kept using my name, half the crowd would know it. I wasn't sure I liked that.

"Then what exactly are you, Mr.—?"

"Me? Why I'm nothing but a businessman." He still wasn't answering my questions.

"And what business would that be?"

"Why, I buy and sell things."

"Things? That's sort of a broad category."

"Let's just say anything that will turn a profit."

"That always struck me as a good plan."

"Yes, I think so. Can I buy you another drink?"

"Sure, why not."

He motioned to the barkeep, whispered something in his ear when he came to take the order.

"You were here, though, weren't you?"

"As long as you're buying, yes, I was here."

The barkeep returned with two glasses of amber liquid. No ice. There was something funny about the drink. It didn't look right. It didn't smell right either. I took a tentative sip. I was right. It was Scotch, the real deal, two hundred fifty dollars Crockett on Star City.

"Thanks for the drink," I said, holding up the glass in a silent toast. "Just what is your interest?"

"Curiosity, Mr. Sladek. It's just possible I may have had business dealings with the man that was murdered."

"I'm afraid I can't help you. I never saw the man before in my life."

"I'd have been surprised if you had. He was a new arrival on Star City."

This was news to me. As far as I knew, even the cops weren't aware of the identity of the dead man.

"He wasn't, by any chance carrying something with him, was he?"

"Not that I could see. He just came in, asked for some red-headed dame and got shot. Three times."

"So the other man, the shooter, he didn't pick up something that the dead man had brought in?"

"No. He just said 'Yano,' shot the guy, picked up his sample case, and walked out."

"Sample case? Oh. I believe that is where the shooter carries the tools of his trade."

"You know the shooter?"

"By reputation only. I personally find such tactics bad for business."

"I'm sure the dead guy feels the same way. Just what is this item that you thought he might have had on him?"

"Oh, just a piece of merchandise that I have an interest in acquiring. You wouldn't, by any chance, have any idea of where the item is, would you?"

"Look, mister. I appreciate the Scotch. But I don't have the faintest idea of what you're talking about. I saw a guy get drilled. That's all I know."

"You wouldn't have any idea, then, of where the red-headed woman is or how I could get in touch with her?"

"No. Like I said, she didn't come in here."

"I'm sure she didn't. But, if you should hear anything I would be interested in finding out, Mr. Sladek. It would be worth your while." He handed me a card on which was printed a communicator address and nothing else. "Cheers." He drained the remains of his drink and got up to leave.

"And Mr. Sladek—I'd be careful who you dealt with. There are some dangerous people out there." With that he walked out the front door.

At this point, my curiosity was starting to get the better of me. It would have been safer if it hadn't, but then, that's life. I was wondering just what this "item" was that the woman had been trying to unload and my friend from the bar seemed interested in acquiring. Obviously, the dead guy had been interested, too. With the shooter, that made at least four involved factions, none of whom I knew from experience or reputation.

In my line of work, it pays to know the players, and I pride myself on being good at what I do. I was pretty sure that the shooter and the dame weren't local, and the dead guy and the Scotch drinker didn't appear to be from Star City either. I was just wondering who else might be involved, as it seemed a safe bet there might be more players. And of course, the big question. What was the item?

When I got back to my apartment, the front door was unlocked. I still wasn't packing, but that was beginning to look like a mistake I'd have to remedy if I survived.

I opened the door to find Latimer and Rossetti sitting in my good chairs. They were sipping some of my whiskey, too, but considering the quality of the stuff I could afford, that didn't bother me.

The bag I had stuffed the red-head in was sitting on top of the table in front of the chairs. They'd opened it, and the contents were laid out on table top.

"Is there something you haven't told us, Sladek?" Latimer asked.

"Like maybe you like a bit of dress-up?" Rossetti added with a laugh.

"Maybe I was thinking of going to a costume party." I said.

"I don't think they're your size, Sladek. But it might be interesting to have you put them on before we take you down to the station."

"OK. The dame was here. She somehow found out I'd been present at the shooting. I told her what I knew, which was nothing. Except that the dead guy had asked about a red-head in a black dress and boots. She walked out of here a blonde wearing something pink and skimpy and left those souvenirs. That's all I know. She didn't give a name or address or anything."

"Do you expect us to believe that cock-and-bull story, Sladek?" Latimer asked tersely.

"I don't care what you believe, flat-foot. It's true. She said she had arranged to meet this guy but got held up. They hadn't met before. The wig and dress were so he could recognize her.

Maybe if she had showed up on time you'd have had two corpses. But that's women for you. Always late."

"So's the dead guy. Did she say who he was?"

"No. She said she didn't know. It sounded to me like a blind meeting where they were going to exchange something."

"What?"

"She—," I started to say.

"Let me guess," Latimer interrupted. "She didn't say."

"You seem to know all the answers, Latimer. I sure as hell don't."

"Did she say how you could contact her?"

"No, but she said she'd be in touch. She knows where I live."

"So do we, Sladek."

"I'll keep that in mind, Latimer. Look. I don't know nothing. Nobody's hired me. I was just a guy in a bar drinking a drink in the middle of the afternoon."

"You're just dumb enough for that to be true, Sladek," Latimer said. "Let me know if she contacts you again. I mean it. The powers that be don't like the idea of professional assassins going around putting the hit on city visitors. It could give Star City a bad name. They're putting pressure on me, so I'll put pressure on you if you play games with me."

Latimer got up, kicked Rossetti's feet off the table and headed for the door.

"Do we understand each other, Sladek?"

"I understand you, Latimer. I just hope you understand me."

The two left. They hadn't even bothered to take the dress and boots with them. I stuffed them back in the bag and put it back in the closet. I didn't bother to put it up on the shelf behind the tennis racket.

I checked my communicator and there was a new call from a number that I didn't recognize. It was a text asking me to call back. The name was Johanna Smith. It might have been her real name. Stranger things have happened. Half of my clients didn't use their real names. As long as they paid me in real money, I didn't mind.

I called the number. It was answered immediately by a woman with medium length brown hair. She was dressed in the current conservative business style. She was sitting in what appeared to be a hotel room. The lighting was bad and her face was in shadows.

"Thank you for returning my call so promptly, Mr. Sladek."

"Miss Smith, I presume?"

"Yes, that name will do for the moment."

"What can I do for you Miss Smith."

"I'd like to engage your services, if you are available, Mr. Sladek." The voice was familiar, but I couldn't place it, but then communicators have limited fidelity.

"What exactly did you have in mind, Miss Smith?"

"I'd rather not discuss the details over a public communications channel. Such things are better handled face to face. Do you know the Coffee Room at the Rigel Royal?"

"I can find it," I answered.

"Shall we meet there in, say, one hour?"

"The Coffee Room at the Rigel Royal in one hour. Should I wear a white carnation?" I could tell that her strictly business attitude was starting to annoy me by the comment I'd just made.

"That won't be necessary, Mr. Sladek. I know what you look like." The communicator went dead.

I changed into a more professional jacket. I also slipped a gun into the special pocket I had had put in, a small Baretta 25 kilojoule laser. It's good only for short range work, but then I rarely get into all out gunfights. The nice thing about it was that short of a full body scan it was virtually undetectable when tucked in the pocket.

I caught the tram and headed uptown.

The Rigel Royal is a respectable hotel of the sort favored by businessmen travelling on expense accounts. Most of the clientele are on layovers waiting to make connections. It does not cater to tourists or the extremely wealthy, but it does have a good reputation. It also has a prime location just off the corridor from the main passenger docks.

The Coffee Room is a large, cheerfully bright expanse of small tables in artistic colors. It serves a variety of non-alcoholic beverages, pastries, salads and light sandwiches. The coffee is made from real beans imported, if not from Earth, at least someplace where they actually grow such things in the ground. Not my sort of place, but it makes a great place for a meeting when the two parties aren't quite sure of each other. The security is, as to be expected of such an establishment, discrete, but that doesn't mean that it isn't efficient. As I entered, I could spot at least five observation cameras, three that were plainly visible to reassure the patrons and discourage would be criminals, and two that were not nearly as obvious. I suspected that there were several that I hadn't made.

Miss Smith was sitting at a table against the far wall where she could see everyone that entered. Maybe she was making sure that she didn't miss me, but I was starting to doubt that. She caught my eye discretely, with no outward gesture. As I approached the table I thought she looked familiar. Then it came to me. Miss Smith was the red-head in the black dress, and the short-haired blonde.

"Miss Smith," I said politely as I sat down across from her.

"Thank you for coming, Mr. Sladek."

"I have some things of yours that you left behind last time we talked."

"Oh, I don't think I shall be needing them again."

"That's a pity. Black and red is one of my favorite color combinations."

"But perhaps too well known."

"You'd know best. Now what can I do for you, Miss Smith?"

"Not here. I suggest we discuss the arrangements somewhere more private."

"That's too bad. I was looking forward to a cup of coffee."

"There will be time enough for coffee later. Why don't we adjourn to the Promenade?"

"I never reject an invitation to go out walking with a lady."

"I never said I was a lady. Shall we go?"

The Promenade is a sort of gallery that extends out past the passenger docking ring. It's in the form of a ring about five kilometers in diameter, twenty meters thick, and about fifty meters wide. The wall facing away from Star City is one long window. It's one of the few places on Star City where you can actually get a view of space. A favorite hangout of the wealthy and powerful, its where they go to stroll so that they can see and be seen. By its very public nature, it is a great place to hold private conversations.

Access to the Promenade is strictly controlled. First class passengers, Star City's elite, and a limited set of others have unrestricted access. The respectable can enjoy it for a small fee. Working stiffs aren't welcome unless they're sweeping the floors or washing the windows.

Needless to say, I've rarely been there. Frankly, I think space is over rated. Particularly the space around Star City. Unless a star liner is making an approach or departure, there's not much to see. The brown dwarf that serves as Star City's primary is best observed in the near infra-red, and none of the other planetoids amount to much. No ringed worlds or comets nearby, no big clouds of luminous gas. Sure, there are some bright lights in the distance, but I'm no astronomer.

Miss Smith had a pass that got her waved through the security at the elevator at the top of one of the four spokes that held the Promenade to the hub. I wasn't terribly surprised at that. It got me through, as well, which was a little more of a surprise. I'm not exactly on Star City's "A" list.

We got off the elevator and walked a bit until there was no one within fifty meters of us. It was evidently a slow time for the Promenade, as only a few strollers were evident in the section that was visible before curving up out of view.

"Shall we get down to business, Mr. Sladek?"

"Please, let's, Miss Smith," I said a bit snarkily.

"I'm here on Star City acting as a sort of middle man. In light of recent events, I find it might be wise if I were to be supported by someone of your talents and experience."

"Recent events being the sudden demise of the unnamed party in the Blue Moon?"

"In a word, yes."

"You want a bodyguard?"

"Not exactly. I would much rather avoid embarrassing incidents than confront them. You have local experience and contacts which I don't. I would like to draw on those."

"A nice way of putting it." We kept on walking. "Exactly what are you involved in?"

"There is an item arriving at Star City shortly. I am to take possession of it and arrange for its transfer in exchange for a rather large sum of money."

"Won't Interstellar Express do the same thing?"

"In this case, both the supplier and receiver would prefer that the transaction remain a secret."

"I can appreciate that. Exactly what is this 'item' you keep referring to?"

"Frankly, Mr. Sladek, I don't know. It has been described to me as a short, metallic cylinder about twenty five centimeters long and five centimeters in diameter weighing about a kilogram."

"But you don't know what it is or why it appears to be of interest to so many people?"

"That is correct. All I know is that if the transaction is successful, one million dollars Crockett will be credited to my account. If you support me I am willing in turn to credit five percent of that amount to you account."

"Fifty thousand Crockett dollars is a lot of moola. And if you fail to deliver?"

"As they say, failure is not an option."

"Do you do this sort of thing often?"

"Occasionally. But I admit, never when the stakes have been this high."

"What went wrong at the Blue Moon?"

"I was supposed to meet the dead man to arrange the final details of the transfer, but I was held up. There was a problem. The ship that is bringing in the item had drive trouble and was delayed. I was waiting for word on the new schedule. Somehow word must have gotten out, presumably from the other end."

"Any idea who the shooter is?"

"I think he is a man named Vogel. A professional hit man. I know him by reputation only, and frankly, until the incident at the Blue Moon I didn't believe he existed."

"Who is he working for?"

"I believe there are other parties interested in the item."

"Evidently. And Yano?"

"You mentioned that before. That before he shot my contact the shooter said that word. I've no idea."

"Great. I should mention that there was another party expressing curiosity about the incident."

"Oh?" For once Miss Smith seemed surprised. I described my encounter in the Blue Moon earlier in the day. "I see. I'm not familiar with the gentleman, but I find I'm not surprised."

"One more question, Miss Smith."

"Yes?"

"Are you armed?"

"I have a small stunner. I don't believe in violence. Why?"

"If you will not look back about seventy meters you will find a man. He's been following us since we left the elevator. He's been much more interested in us than in the splendors of space."

"Do you think he is going to try and kill us?"

"Hard to say. But judging from the size of the bulge under his jacket I'd say he's packing a weapon, probably a long range laser pistol."

"I see. What would you advise? And am I to take it that you will accept my proposal?"

"We can talk about that later. Let's keep walking towards that kiosk up ahead."

About fifty meters ahead and to our right was a refreshment kiosk which might provide a bit of cover. There was only one other person in sight, a man coming from the other direction. I was about to ignore him when I noticed his hand reaching inside his jacket.

"When we get even with the kiosk, dive behind it." We were only about a dozen steps away.

As we came even with it, Miss Smith moved as I had asked. From somewhere a small stunner the twin of the one I had found in her bag appeared in her hand. Not that it would do much good at this range.

A chip flew off the corner of the kiosk as she made its cover, blown off by a laser shot from the man that had been following us. My own laser was out and I fired a shot in his direction. It missed, but he must have sensed it. He turned his bigger weapon towards me. One problem with higher powered lasers is that they take longer to recharge after a shot. Mine recharged first. I caught him in the chest. At that range it probably wasn't lethal, but it would certainly give him something to think about.

During the shooting I'd lost sight of the other man. When I looked around he was only ten meters away. He had pulled out his weapon, a directed energy pistol of the kind commonly called a blaster. Strictly a military type weapon. He was hesitating, not sure whether to go after me or the girl. That gave me time to put the kiosk between us.

Miss Smith was slumped down with her back to the kiosk. The stun gun was in her hand but down by her side. Her face was white.

"OK. I got the guy that was following us. The other one is out front holding a cannon. I'm going to count to three and then try and draw his fire. As soon as I move, you start running to the next elevator and don't stop for anything. Do you understand?"

She nodded.

I counted, "One, Two, . . ."

She moved first, up and running ahead. I moved around the other side. The guy with the blaster was indecisive again. He split the difference and the kiosk disappeared in a gout of flame. My shot hit him dead center in the chest at five meters, drilling a hole in his heart.

I stood up and walked towards the man that had been following us. He was still down on the tile floor. I kept walking away from the direction the woman had run.

I dropped my gun in the first trash container I came to. The elevator was empty on the ride back to the hub. No alarms were sounding and no guards barred my way. I didn't see the woman, either, as I stepped off the elevator. I gave my shoulders a mental shrug and took the tram home.

I was debating whether to return to my apartment or step into the Blue Moon for a quick shot when a car rolled by. It didn't take a genius to spot it as an unmarked police vehicle. I tried to ignore it, but as it slowed, then backed up next to me, that was hard to do. It was even harder when Latimer's ugly head reared up out of the driver's side window.

"Sladek, get in. I got some questions for you."

The rear door popped open. Inside I could see Rossetti sitting on the far end of the back seat with an ugly expression on his face. His hand was holding a stun gun pointed at my chest. There didn't seem to be any point in resisting. I got in.

"What do you want to know, Latimer?" I asked ignoring Rossetti.

"Not here, Sladek," Latimer answered. "Up at headquarters. We're going to do this nice and official."

Latimer stuck to his driving while Rossetti played the Sphinx, all the time the stun gun aimed at my ribs. It was a quiet ten minutes before we pulled into the police garage. It was dark and empty, the only lighting provided by widely spaced glow strips. If Latimer wanted to finish me, no one would be the wiser.

Instead he pointed towards the elevator pod in the center of the garage. We took a car up to the eighth floor. From previous experience I knew that was the detective department. It appeared I wasn't being arrested. Yet.

Latimer didn't say anything until we entered one of the interrogation rooms. Rossetti closed and locked the door behind him.

In a bored voice Latimer repeated the stock phrase, "This session is being recorded. Anything you say or do may be used against you. Do you understand?"

Latimer was playing it by the books. I wondered what was up.

Rossetti patted me down, shaking his head when he was done.

"Have a seat," Latimer said pointing at a hard metal chair on one side of a bare metal table. He took the chair on the other side. I noted it had a cushion at least a centimeter thick. Rossetti continued to stand in front of the door. He actually looked like he was a bit frightened.

"You aren't packing," Latimer remarked.

"I rarely do. Guns are dangerous. People can get hurt."

"Like the two dead guys on the Promenade?"

"Oh? I hadn't heard." I tried not to show surprise, but they had picked me up less than half an hour after I left the Promenade.

"Yeah. Both of them shot in the chest by a low powered laser."

"That's too bad. And on the Promenade! What is Star City coming to?"

"Cut the comedy, Sladek. We know you were up on the Promenade with a woman."

"I was showing my cousin the sights. She's from out of town."

Latimer's fist slammed down on the table. The small room rang with the noise.

"Can it. I want answers, Sladek."

"Isn't there a recording of what happened? I thought there were cameras everywhere on the Promenade?"

"There are, but the memory's been erased. We know you went up, but after that it's a blank. I want to know what happened."

"Like I said, I took my cousin to see the view. Turns out she's got vertigo, so we came straight down. I didn't see any shoot out."

"This cousin wouldn't happen to be a red-head in a black dress, would she?" Latimer asked.

"No. She's a brunette. Kind of prim looking. Like a school teacher."

"So where's your cousin staying?"

"I don't know. We're not that close. Truth is, she's only my second cousin. She gave me a call. We met at the Rigel Royal Coffee Room. I suggested she should see the view. She was only going to be here a few hours until her connection left. She may be gone by now."

"Sladek, that story is a load of hooey."

"It's the only one I got."

"Well I've got another one. Two guys, one with a high powered laser pistol and the other with a directed energy weapon let loose on the Promenade. Both of them are dead and there's a refreshment kiosk blown to hell. The powers that be don't like it. If the energy beam had been aimed at the window the whole Promenade would have been evacuated and a bunch of innocent people killed. Possibly important people. That kind of thing might be acceptable down in New Minglewood, but it ain't going to fly uptown."

"I can't help you. I don't know anything about two guys trying to shoot each other on the Promenade."

"Who says they shot each other?"

"Stands to reason, doesn't it. From what you tell me, they sound like pros. If they weren't aiming at each other, I'd have thought you'd have more than two bodies on your hands."

Latimer looked up at the dingy ceiling. I knew then he didn't have anything on me. He knew it too.

"Either that, or they ran into someone who's even better with a gun. You're pretty good from what I hear."

"You must have heard wrong. I don't go in for rough stuff. I leave that to the cops."

Rossetti looked for a moment like he was going to take a swipe at me but Latimer gave him a look.

"So, you seen your red-head friend lately?"

"You know yourself that she wasn't really a red-head."

"Yeah, we know. She's a blonde. Or is she?"

"You've got me, Latimer. I don't know any more about her than you do."

"Look, Sladek. I've got nothing on you now. But if this thing, whatever it is, goes bad, you're in a lot of trouble. You hear anything. You let me know."

"You'll be the first. Can I go now?"

"Get out of here," Latimer said in disgust.

I decided to forgo a stop at the Blue Moon on the way home. The fact was that I was tired. Tired of being shot at, tired at being lied to, and just plain tired. Besides, I had a bottle at home.

I knew when I opened the door to my apartment that I wasn't alone. It wasn't anything in particular, no sound or smell. I just knew that there was someone in the apartment besides myself. I shut the door as quietly as I could, regretting that I had dumped my laser on the Promenade.

I heard a noise from the kitchenette, the sound of liquid being poured.

"Do you want ice, or do you prefer it straight?" came from the kitchen. I recognized the voice. Why wasn't I surprised?

"With ice."

I heard the cubes splashing in the glasses. A moment later she emerged from the kitchen holding two glasses, one of which she handed to me before taking a seat on the sofa.

Her hair was pink this time, just long enough to reach her chin with bangs that touched her eyebrows. She was wearing a bright orange form-fitting cat suit with low boots that matched her hair. It should have looked hideous, but somehow it didn't. She patted the sofa next to her.

"Come sit down. We have a lot to talk about."

I sat. I drank. It was bourbon, the real stuff. She must have brought her own bottle.

"I'm glad you got away all right," she said when I put the glass down. Her own she was cradling in the cup of her left hand while the fingers of her right grazed the rim.

"So am I. The police picked me up. Latimer and Rossetti. I didn't tell them anything. I said I was showing my second cousin the sites, but she has vertigo so we left before the action. Someone wiped the security-cam memory."

"Yes. I suspected as much."

"Who were those guys? I didn't recognize them. I don't think they were from Star City."

"No, they weren't. You've probably guessed that there is more than one interested party."

"So I've gathered. Let's see. There's you."

"I'm just a middle man. A facilitator."

"OK. So there's whoever you are working for. There's whoever hired the travelling salesman who made the hit in the Blue Moon. There's whoever hired the two gunmen on the Promenade. I assume that they weren't working for the same party."

"I think that's a safe assumption," she said as she took a sip of the Bourbon.

"So that's three parties at least in competition," I didn't mention the man who had bought me a drink in the Blue Moon. I wasn't sure where he fit in the whole scheme. "Are there any other players that you know of?"

"At least one more. But I don't know anything about him. He hasn't shown his hand."

"It's all getting too complicated for me. You can't tell the players without a scorecard and no one is handing out programs."

"These things happen," she said. Her drink was finished. I looked down. So was mine. "That's what makes it fun. That, and the money."

"Not my idea of fun," I said.

"There's still the money. I liked the way you handled yourself on the Promenade. I'm willing to bump my offer to twenty percent. That's two hundred thousand dollars Crockett if we make the delivery."

Two hundred GCs was a lot of dough, particularly for a two bit dick just this side of New Minglewood.

"So the delivery is still on?" I asked.

"I got the word after our little sight-seeing jaunt. The ship bringing the item is arriving in eighteen hours. I pick it up and deliver it an hour later."

"Just like that?"

"Just like that. I just need someone to watch my back while I do it. Can I count you in?"

I thought about it. Maybe it was the bourbon. Maybe I was tired. Maybe it was the curves on the dame next to me. Even in orange and pink she looked good.

"I'm in."

"Good. One more thing. I need a place to lay low until the meet. I haven't slept in thirty-six hours and I'd rather not have to depend on chemicals to stay awake. It would help if I could stay here."

"I've only got the one bed."

"That shouldn't be a problem. Do you want another drink?"

We decided against another drink. We both got some sleep, too, eventually. I never did find out what her natural hair color was, though. When she came out of the shower it was shoulder length and black with just a hint of a wave.

"Do you have a gun? I'm afraid I ditched mine on the Promenade."

"I might. Stunner or laser?"

"I don't care as long as it's small and lethal."

I have a safe in the spare room where I keep my weapons. It doesn't pay to let them lying around loose. Too many accidents happen that way. I pulled out a small needler and a 25kW laser.

"Take your pick."

She chose the needler. Probably not a bad choice. They're small and quiet, and as the incident at the Blue Moon had shown, deadly.

"What about you? You are going armed, aren't you?"

"Are you one of those dames that get's off on guns?"

"Call it professional curiosity."

I'd been debating what to take. There was a good chance that whoever we might come up against would be heavily armed.

There was no telling just what the travelling salesman carried in his sample case. Finally I made a choice.

"What's that? I don't think I've ever seen one of those before."

"Probably not. It's an antique."

"Where's the energy pack?"

"There is none. It uses chemical explosives. It's a .45 caliber automatic."

"A real ballistic gun? You are retro."

"The clip holds eight rounds. No recharge time. The projectiles will penetrate any electronic armor and it can't be jammed."

"It still seems horribly old fashioned."

"Like my uncle told me once, 'you can get killed just as dead by a pointed stick as by a blaster.' He's the one who gave me this gun."

"You must have a fun family."

"He was an Interstellar marshal. He died on Paradise when a bomb blew up his vehicle."

She must have recognized she had touched a raw nerve. "We need to get going soon, and I have to get dressed." She ducked back into the bathroom.

When she emerged from the bathroom she was dressed all in black to match the new hair color. The outfit was tight and form-fitting but looked suitable for action. I hadn't noticed that she had brought any luggage with her, but then I hadn't been looking. I also wondered what embarrassing bits of wardrobe she was leaving behind for Latimer and Rossetti to find. I was pretty sure that no matter how the pickup went she wouldn't be coming back.

We were to meet the incoming courier at the down end of Star City where the freighters dock. It's the part of the city that tourists and star liner passengers never see, a dark grey world of chemical factories and warehouses. Parts of it even make New Minglewood look good.

The docking ring for freighters is a twin of the one at the other end of Star City where the liners berth, except, that is, for the high class hotels and restaurants, clean waiting rooms and other amenities that cater to the passengers trade. What there are in their place are a few dive saloons, hotels that offer cubicles by the hour and a steady supply of "working girls" of various genders and preferences. These, however, take up only a fraction of the down end. The rest is given over to warehouses and parking racks for shipping containers. Most of the cargo is handled by robots. One can go for blocks without running into anyone living. The robots don't need light, so illumination is supplied at a bare minimum. Streets, alleys, and passageways are all geared to the moving of cargo around and tend to be narrow and irregular.

All this makes the down end a perfect place for a rendezvous which the participants wish to keep low profile. With that much cargo, of course, there are plenty of security sensors, but Down End is a big place, and security is apt to respond to only the most obvious transgressions.

I let Johanna—if that was her real name, which I doubted— lead the way from the tram line. As we meandered through the dark alleys, I could say that I became hopelessly lost, but the fact is, it's hard to get really lost on Star City. One only has to look overhead to the spar that ran down the central axis to hold the glow tubes that provide what passes for daylight to get one's bearings. Finding one's way is sometimes a different matter.

We came to the door of a warehouse that looked just like every other warehouse on the street. There was no sign, but it did have a plaque with an identity number for the robots to read. The door was unlocked. Normally, this would have made me suspicious, but plans had obviously been made in advance for the meeting.

If the outside had been dim, the inside was downright gloomy. Only a few widely spaced light globes on the twenty meter high ceiling provided any light. The fifty by hundred meter space was largely empty, but there were enough crates and shipping containers spread out over the floor to create plenty of places to hide and lots of shadows to hide in. Me, I always like brightly lit spaces with lots of people to make an exchange. It's safer.

I gave the space a once over, but there was no way to do a thorough job. I'd just have to trust that my client had done her homework.

"What now?"

"We wait," she said. "It shouldn't be long."

It wasn't. After about five minutes a door at the other end of the space opened slowly. After a second a spacer entered carrying a shoulder bag. At least he was dressed in the type of one-piece coveralls favored by spaceship hands. The coverall carried no indentifying patches or logos, but that wasn't unusual for casual hands. He was of medium height and build, hair cropped short. In a word he looked like any one of a thousand other space hands on the docks that night.

He walked to the center of the space. We did the same. As far as I could see in the dim light he was unarmed, but he could have been hiding a hand cannon in the bag that hung from his shoulder.

"You got the credits?"

"Here," Johanna said. She handed him an exchange card. He waved it over his communicator. He must have been satisfied because he reached into his bag and pulled out the item. This was, as advertised, a cylinder about twenty five centimeters long and five in diameter. It was made of some silvery metal that looked liked brushed aluminum, but might not be. There were no visible cracks or seams. When the exchange was made it looked like it might mass about a kilo.

"You should leave first," Johanna said. "We'll wait until you're gone."

The spacer turned and left through the door he had come in.

"How much did he get paid?"

"5 GC. He didn't have any idea what he was transporting."

"Do you?" I asked. I sure as hell didn't.

"I know it's worth a lot more than five thousand Crockett dollars."

"So we wait here?"

"No. The exchange is to be made at another place. In half an hour."

I was starting to wonder about the deal. OK I had been wondering from the first, but Johanna claimed that she was getting paid a million DC, yet the "item" was going to be in her possession for less than an hour. I could understand the two parties wanting to keep their identities secret from the other, but that seemed excessive. Particularly considering it appeared that at least three other groups seemed to be aware of that an exchange was taking place. I may be just a local rube, but it didn't add up.

We hung around for maybe fifteen minutes, and then left by the front door. More alleyways and dark passages and five minutes later we found ourselves in another warehouse that could have been a twin of the first one except for the fact that there were a few more containers cluttering the floor.

Again, we appeared to be the first to arrive, but there was really no way to be sure. You could have hidden an elephant in some of the shadows, whatever an elephant is.

Again we waited. This time about ten minutes. Again, a man entered through a door other than the one we had used. This time the courier was dressed as a maintenance man. He carried a toolbox in his left hand. It looked just big enough to carry the item discretely.

"Do you have it?" he asked. This seemed unnecessary as the cylinder was clearly visible in Johanna's left hand.

"Check for yourself."

He pulled a device out the toolbox. It looked to be some sort of scanner or meter. He passed it the length of the cylinder and then checked a readout on the scanner.

"It's legit."

"The payment?" Johanna asked.

He tapped out a code on his communicator. Johanna looked at hers, waited a few seconds, and then nodded.

"It's all yours." She held out the cylinder.

Just as his hand touched it a line of holes stitched his chest. A needle gun. The courier collapsed on the floor.

"I'll take that," came a voice from the gloom. It was the travelling salesman from the Blue Moon. His sample case was in his left hand. A needle gun was in his right.

"I wouldn't try anything. Either of you. You know I can hit what I aim at."

I let my hand fall from where it had been reaching for the automatic in its shoulder holster. Johanna stood still, the cylinder in one hand, her communicator in the other.

The salesman walked slowly toward us. He examined the body on the floor with professional detachment. A small pool of blood was collecting underneath the body from where the dart had torn through the heart.

He plucked the cylinder from Johanna's hand, and then motioned her back a step. He set his sample case down on the fused silica of the floor, worked a catch and opened up the case. It was a little marvel. I counted half a dozen weapons, each neatly arranged, from a pocket stunner to an energy beam pistol. There was also a form fitting pocket that looked to be just the shape and size to hold the cylinder. He set it gently in this space and moved to close the case.

One drawback of a plasma rifle is the crackle of ozone that comes just before the weapon is discharged. All three of us must have detected it at the same time. In any case, we all reacted the same way—that is we jumped for cover. I'll take my chances with a needle gun. Plasma rifles are messy, indiscriminate things good only for making craters.

I was scrambling for cover when the blast went off. For a moment the warehouse was lit like the sun, and then it plunged into darkness. Whatever dark adaption my eyes had was gone. All I could see was the after image of the plasma burst. I had found cover behind a shipping container more by touch than sight.

I waited while my eyes readjusted. Depending on the size of the power pack, I might have as much as a minute before the rifle could fire again. Of course they might have other weapons, but the container would probably shield me from them.

As the scene came back into focus, I could see that there was a small crater in the floor about a meter in diameter. Half of the dead man was next to it. I assumed the other half had been in it and was gone. Neither Johanna or the salesman were in view. Miraculously, the salesman's case and the cylinder were sitting there still intact. That meant the salesman only had his needle gun at hand.

I tried to spot where the guy with the plasma rifle was. I thought he was to my left, but that wasn't very specific. For the moment no one was moving, everyone hunkered down behind the nearest crate.

I realized the automatic was still resting under my armpit. I got it out. I had eight shots in the gun and a spare magazine. The question was, did the plasma rifleman have a partner?

He did. Armed with a laser. A beam flashed harmlessly against a container to my right, the direction I thought the salesman had gone. Meanwhile, I could hear the sound of someone climbing up on top of one of the crates to my left. It was probably the guy with the plasma rifle trying to get a vantage point from which he could pick us off.

The gunman with the laser pistol was circling around, counting on the plasma rifle to give him covering fire if necessary. They seemed to be most concerned with the salesman, which was probably the smart move. I began to crawl to my left, away from the gunman.

I still wasn't sure where Johanna was. I thought I knew where the plasma rifle was. He was on top of a pile of crates about five meters high and maybe fifteen feet in front of me. The salesman was to my right, maybe ten meters. The laser gunman was between the rifle and the salesman, maybe twenty meters back working his way around a line of boxes.

I didn't think things could stay the way they were for long, and I was right. The laser gunner got around far enough so that he could see the salesman. Of course, that meant the salesman could see him. There was the soft fwack of the needle gun, one shot, followed by a laser beam which had been fired wild up at the ceiling. I heard a groan, then another soft thud of a dart hitting a body.

I saw the plasma rifleman stand up and aim in the salesman's direction. I had a clear shot and let off three quick rounds. The shots echoed through the cavern of the warehouse. I didn't think I had hit him. A second later I was sure as the plasma rifle went off, but by that time the salesman had reached cover.

I could smell the plasma rifle cycling again. I took my chances and stood, the pistol braced with my left hand. I could see the barrel of the plasma rifle pointed directly at me, but the power pack was still charging the capacitors. I fired, once, aimed again and fired a second shot. It hit and the rifleman was knocked off his tower of crates.

"Nice shooting, Mr. Sladek," came a voice from behind a crate. "I admire your skill. Too few in our profession bother to acquire it and rely on gadgets instead. If you walk out now, I won't hinder you. You can even take the woman."

"Don't listen to him," Johanna called out. "You can't trust him." She was probably right.

"I'll make you the same offer. Leave the cylinder and I won't stop you."

"Don't be foolish, Sladek. Do you think you can trust her?"

"I made a deal," I replied.

"I admire your ethics," the salesman said. While we had been talking, he had been circling towards the right, trying to flank me. I moved to put the crate between us. I had three bullets left in the gun. I debated changing clips, but decided against it.

For a big man he was quiet on his feet. I knew if it came down to a straight shoot-out I was a dead man. Twice I'd seen him drop three needles in a space the size of fist from ten meters or more. He was quicker and more accurate than I was.

The advantage I had was that a needle gun dart is easily stopped by metal or a thick enough piece of plastic. Not so much with a .45 slug at close range. All I had to do was figure out where he was and shoot through whatever cover he was using.

It sounds easy. It wasn't. It was only when Johanna shouted a warning that I knew where he was. I popped the last three rounds in the gun in a line chest high through the box he was behind and hoped that it wasn't holding something dense enough to stop the slugs. It wasn't. I heard the sound of the salesman's body falling, his needle gun sliding across the floor of the warehouse.

I walked cautiously over to where he lay. One of the bullets had got him solid in the torso. The salesman was dead. There was no doubt about it.

I straightened up, the automatic still clutched in my hand. I walked over towards his sample case where the cylinder lay in its cradle. It looked so innocent, just a piece of metal. Yet seven men had died because of it. And I didn't even know what it was.

"Step away from the case, Frank." The words were chilling in their coldness.

"Whatever you say," I said, taking a step back.

"I'm sorry Frank, I have no choice." I could see the needler, my needler, held in her hand pointed at my chest.

"Take it, Johanna, or whatever your name is. I don't want it. I don't even know what it is."

"I wish I could take a chance, but I can't. Good-bye, Frank."

There was a blast. Where her head was there was just an empty space. "Drop the weapon, Mr. Sladek." It was the man that had bought me the Scotch in the Blue Moon.

"It's empty."

"Maybe. I'm unfamiliar with the type. Drop it so I don't have to do anything regrettable."

I placed the automatic on the floor and kicked it away with my foot. It slid noisily across the fused silica.

"Now step back from the case."

I took two steps back.

The Scotch drinker moved forward and picked up the cylinder in his left hand. The weapon he held in his right was pointed straight at me. I didn't recognize it, but I had seen what it could do.

"I admire you, Mr. Sladek. You kept your head while those around you lost theirs." He examined the cylinder and seemed satisfied.

"I apologize for the pun. It was in poor taste. If it's any consolation, she never would have collected the million dollars. Nor would you have gotten your fee."

"I see. Well that happens some time," I said. "Do you mind telling me just what that thing is?"

"I'm afraid I can't do that, Mr. Sladek. But, I will make a deal with you. I'm going to walk out of here in a moment. Don't follow me. If you heed my instructions, I'll let you live. I'll even credit five thousand dollars Crockett to your account. How does that sound? Do we have a deal?"

"That sounds just fine to me."

"Good. I'm glad someone is showing some sense."

He backed towards the door, all the time pointing his weapon at me. When he reached the door he put away his gun and vanished.

I walked slowly over to where Johanna's body lay. There was nothing left of it above her breasts. I thought idly that I would never know what color her hair really was.

Latimer and the cops showed up a couple of minutes later.

"Jeezus, Sladek, what you been doing? Rehearsing the last act of Hamlet?"

"It was just supposed to be a meeting. Then people pulled out guns."

"So how many of them are yours?"

"Just the guy with the plasma rifle and the one over there. He's the one that shot the man in the Blue Moon."

"Plasma rifles are illegal. So is murder. You trying to do my job for me? What about the dame?"

"She was the woman with the red hair and the black dress."

"She got no hair now," Rossetti said. Latimer gave him a dirty look.

"Who got her?"

"I'm not sure."

"I don't recognize the wound type. Messy."

"What about the other two?"

"The salesman shot them."

"I guess that accounts for all of them. What the hell was this all about, Sladek?"

"I wish the hell I knew."

When I got home after answering questions at police headquarters for a day and a half, I took the pink wig and orange cat suit and put them in the bag with the black dress and the red wig. Then I took the bag and dropped it in the disposal.

Oh, there was five grand deposited in my account. No ID on the depositor. And I still don't have a clue what it was all about.

THE NEW
MINGLEWOOD
BLUES

THE NEW MINGLEWOOD BLUES

They say that there's nothing new under the sun. I wouldn't know. I've never seen the sun, or any other real star for that matter, that was close enough to be more than a point of light in a black sky. Star City, the interstellar space station where I was born, occupies the hollowed out center of a hunk of rock that orbits a brown dwarf that you can just make out if you know exactly where to look. But that's neither here nor there.

The gist of the saying is that things just keep repeating themselves. The point of this story, if it has a point which it may not, is that bad things can happen when a man loves a woman and she doesn't love him back. That's a story that's been happening since humans were living in caves back on Earth, and it's been repeating itself ever since. New players, new locations, but always the same old predictable results.

The story started, where so many of them do, in The Blue Moon. I don't have a regular office. That's too much unneeded overhead in an on again, off again business like being a private detective. So much for the clichés of the door with my name painted on the frosted glass and the battered desk with a bottle of the amber juice in the lower left hand drawer. Instead, when I need to meet with a prospective client, I tend to pick someplace public yet quiet, like The Blue Moon, which is the bar across the street from the apartment building which I happen to call home.

The Blue Moon is an old-fashioned sort of bar, a bar of the kind that has been out of style since before the first rocket left the surface of the Earth. It's dark, it's quiet, and in the middle of the afternoon it's mostly empty except for a few regulars sitting at the bar sipping their tumblers of brown or clear depending on their personal preference. The neon sign out front proclaims "cocktails" when it's functional, but The Blue Moon doesn't really go in for fancy drinks; not that the barkeep won't add an ice cube or a splash of soda water to your drink if you insist. The signature drink is, not surprisingly, something called "The Blue Moon," which is in fact blue, and does have a tendency to glow faintly. I've never had the inclination or the courage to try one, so I can't tell you what's in it or what it tastes like.

All of which is besides the point, but makes The Blue Moon as good a place as any to do business when you want witnesses that will back your story or play dumb depending on the situation. I'd received a call from someone who said his name was Felix Shotmeyer. He said he wanted me to find something for him. I didn't know if he'd made up the name or was just unfortunate in his choice of parents. Over the phone he'd sounded like it might actually be his real name. I'd arranged a meeting him at The Blue Moon to discuss his case.

I entered the bar right on time, one of the advantages of living across the street from the place. As I let my eyes adjust to the gloom after stepping through the door, I gave it the once over. Nothing seemed out of place. Charlie was at the end of the bar drinking brown, Zelda was in the middle drinking a glass of clear. The bartender was new, but that wasn't unusual. The good bartenders go where the tips are better; the bad ones just don't last. There was a short, skinny guy in a business suit sitting in a booth staring at a mug of what passes for beer on Star City that I figured was my client. I ordered a glass of what they call "whiskey," but most just call brown, with a splash of soda and ice just to be sociable and went over to introduce myself.

"Are you Felix?" I said, sliding into the booth.

"Mr. Sladek?" he asked. His voice betrayed some nervousness, like he wasn't used to conducting business in a joint like The Blue Moon.

"That's me. Over the phone you said there was something you wanted me to find."

He seemed to hesitate, like he was thinking over just what he wanted to tell me. I took the opportunity to give him the once over. He was a skinny guy just under medium height, with thinning hair of some indeterminate color that was neither brown nor blonde. His eyes were a washed out blue. The suit he was wearing hadn't been cheap five years ago, but didn't fit him particularly well. I didn't get the impression he was on hard times, though. It was more like he just didn't care. In short, he looked like an accountant or a better class of tech.

While I was making these observations, he was giving me the once over, too. I hoped he liked what he saw, a guy pushing forty, a little over medium height, athletic without being muscular, handsome in a rugged sort of way. Of course, I'm not sure that's what he saw. We all have a skewed image of ourselves. Whatever he saw, he must have been satisfied.

"Actually, it's not something, it's someone."

"Doesn't matter," I replied. "The rates are the same. A hundred a day plus expenses, three days up front."

"Her name is Velma, Velma Schmitz," he said. The name meant nothing to me except that parents should have more respect for their children's futures.

"And why do you want to find this Velma Schmitz?" I asked.

"Because I'm in love with her." Somehow I got the feeling the sentiment might not be reciprocated, but it wasn't my dime and business had been slow lately.

"So what can you tell me about Velma, and how did you misplace her?"

"She works as a waitress in one of the lounges at the Casino. That's where we met. I eat there a lot because it's where I work. Here, I've got a picture of her."

He flipped his phone around so I could see the screen. I started. Velma deserved a better name than Velma Schmitz. Not that she was really beautiful, but she was certainly no slouch in the looks department. She had a cute nose, prominent cheek bones, and certain other prominent attributes if you get the picture. The face was framed by shoulder length hair, blonde though it wasn't clear that was her real color. It wasn't clear whether the loving looks she was giving to Felix in the image were real, either, but I could see where they might be enough for the little guy.

"So when did she go missing?"

"Wednesday, she didn't come home after work." It was now Friday, not a long time, but enough to be suspicious that it might turn permanent.

"And you two were living together?"

"Yeah. She'd been sharing my apartment for four months." That put a slightly different spin on things. A couple of days, even a week, and Velma might have just gotten cold feet or come to her senses, but four months was a long time to live with someone casually.

"Did she take any of her things with her?"

"I don't know. Maybe. I guess I don't pay a lot of attention to that girly stuff. All I know is that at least some of her clothes are still at my place." OK, I thought, that was ambiguous at best. If she was moving out permanent she would have slipped out with all her stuff while Felix was at work. If something had happened to her, none of her stuff would have been missing. If she had taken a few things it could mean anything. Like she was staying with a sick aunt. Or a friend.

"You're not giving me much to work with, Felix," I said, trying not to sound too harsh. "What do you think happened to her?"

Again, he hesitated. I couldn't tell whether it was from embarrassment or something else. Finally, he spoke up, "There was this guy, Jason, that Velma used to see, back before we got together. He'd been hanging around lately. Velma told me not to worry about him, that it was all over. I believed her."

"Sure you did, sucker" I left unspoken. Instead I asked, "This Jason, does he have a last name?"

"I'm sorry. Velma never told it too me."

"Any idea what he does for a living? Where he lives?"

"Velma never told me what he did. I kind of think he might be unemployed." He said the latter like it was a sin. Me, I'm unemployed whenever I'm not working. "But I think he lives in New Minglewood."

That put a different spin on things. If Star City has a ritzy district, New Minglewood isn't it. A geezer once told me that in the original plans, the area known as New Minglewood was going to be a park and recreational facility for all the working stiffs, a place with trees and shrubbery and playing fields and grass that the people that cleaned the streets and worked in the air plant and that kind of thing could go to and relax when they weren't working. Of course, that never happened. Instead, it had started out as low rent housing that quickly went downhill, something of a feat when you consider all of Star City is built on the inside of a spinning hunk of rock orbiting a failed star.

Over time, it became the home for all the cast offs, two bit grifters, losers and low-lifes that a space station stuck in the middle of nowhere but on the way to everywhere can attract but somehow never get rid of. Even the police won't enter in groups of less than four, and then only with backup. I knew all about New Minglewood, of course. Half my business involved things that passed through or got lost within its boundaries. That's part of the reason I live just outside its border. That and the fact that the rent is cheaper.

I was beginning to think that maybe my friend Felix had been the victim of some kind of con. A pretty girl, a little nebbish of an accountant, a low-life ex-boyfriend. What else was I supposed to think?

"Felix—and I'm asking this only because I'm being thorough— you haven't lost any money from your bank account or lent any to Velma, recently, have you?"

"No!" he said, sounding insulted. "I'm not stupid. I checked. It's all there. Velma's even been paying half the rent."

"I'm sorry I brought it up," I said trying to placate him. "I'm just doing my job. It sounds to me like maybe this Jason lured Velma into New Minglewood under some pretense and maybe he's holding her against her will." OK, I wasn't proud of that, but I was running a little behind at the time. At that moment three hundred looked like big money.

"Yeah, that's what I thought. So will you take the case, Mr. Sladek? All I want is to get Velma back."

"You haven't given me much to work with, but I'll look around, see what I can turn up. Is that OK with you?"

"Yeah, sure, Mr. Sladek. And I've got your money, right here." He reached inside to his jacket pocket. My reflexes being what they are, it was all I could do to not duck under the table, but Felix just pulled out a small envelope. I looked inside and counted five crisp hundred Crockett dollar bills.

"This is too much, Felix," I said, suddenly feeling sorry for the shlub. "My minimum is only three hundred.

"I want you to look real hard for Velma, Mr. Sladek. Real hard."

"Sure thing, Felix. Is there anything else you can tell me about Velma? Or this Jason?"

"No, not that I can think of. I'll be going, now. I've got to get back to work." He got up and walked out of the bar. I counted the money again and tucked it into my jacket pocket, then looking down at the table, I realized that I hadn't touched my drink. What the hell, I thought, it was still early in the day. I could start looking for Velma when it was finished.

I'd met Cindy a few years back while working on a case. I'd been sitting in a bar waiting for the subject of my investigation to show up. To avoid attracting attention I pretended to be a guy sitting in a bar trying to pick up a woman. I'd bought Cindy a drink and started to talk to her while I waited. The guy I was interested in never showed. I learned later his body was found in an alley the next morning, a needle gun wound just above the bridge of his nose. One drink led to another, and when it became obvious my target wasn't going to show I let Cindy persuade me to spend the night at her place.

After that, we saw each other off and on for a few weeks, but after a while we both came to the conclusion it wasn't going to lead to anything more. We parted on more or less amiable terms. That would have been the end of the story, except that it turned out that Cindy worked in Star City's Personnel Department in a capacity that gave her access to the records of anyone gainfully employed, and that she wasn't averse to occasionally providing supposedly confidential information in exchange for dinner and a few drinks.

After my meeting with Felix I had given her a call and arranged a date for that evening along with passing her Velma Schmitz's name. As an afterthought I mentioned Felix's as well.

We'd agreed to meet in the bar of a little restaurant called "Roma Gardens." It was a decent place in a respectable part of town, far enough from the big hotels so that most of the clientele were locals and not tourists. On the plus side Cindy liked the food and the prices were reasonable.

Cindy isn't what many people would consider a beauty, but that doesn't mean she isn't pleasant to look at. She knows how to dress and makes the most of what she's got. She smiled when she saw me. I smiled back. I knew her tastes and already had a drink waiting for her on the bar. She took the stool next to me and finished half the drink in one long swallow.

"Thanks, Frank. I needed that."

"Rough day?" I asked. I motioned to the barkeep for another round.

"Yeah. They've been running me ragged with information requests. I think something must have gone down at one of the casinos. Everyone seems tense and Security at all of the hotels and casinos are running background checks on all their employees."

That was news to me. I rarely deal directly with that level, but if something was up word hadn't trickled down to the street.

"Don't worry. I got what you asked me about." She reached into her purse, pulled out her handheld and slid it over to me.

I keyed the screen and brought up the file on Velma. She was a local. Her mother had been a dancer at one of the hotels who'd ended up a waitress when her legs had gone. Her father, and presumably she'd had one, was unknown. The mother was dead. She'd worked as a waitress at a number of different places once she'd left school at eighteen. Mostly places that served more alcohol than food. No criminal record. Five months ago she'd gotten a job at The Casino. That I found interesting. The place she'd been working just before that probably paid better and gave the chance for better tips.

Four months earlier she'd moved in with Felix Shotmeyer. A month later the two had signed a five year marriage contract. Now that was a surprise. Why sign a long term contract and then disappear three months later? Either she had been serious about the guy but then the bloom had fallen off the romance as they say—or she had never intended to stick it out and had been planning to take a powder from the beginning. But if the latter was the case, why?

Known associates included an ex-boyfriend name of Jason Rico (no details). The file didn't have much else in it. Height, weight, vaccination history, school grades, employment history. Nothing of note or interest. It's strange how little some people disturb the fabric of the universe.

Felix's file wasn't much more detail. He'd been born on some planet I'd never heard of. He actually been educated at some minor technical school on Crockett, which in itself was sort of impressive. He'd graduated thirteenth in his class (it didn't say how big the class was.) He'd been hired right out of school to work in the Entertainment Department of The Casino, which is where he had worked ever since. His position was listed as a programmer in 'games development,' he made a modest but decent salary, he rented an apartment whose rent he could easily afford, and his bank account was about what you'd expect. The five hundred he had paid me on account had made a sizable dent in his savings but hadn't cleaned it out. No previous serious relationships with women were listed.

"Thanks." I slid the handheld back towards Cindy.

"Done?" she asked. When I nodded she erased the files. Cindy is the careful type. It's one of the things I like about her.

"I've reserved a table upstairs," I said as I finished my drink.

Cindy smiled. "You do know how to treat a girl. Shall we?"

One of the nice things about Roma Gardens is that they have a rooftop dining area. Once the light pipes that run down the central axis of Star City go off for the evening you can see past them to the other side of the cylinder. The lights of all the people living on the other side of the city show as a twinkling arc overhead. It's actually quite attractive in its own way. Cindy seems to like it.

We had dinner and split a bottle of wine. It was a pleasant evening. The food was good, the wine was red. There was no more talk of business or personnel files. By mutual consent we went our separate ways afterwards. As we left the restaurant I slipped a twenty dollar Crockett piece into her hand. She gave me a little smile, a wave of her other hand, and walked off in the direction of her apartment.

I woke up the next morning alone in the bed in my apartment. If I had had any dreams I couldn't remember them. I fixed a full breakfast. I had a busy day ahead of me and I didn't want to be bothered by hunger pangs.

You'd think that finding someone in an area that was maybe ten blocks by fifteen wouldn't be that hard. You'd be wrong, at least if the area were New Minglewood. The people who live there don't particularly like questions, especially when they are coming from outsiders, which was what I was even if I only lived a few blocks from the edge. Half the people in New Minglewood are there because they have no place else to go. The other half are there because they don't have any place outside of New Minglewood where they can stay. It has its share of thieves, crooks and grifters, also drunks, addicts, and those too far gone on intoxicants legal or otherwise to make a living. The whores are considered to be gainfully employed and respected for it.

The police rarely go in without numbers, and to too many of its inhabitants a private dick looks much like a cop. I debated whether to pack or not. Carry something too obvious and it was an open invitation for a confrontation. Go in unarmed and you were taking the chance of running into something you couldn't talk your way out of. I settled on a small needle gun and slipped it into a shoulder holster that I could hide under my jacket. You could barely see it unless you knew what to look for, and those that did were usually smart enough to pretend they hadn't seen anything.

An outsider can't just walk into New Minglewood and start asking questions expecting to get answers. What he can expect is to end up injured or worse. I'd worked that side of the street enough to know that. Fortunately, I'd also managed to establish a few contacts along the way. Not friends, exactly, but people who would at least take the time to listen if I waved a finn in front of their noses.

Stubby Smith was one such contact. He ran a small shop that sold personal electronics and accessories like vid sticks and music cubes. Some of it was even legitimate merchandise. Right! Anyway, his shop was just inside the boundary, so he was first on my list.

He's called Stubby because one of his arms ends in a knob instead of a hand. There's something about his gene code that prevents regeneration. Besides that, he's short, bald, and has a mouth that would make a sailor blush. I've never actually met a sailor, so I'm not sure what that would take. I walked into the shop and pretended to be interested in some bootleg Jive Samba cubes.

He greeted me with, "So, what you doing in Minglewood, shamus? Slumming? Or have you finally gotten yourself kicked out of high society?" Shop keepers in New Minglewood are not known for their customer skills.

"Looking for some music. Got any Adderson?"

"You're dating yourself, Sladek. No one listens to that crap, anymore. Got some Niles Quintet that might be more your speed."

"Nah," I said. "She's ok, but not what I'm looking for."

"What are you looking for, then? Or are you just trying to ruin my business?"

"Actually, I'm looking for a woman."

"Aren't we all?" he answered.

"For a client. Name is Velma Schmitz. The woman, not the client."

"What do I look like? I sell tech and recordings, not info. Particularly to a two-bit Shamus."

"There's a double sawbuck in it for whoever gives me a good lead."

"Get outta my shop, Sladek. You're scaring the honest customers away." Like there'd be any honest customers in New Minglewood.

"You got my number," I said as I moved on. I wasn't discouraged. Stubby's response had been part theater and part protection. Snitches don't last long in New Minglewood. I knew he had my number if anything on Velma turned up.

The rest of the morning was pretty much a repeat performance with each of my contacts. At least the word was getting out. There wasn't much else I could do. As I came out of the last places on my contact list I noticed two young toughs loitering about in the street. I thought they might have been hanging about one of my earlier contacts. When I spotted them after my last stop I decided it was time to leave New Minglewood. They didn't have the look of professional muscle, but amateur thugs can kill you just as dead.

Besides, it was almost noon and despite breakfast I was feeling hungry. As I crossed the street that marks the unofficial boundary of New Minglewood, my two tails turned around and slinked back into the shadows. I took that as a sign that they were probably just some local talent who thought they had spotted an easy mark rather than parties with a professional interest in my comings and goings.

I walked to a diner that I frequent and ordered a fried meat sandwich and a cup of joe. The former had never seen the inside of any animal while the joe, that ubiquitous drink of Star City, looked and tasted almost completely unlike the beverage it is supposedly modeled on. The only similarity between the two is the presence of caffeine. I didn't care. I was hungry, and I'd been eating and drinking the stuff all my life. It's what I was used to.

While I was sitting at the counter, my communicator went off. It was Felix wanting to know if I'd found Velma yet. If there is one thing I hate, it's clients that try to micro-manage a case. I told him that I was working on it and would let him know when I found anything out. He didn't seem too happy with that. I didn't care and disconnected. The rest of my meal was finished in peace.

After lunch I decided on doing the gumshoe bit outside of New Minglewood. Felix had said that he thought that was where Velma and her boyfriend were holed up, but there were a lot of other places on Star City where the rent was cheap and no questions were asked.

Interesting term, gumshoe, one who's origin, like many other terms and phrases, is lost in antiquity. One learned drunk that I knew had mentioned that he thought it referred to a curious artificial substance called gum that people used to chew back on Earth. It seems that this stuff had neither taste nor nutritive value and after people had chewed it for a while they would discard it wherever convenient, such as the sidewalk. As it was still sticky, people who walked a lot like policemen and detectives would pick it up on the bottom of their shoes, hence the term "gumshoe." Personally, I thought his story was a bunch of hooey, but I've got no better explanation.

I spent the rest of the afternoon hoofing it from one cheap hotel to another flashing images of Velma and Jason Rico. Nowhere did they produce any flash of recognition even with the promise of a five spot. If I was being tailed, they were good at their jobs, because I didn't notice them.

I decided to knock off about 17:00. My feet were sore and my throat parched. My lunch was still producing an after taste in my mouth, so I decided to take care of both problems with a stop at the Blue Moon for a drink. It was dark and quiet and nobody disturbed me. As I seemed to be on a roll, I ordered another.

As the black limousine pulled up next to me in the street in front of the apartment building where I lived, it occurred to me that I needed to start varying my routine. I was becoming too predictable which one of these days was going to prove to be a liability. When two large gentlemen disembarked from the vehicle, I wondered if this was going to be that day.

I didn't recognize either of them, but then I try to avoid those circles which they might frequent. They were dressed in expensive dark suits. Their tailor must be very good, I thought, because I could barely see the bulges of the needle guns in the shoulder holsters that each wore.

"Mr. Sladek, Mr. Anthony would like to see you," the nearer of the two said. His voice was quiet and surprisingly deferential. The other didn't say a word, but had positioned himself to make my escape unlikely.

"That's nice," I answered. "He can have his secretary call and make an appointment."

"I believe the appointment is for now," the spokesman said, taking my upper arm in a firm but not yet painful grip that would have prevented me from reaching for a piece even if I had been packing at the time, which I wasn't.

"Fortunately, my schedule seems to be free. I assume transportation is provided?"

The other goon just smiled and opened the back door of the limousine. The spokesman motioned me into the seat and then sat next to me. His companion walked around to the other side of the vehicle, and I found myself sandwiched between the two of them. It had all been done very professionally, no rough stuff and nothing that would cause any onlooker to question. The spokesman rapped on the glass partition between us and the driver and the limousine sped off.

I hadn't questioned who Mr. Anthony might be. There was no need to ask which Mr. Anthony. There was only one, just like there was only one "Casino," the operation which he ran for some unnamed entity. Sure, there are other casinos and gambling houses on Star City, just as there might be other men whose last name was Anthony, but when the spokesman had said the name, I knew who and what he meant. The Casino was the largest gambling house on Star City positioned prominently on the fancy end of that rock. There might be other casinos that were more exclusive or ritzier, but none were bigger and more profitable.

Mr. Anthony was the man in charge of The Casino. If he had a first name, it was never mentioned in public. I certainly didn't know the sort of people who might be in a position to use it. Nor, to my knowledge was he referred to as just "Anthony" without the prefatory Mr. He was that sort of guy, and The Casino was that sort of place.

I wasn't surprised when after a short drive, can there be any other kind on a rock that is only a dozen kilometers long, we pulled into a private garage under The Casino. Out of the corner of my eye I caught sight of the door to the garage lowering ominously behind us.

My escorts directed me into a small elevator. There were only two buttons on the control panel. I assumed one was for the garage level and the other for our destination. The door of the elevator shut and there was a barely perceptible sensation of motion. The trip was brief, but I judged that we were on one of the top levels of The Casino.

The elevator door opened on a small, tastefully furnished reception area. The tasteful furnishings extended to a trim blonde sitting behind a spotless desk. She was dressed in the sort of expensive business attire one might expect in the upper offices of any major corporation. On her it looked good.

"Mr. Anthony is expecting you, Mr. Sladek," she said in alto voice as smooth and polished as the surface of her desk. Indicating a door behind her she continued, "Please go right in."

I shrugged and took the cue, my two companions following behind me. The door led to an office. It was smaller than I had expected, though anything but cramped. It was furnished comfortably; a desk with two chairs in front that looked like they actually would be comfortable to sit in, a sofa flanked by low tables along one wall, a nice but not extravagant entertainment unit across from it. One wall of the room was taken up by a window that provided a stunning view of the interior of Star City. Fortunately, the shabbier parts at the far end of the city were obscured by haze and the distance and so didn't mar the view.

I'd never met Mr. Anthony in person before, but I'd seen enough images to know that he was the man sitting behind the desk. He didn't rise to greet me or extend a hand to shake, but he did say, "I'm glad that you accepted my invitation, Mr. Sladek."

"Did I have any choice?"

"We all make many choices every day. Some good, some bad. Fortunately for you, you made a wise choice. Sit." The latter was more of a command than an invitation. I sat.

"Bruno and Guido, you can wait outside to drive Mr. Sladek back when we're done here." My two escorts left the room.

"Are those their real names?" I asked.

Mr. Anthony flashed a mirthless smile. "No, merely convenient labels. I could refer to them as Chauncey and Edgar, but you must admit, it wouldn't be as effective."

"No, I guess not," I responded. "Just why did you ask me here, Mr. Anthony?"

"Direct, I see. Good enough. I'll be direct, too. I understand that you are in the business of finding things, Mr. Sladek."

"That's as good a description as any."

"And that at the moment you are looking for one Velma Schmitz at the behest of Felix Shotmeyer."

"I don't usually discuss my client's business with other people, Mr. Anthony. Professional ethics, you understand. For instance, if you were to employ my services I wouldn't discuss them with others."

"Ethics are good, Mr. Sladek," he said, and then paused, "up to a point. It turns out that both of these people are employees of this establishment, so in a way it is my business."

"OK. If we grant for a moment, hypothetically that is, that I'm looking for this Velma for this Felix, why should it interest you?"

"Are you familiar with the game 'Comets and Meteors,' Mr. Sladek?"

"As a rule, I don't go in much for gambling. It's too much of a gamble."

"Very wise, Mr. Sladek. Fortunately, there are a lot of people that feel otherwise, or this wouldn't be a very lucrative business. 'Comets and Meteors' is a very simple game, actually. The player catches either a comet or a meteor. The bigger the comet, the more they win. The bigger the meteor, the more they lose. Play is quick, there is no real strategy, and normally the game makes a great deal of money for The Casino. Currently there are nearly a thousand of the games in operation in house."

"I take it that this hasn't been the case lately?" I observed.

"Very astute of you, Mr. Sladek. Theoretically, the odds are set slightly in the houses favor. Quite honestly, I might add, and no different than any other game. The outcome is determined by a random number generator in the computer and the house wins about one percent more than it loses. Except that recently it hasn't. It's been more like a half a percent."

"And you think someone has rigged the games against the house?"

"I know it. But only for certain players. That's why it took us so long to spot that something was wrong. For most players, the odds are what they should be. But certain players always walk away winners. Oh, they win some games and lose others, but over a session, they always win. Maybe not much, a few hundred credits, not enough to attract attention, but they win."

"Are you sure it isn't just a run of luck?" I said, not terribly sympathetically, I admit.

"No, Mr. Sladek. It is not a run of luck. We did some investigating. The winners always have their winnings deposited in accounts with a certain credit operation, an operation that makes high interest loans to individuals with poor credit. The money goes into their accounts and gets withdrawn to pay off their debts. I think the rate is for every two credits they win one credit of their loan is eliminated."

"Pretty raw deal for them," I commented.

"Not if they know they are going to win. It's a great way to siphon money from The Casino into someone else's pocket without being detected."

"Just as a point of reference, how much money are we talking about?"

"Roughly three million credits," Mr. Anthony announced flatly. That was a lot of dough, I thought, nearly two million and change in Crockett dollars.

"So why don't you just stop offering the games, at least until you find out how it's being done?"

"It appears you don't understand the economics of running a gambling house. You don't make your money in the high stakes games, that's just window dressing. The bread and butter is in the mass games, those with low stakes but plenty of plays. If we stopped 'Comets and Meteors' it would take a big chunk out of our bottom line. Our investors wouldn't be happy."

"I can see that," I said. "This is all very interesting, Mr. Anthony, but I guess I don't see what this has to do with me or Felix Shotmeyer or Velma Schmitz for that matter."

"We were able to trace where the money was going, Mr. Sladek. It was funneled into the account of a Jason Rico. Now Jason Rico up until about four months ago was a friend of Velma Schmitz, the wife of your client."

"Let me guess, Felix Shotmeyer has something to do with the programming of the 'Comets' game."

"Exactly."

"So why don't you deal with it?"

"We know where Felix is, but it would appear he doesn't have the money. He wouldn't have hired you to find Velma, if he did. Rico probably has it, but we don't know where Rico is."

"And you want me to do what?"

"You're looking for Velma. Velma is probably with Rico. Rico has the money. I want you to find Rico and the money. When you do, tell me. I'll take care of the rest. You will be suitably rewarded."

I had a pretty good idea of what Mr. Anthony meant when he said he'd 'take care of the rest,' and I didn't particularly like the idea of fingering someone, even if they were a two bit grifter and a two-timing broad.

"I'm sorry to disappoint you, Mr. Anthony, but I make it a practice to only take on one client at a time. Professional ethics, you know."

"That's unfortunate, Mr. Sladek. The Casino will get its money back, and we will deal with the people who stole from us. Remember that if you should recover the money and find yourself tempted."

"I'm not crazy. I was hired to find Velma Schmitz. That's what I'm going to do. If I run across your money, I'll let you know."

"Be sure you do, Mr. Sladek. Be sure you do. I think our little meeting is done now.   Bruno will see you back to your apartment."

The door to the office opened and Bruno appeared in it. It turns out Bruno was the one who had done all the talking earlier. He didn't do any now. I got up and followed him out.

On the ride back I had time for thinking. It seemed pretty clear to me. Rico and Velma had cooked up this scheme between them. Velma would get in tight with Felix which couldn't have been hard for a broad like Velma. She'd talk him into rigging the game. Rico would be brought in to funnel the winnings out of the casino and into some more transportable form of wealth like a credit stick. By doing it a few hundred credits at a time, they would avoid attention. When the time came to close up shop, Velma disappears with Rico into New Minglewood along with the money. They'd hide out there until they could arrange to get off Star City in a space ship. And poor Felix would be left holding the bag when the casino caught on.

Bruno and Guido dropped me off in front of my apartment building right where they had picked me up. It was almost like my visit to Mr. Anthony had never happened, except that it was late enough that the glow tubes that run the length of the spar that runs down the axis of Star City had been turned off to create "night," just like they do every day. The smart guys will tell you that the daily cycle of fourteen hours of light and ten hours of dark are a physiological necessity dating back to our origins on Earth, and without which we wouldn't be able to sleep, procreate, or digest our food. Me, I think it's just a way for the people who run Star City to cheap out on energy consumption.

I thought about a nightcap at the Blue Moon, but I was tired and my feet were sore. Besides, I had a bottle in the apartment. The elevator wasn't working, and I had to walk up the three flights of stairs to the fourth floor where I had my apartment. I swiped my key in the lock and opened the door. There was a light on in the living room. It hadn't been on when I left.

I keep a loaded needler in the drawer of a table next to the front door. As silently as I could I opened the draw, grabbed it and quietly tip toed down the hallway. I needn't have bothered. Sitting in my favorite chair, highlighted by the glow of a reading lamp, was my favorite cop, Latimer. He had made himself at home. A glass with ice cubes and an inch of brown was in his hand. A bottle of my best local booze was on the table next to the chair. Latimer's hat was next to it.

I put the gun in my pocket. "What the hell, Latimer?"

"I heard your apartment might be available," Latimer answered. "I thought I'd check it out. Nice place." Latimer is a detective with the Star City police. He's more honest than most. We're not friends, but we aren't enemies either. At least he hadn't brought Rossetti with him. Rossetti was his partner. We don't get along.

"You heard wrong." It was a lame thing to say, but I was tired.

"It's just that people who get picked up by a couple of Mr. Anthony's goons sometimes don't come back. What gives, Sladek?"

"It was business. Mr. Anthony enquired about hiring me to find something that went missing. I declined because I had another client. The twins drove me home."

"There's more to it than that, Sladek. Mr. Anthony wouldn't be involved unless it was something important. And if he's interested, I'm interested."

"There is such a thing as client confidentiality, Latimer."

"And there's such a thing as an interrogation room at headquarters. I came here as a friendly gesture, Sladek. I figured we could do this on the QT. I'd hate to think I was wrong and Rossetti was right."

"Rossetti's never right. He hasn't got the brains," I commented. Like I said, Rossetti and I don't get along.

"That's my partner you're talking about," Latimer said, taking a sip of his drink. His opinion of Rossetti isn't much better than mine. "Look, I can sit here all night drinking up your booze or you can clue me in on what's up. If it's none of my business, than it never needs to leave this room."

I looked at Latimer sitting in my chair, my booze swirling in my glass. Latimer could be tenacious when he needed to be, and it wasn't like I had any way to chuck him out.

"Look, it's like this. Some grifter figured out a way to bilk the Casino out of some big money a few hundred at a time. There's a dame involved. She happens to be the wife of my client. He wants to find her. Mr. Anthony wants his money back. The grifter is probably toast if Mr. Anthony finds him. Maybe the dame and my client, too, for that matter. I didn't feel like being the fingerman for a hit, so I declined Mr. Anthony's offer, but I said I'd return his money if I found it."

"You do seem to have managed to get yourself into a pickle, Sladek," Latimer said when I'd finished explaining.

"What you going do?" I said with a shrug.

"Any chance you could let me know where these people are before Mr. Anthony gets to them?"

"I don't know where they are. I'm still looking. I just promised to find the dame."

"Any chance you could give me their names?"

"The grifter is called Jason Rico. He was involved in high interest loans."

"And the dame?"

"I think I'll keep that confidential for now. Ethics, you know."

"Have it your own way, Sladek," Latimer said as he dropped his hat on his head. "Thanks for the booze." He emptied his glass and stood up. "I'll be seeing you."

"I suspect so," I answered with resignation. It was getting late and I was too tired for anything more witty.

Latimer let himself out. I went to bed.

Nothing much happened the following day except for several more calls from Felix Shotmeyer demanding to know if I had found his Velma yet. He seemed to be growing more anxious by the day. It made me wonder whether he suspected that Mr.

Anthony was on to him. From my perspective, it was getting to be annoying.

The next morning there was a text message on my communicator. It read, "I have the Adderson recording you were looking for. Please stop by to pick it up." It was unsigned, but from the contents I knew it was Stubby Smith letting me know he had some information for me. I guess if you live in New Minglewood you can never be too careful. I checked my needler and slipped it back into its holster.

I was cautious on my way to his shop, but I didn't see any sign of my shadows from the last visit. Stubby didn't seem that glad to see me, but then he treats all his customers that way. "I got that Adderson you were asking about, though what you want with it I don't know." He seemed nervous and kept glancing outside. I didn't see anyone, but if they were good, I might not.

He slipped a music cube into a bag along with a receipt. Stubby never gives receipts. Or bags for that matter. "That'll be twenty five dollars Crockett."

I'd promised him twenty. I guess he figured the extra finn was for the cube. I slipped him the bills and left, glancing up and down the street. Nothing. When I was around the corner I opened the bag. Written on the back of the receipt was an address on L Street and the notation "third floor, room in the back." Out of curiosity I looked at the label on the music cube. It actually was an Adderson recording, one I didn't have. Will wonders never cease?

L Street was a couple of blocks over. The way things were playing out, I thought I'd check it out before letting Felix know. The address proved to be a building with single rooms to rent. No cooking facilities and a shared bath for each floor. Actually for New Minglewood it was fairly posh. There was no reception desk, just a sign saying "manager" on one of the doors off the first floor landing. I didn't feel the need to announce my presence.

A narrow staircase led up along one side of the hall. I started up it trying to be as quiet as possible. The second floor was laid out much like the first with the exception that a front facing room replaced the entry. There was a narrow hallway lit by two dim ceiling globes with another set of stairs leading up to the next floor. The other side of the hallway had four doors. That, plus the front and back rooms gave six rooms to a floor. A door labeled "bathroom" was located on the same side as the staircase towards the back of the hall.

So far, I'd aroused no sign of life. There were no sounds coming from any of the rooms. The worn carpet did little to muffle the sounds of my footsteps, but no curious heads popped out of any of the doors. In New Minglewood, people learn to mind their own business.

I took the steps to the third floor. As I expected, the layout matched the one below. I poked my head in the staircase leading to the next floor, but there was no one there.

Something about the situation caused me to reach inside my jacket for the gun nestled there as I moved towards the door to the room in the back. Placing my hand on the door handle I gave it a gentle pressure. I was a little surprised when it turned and the door swung open. I hadn't been ready for that.

The room was about what you'd expect. There was a small window giving out onto the alley in back. The walls were some unidentifiable shade of brownish-gray. The furniture consisted of a broken down bed, a small table and a chair. Someone was sitting in the chair facing the window. A man. He didn't move as I entered and shut the door behind me.

The reason was clear as I moved around him. There was a neat, barely visible hole burned into his forehead just above the bridge of his nose. It looked like the kind of hole made by a low power laser pistol, the kind some women carry in their purse. Also some assassins. There was enough light coming in through the alley window for me to recognize the corpse in the chair. It was Jason Rico. He had a look of surprise on his face.

I gave the room a search. It didn't take long, as there weren't many places to hide things. There was a small bag stuffed under the bed, but all it contained was a couple of changes of clothes, all male, and all about the right size for Rico. There weren't any women's things, nothing to indicate that Velma Schmitz had ever occupied the room except a smear of lipstick on one of the two glasses on the table. I checked the corpse, too. The only thing I found was the room key and a wallet with about twenty credits and five dollars Crockett. No sign of a credit stick.

There didn't seem to be any point in hanging around. I let myself out. As an afterthought, I locked the door with the room key and tossed it into the waste-basket in the bathroom next door. I didn't even think of calling Latimer. What was the point. It was just another corpse in New Minglewood. Somebody would be sure to find it in a few days, if only from the stench.

I thought about stopping for a drink at the Blue Moon, but it was still early in the day. Instead, I went up to my apartment, put a couple of ice cubes in a glass, poured a couple of centimeters of brown in after them, and dropped the music cube Stubby had sold me into the player in the living room.

As the slow, sensual sounds washed over the room I tried to figure out where things were at. It didn't look encouraging. My one clue to locating Velma would appear to be a dead end, no pun intended.

Rico was dead and the credit stick was missing. The question was who had killed him? Had Bruno and Guido caught up with him? It almost seemed too neat a job. You'd expect a little more violence, if only to leave a message for the next guy who thought to pull one on Mr. Anthony. And if it had been them, where was Velma? Why leave her alive?

That led to the next possibility, Velma herself. Rico had been shot at close range. There had been only a few steps between the chair and the rear window. There'd been no sign of a struggle. Rico had clearly known the person who shot him. It made sense. A double cross. In New Minglewood. What would be more natural? But that didn't seem quite right, either.

Who did that leave? Felix? Maybe. It's always hard to read guys like that. They seem like they wouldn't hurt a fly, but inside there's a lot of repressed anger bottled up. Was it a lover's triangle? Or had Felix tracked down the pair and killed them for cheating him? But then, where was Velma? Or had he and

Velma planned to cut Rico out from the beginning, and were now trying to make their escape with the casino's money?

Or was there an outside party? Someone who had found out about the scam and knocked off Rico just for the credit stick? A credit stick like that was negotiable anywhere in human space and almost impossible to trace once you got it off Star City. Two million dollars Crockett was a mighty tempting target.

But if that was the case, it came back to the same question, where was Velma? Why hadn't her corpse been in the room with Rico? Had it been luck? Had she been out getting food or a bottle only to come back to find Rico dead and the money gone? Had she split in panic when she discovered her partner dead? Or had she fingered him to this outside party for a cut of the take?

I realized that my drink was empty. The recording had played through and I hadn't heard a note. So where did that leave me? I hadn't a clue. On Star City, any of the scenarios were possible. If we had one, the double-cross would be the national sport.

I was pondering restarting the Adderson when my communicator buzzed. It was Felix. I answered the call.

"What progress have you made, Mr. Sladek?" he asked. He didn't seem as anxious as he had been.

"I found Rico. He's dead."

"Oh," his voice was flat, emotionless. "What happened?"

"He was holed up in a flop in New Minglewood. Somebody put a laser beam through his brain. You wouldn't know anything about that, would you?"

"No. Why should I?"

"No reason. It's just that I don't know who killed him. He'd been dead some time when I got there."

"Did you find anything on him?"

"Like what?" I asked. Felix wasn't supposed to know that I knew about Mr. Anthony's money.

"I don't know. Like money."

"I searched the room. All he had on him was about twenty-five credits in cash."

"I see."

"Do you want me to keep looking?" I asked.

"Looking?" he replied sounding puzzled.

"For Velma. Do you want me to keep looking for Velma?"

"Yes, please." Then he disconnected.

At the time I just thought the guy might have been in shock because things weren't going as he expected. Later, when I replayed the conversation in my head, there was something I should have noticed. It would have saved me a lot of grief. Not once during the call had he asked about Velma.

The buzz of my communicator woke me. It interrupted a dream. As I moved to full consciousness the only thing I could remember of the dream was a chorus line of dancers, each one of which had had a little red dot on their forehead. All of the dancers looked like Velma.

The ID of the caller had been blocked.

"Sladek, here," I answered groggily.

"Mr. Sladek, I need your help." It was a woman's voice. One I didn't recognize.

"Who is this?"

"Velma. Velma, Schmitz." Her voice quavered.

"What's seems to be the problem, Ms. Schmitz?" I asked. I didn't want to let on any more than I had to.

"Some men are after me."

"Who are they?"

"I don't know. All I know is that they've already killed someone I was with."

"How did you get my name, Ms. Schmitz?"

"Felix mentioned it. Felix Shotmeyer."

"And when did you talk to him?"

"Tonight. Earlier."

"Where are you now, Ms. Schmitz?" She gave an address in New Minglewood.

"I can be there in half an hour. Will you be ok until then?"

"Yes. I think so." She disconnected.

I know. You think only an idiot would respond to a call like that. I should have known better. Well I did know better, but she had really sounded scared. I'm a sucker for a damsel in distress.

I dressed, including the shoulder holster with the needle gun. As an afterthought, I slipped a 25 kilojoule laser pistol in my jacket pocket.

In some ways, New Minglewood is safer late at night. After midnight, you can pretty much count on the fact that anyone moving about is up to no good and act accordingly. There's not a lot of traffic on the streets at that hour.

I found the address, a five story apartment building. It had been built at a time when New Minglewood still had pretentions of respectability. Now it was just run down. There was no lock or security system on the front door, so I walked right in. The elevator looked like it had stopped working sometime in the previous century, so I took the stairs. The apartment number Velma had given me was on the top floor. Lighting was pretty minimal, but on the fourth floor it had ceased to function all together. There was just enough light coming from the floor above for me to make my way up the stairs.

That should have been a clue. As I started up the steps there was a noise behind me. I felt an explosion in my head and then the lights went out as I sank into unconsciousness.

I came to slowly, still a little groggy, my vision blurred. I recognized the symptoms as the after effects of a neural sap. I had been hit been hit by one once before. The experience hadn't been pleasant.

I found that I couldn't move my arms or legs. At first I thought it was the sap, but then I realized I was sitting in a chair, with my limbs taped to the arms and legs. I seemed to be in a small room, probably the one I had been lured to.

As my vision cleared, I took in my surroundings. About what you'd expect, a small, dingy space about three meters by five, sparsely furnished with a few worn out chairs, a table and a bed against one wall. Velma Schmitz was sitting on the bed. She looked scared.

When enough motor control had returned I swiveled my head to the left. There was a man sitting in another chair. He was holding a gun. It looked like my gun, the little laser pistol. The man holding the gun was Felix Shotmeyer. Somehow he didn't seem to be the same small nervous little figure that I had first met in the Blue Moon. This Felix was self assured, in control of things. Maybe it was the laser. Things were getting interesting, I thought to myself. The memory of having heard that was a curse flickered through the shadows of my mind.

"So you've decided to join us, Mr. Sladek," commented Felix. He didn't sound either deferential or concerned.

"What gives, Felix?" I replied. Not the wittiest comment, I admit, but the cobwebs were still impairing my head.

"Oh, I just needed you for a bit of window dressing," Felix answered.

"You'll have to excuse me, Felix, but I don't understand. My thinking seems to be a little muddled right now. Someone seems to have hit me with a neural sap."

"Very amusing, Sladek. No wonder you are so popular with your clients. Too bad your career is going to come to such a sudden end."

"I still don't understand. What's the point? You've got Velma. I presume you've got the credit stick. Why kill me?"

"Don't you get it, Sladek? The credit stick isn't going to do me any good on Star City. The first time I try to use it, I'm a dead man. Besides, it's only a matter of days before the Casino's goons track me down. It only took you a couple to track down poor Rico."

"I take it you were the one who killed Rico?"

"I would have thought that was obvious."

"So where do I come in? I still don't figure that."

"Oh, it's simple enough. I've got to get off this forsaken rock. To do that, I need a diversion. Rico is already dead. You're probably on the list of suspects. You might easily have worked a double-cross with Velma, here, to kill Rico and grab the credit stick. And what works once, eh? I make it look like you killed Velma and disappeared with the money. They keep themselves busy chasing you while I slip away."

"What makes you think that they'll stop looking for you?"

"Because I'll provide them with a corpse. Suitably attired and disfigured of course. Dead bodies are easy enough to come by in New Minglewood. It doesn't have to be perfect, just create enough confusion so that no one is sure what's going on."

"Clever. It might work, Felix. But it still doesn't get you off Star City. With three million at stake, they'll be watching every passenger leaving this place."

"Oh, I've had that planned from the beginning. I won't be going out as a passenger. I've had a specially equipped shipping container sitting in a warehouse for the last nine months. All the comforts of home, air supply, food and water, entertainment cubes. A little bit cramped, maybe, but it only takes a few days to reach New Shetland. Once there—well three million will take you a long way. Far enough to be beyond the reach of the Casino. Particularly if they're not looking for me."

"I got to hand it to you, Felix. You seem to have thought of everything. Kind of hard on Velma, though, isn't it?"

"I'm sure I'll manage to find someone else."

"But Felix," Velma protested, "I thought you loved me. You said we were going away together. That's why I double-crossed Jason."

"Velma, how dumb can you be? Did you really think I'd want to drag some bleached bimbo across the galaxy?"

"I should have trusted Rico. He wanted to kill you as soon as we got the credit stick. He had it all planned out from the beginning."

"Is that what you really think, Velma? That any of this was Rico's or your idea?"

"What do you mean, Felix?"

"I'd had this planned for a year. I was only waiting until some dupes stupid enough to be sucked in came along. I didn't have long to wait, did I?"

I was beginning to understand what Felix was talking about. It was surprising that it had taken me so long to get the drift. Blame the neural sap. The question was what to do about it. My options appeared limited. The one thing I knew was that the longer I kept Felix talking, the longer I'd stay alive.

"Don't you get it, Velma? Our friend Felix here was playing you for suckers from the beginning. Isn't that right, Felix? You had this great idea to cook one of the casino games a few credits at a time so no one would ever notice. The only thing is, you couldn't work it alone. You needed someone to collect the winnings in such a way that you wouldn't be implicated. That's where Rico came in. He had access to a loan business with a lot of clients on the hook. They were only too eager to help out by playing the rigged game and collecting the winnings for you in exchange for cancelling their debt. Rico would advance them the money to play, give them the code, then when they won a hundred or so, they'd deposit the winnings with Rico, who would knock the advance and their cut off their debt and funnel the balance into his own private account. Who would notice a hundred credits at a time? A perfect scheme. And Velma, here, was just the bait to lure Rico in, wasn't she, Felix?"

"Bravo, Sladek. You do understand. Rico had Velma get a job at the Casino with some vague plan to work a con for a few hundred credits. I spotted them right from the beginning. I let some things slip one night while I was drinking with Rico to plant the idea in his head, and then left it to them to come up with a scheme to 'corrupt' me. I knew I had them hooked when Velma started making passes at me."

"You dirty two-timing rat," Velma exclaimed. "You played us for suckers. And all this time poor Rico thought he was being so smart."

"That two-bit grifter? He couldn't come up with an original idea to save his life. And he didn't, did he? But admit it, Velma, you were ready enough to cash him in when I made the offer, weren't you?"

"Look, Felix. We can still go away together. I'm sure there's room in that shipping container for two, isn't there?"

"A week in a box with just the two of us? Do you think I'm crazy, Velma?"

"You married me, didn't you?" Velma asked angrily. I'd noticed that she'd lost some of the frightened expression.

"That was all just part of the plan, honey," Felix said sarcastically. "It was just to make me look like a poor schlub that could be taken in by a couple of petty schemers like you."

"You're a bastard, Felix," Velma said.

"What did you expect? Well, this has gone on long enough," Felix said. "I've got a freighter to catch. Which one of you should I finish off first, Sladek? You or the lovely Velma? I think we both vote for Velma."

I strained at the restraints, but there was no point. I wasn't going to break free. Instinctively Velma retreated to the corner of the bed. It didn't do her any good. I'll say this for Felix, he was a good shot. The laser beam hit her right in the middle of the forehead.

The weapon swung towards me, the barrel pointing at my, as Felix waited the fifteen seconds for the weapon to recharge. That's the problem with small lasers. It was just long enough. The door burst open with a crash. It was Bruno and Guido. Both had weapons drawn, and theirs were fully charged. Felix didn't have a chance.

"A fine mess you've gotten yourself in, Sladek," Bruno said cheerfully.

"Yeah. It could be better. Don't suppose you could cut me loose, could you?"

"Mr. Anthony didn't give us any orders about that, Sladek."

"Are you just going to leave me here?"

"That depends."

"On what?" I asked.

"Well, first off, where's the money?"

"I think Shotmeyer has it on him." Guido rummaged through his pockets coming up with the credit stick. That seemed to make his day. Funny how a little dongle the size of your pinky finger could cause so much trouble. He also fished out another laser pistol, probably the one that Felix had used to shoot Rico.

"Thanks, Sladek."

"So what's next?"

"You got a choice. Right now you're the only witness to this little tableau. For obvious reasons Mr. Anthony would prefer that it didn't become known that The Casino could be hit up by a bunch of cheap hustlers. He also would prefer that it not become known that Felix here was terminated. It would be bad for the image of The Casino."

"So what are you suggesting?"

"The way I see it, it's like this. You were hired by Felix to find his wife, Velma. She'd run away with her old boyfriend, Rico. Felix found them and killed Rico. You tracked them down, but Felix got the drop on you. Felix and Velma got into an argument over Rico, and they kill each other. You're the witness."

"Sounds reasonable," I agreed. "After all, that's almost what happened."

"I'm glad we understand each other, Sladek. I've got nothing against you personally."

"Glad to hear that, Bruno. So how about you cut me loose?"

"Sorry, Sladek. Can't do that. After all, we were never here. But don't worry. Someone will come to rescue you. Eventually."

Bruno nodded to Guido. The latter wrapped the laser pistol he had fished off of Felix in Velma's hand. He carefully repositioned the body so it almost looked like she could have shot Felix. Very artistic. Professional. The two goons left the room.

I don't know how much time I spent in that shabby little room staring at a pair of corpses. I couldn't check my communicator for the time. It seemed like hours, but it might have only been fifteen minutes. Eventually I heard the clump of flat feet coming up the stairs. There must have been a half-dozen of them.

From where I sat pinned to the chair, I couldn't see the door, but I recognized the voice. It was Latimer.

"Why is it, Sladek, that every time I find you, you're surrounded by dead bodies?"

"I guess I just have a talent."

"Yeah. Any of this your work?"

"Does it look like I was any position to shoot anyone?"

"Guess not," Latimer said. "So what happened?"

"The guy there, his name is Felix Shotmeyer. He hired me to find his wife, the dame on the bed. Her name is Velma. She was shacked up with a guy named Jason Rico. He's dead in a room a few streets over. Felix found them and killed him. I guess Velma and Felix had some marital difficulties that ended badly. They shot each other."

"While you were watching?"

"Yeah. These two. Not Rico. I didn't see that. But I did see the body."

"You know your story is horseshit, Sladek?"

"Yeah, but it's the only one I've got."

"Good thing for you the powers that be want this little matter handled discretely," Latimer said with a shrug. "You'll have to come down to the station and give a statement—"

"Just cut me loose, Latimer."

I gave my statement at the station. Latimer was almost genial. He even offered me a cup of joe. We both knew that the statement was mostly a lie. We both knew that the other knew that it was a lie. I guess we both knew why we weren't about to make waves, too.

As I was signing the printout I asked, "Where's your pal, Rossetti?"

"Rossetti's got a big mouth. He's on other duty." Sometimes I get the feeling Latimer doesn't like his partner any better than I do.

"I was told to handle this whole business discretely. You're not going to cause trouble, Sladek, are you?"

"Me? Why. I was hired to find a dame. I found her. After that, it's not my affair."

"Good. I'm glad that's understood. I was told to tell you there'd be a little something in it for you." Latimer said the last with a touch of distaste. For a Star City cop he's honest, but he's also a realist.

"Look, don't get the wrong idea. I'm not on the take, I'm not crooked, and there are limits to what I'll do. But sometimes it's just better if certain things are handled with a minimum of fuss. The way I figure, Star City ain't any the worse off for the absence of these three grifters, anyway. If certain people want to keep the details quiet, it really doesn't matter, does it?"

"We all got to do what we got to do," I answered.

"Go home, Sladek."

I went home, too, after a stop at the Blue Moon and a couple of shots of brown.

The story, when it came out, was of a lover's triangle that went bad. The Casino was never mentioned in the few brief media pieces. As promised, ten thousand credits appeared in my account a few days later. Not much of a finder's fee for three million, but I'm not complaining. After all, the three million never existed. It said so on the news.

I started out this tale saying that there's nothing new under the sun. I don't know if Rico loved Velma, or if Felix loved Velma, or if Velma loved either of them. In the end, I don't really care one way or the other. It would have ended up the same no matter what. There will always be Ricos and Velmas and Felixes who think they can beat the system and who die trying. And there will always be guys like Latimer and me to sweep the pieces under the rug so the dirt doesn't get on the thousand credit suits of people like Mr. Anthony. It's a living, I guess.

THE
SECOND SHOT

THE SECOND SHOT

Your average citizen has some pretty strange ideas about lethal weapons. Most of that comes from the fact that they get most of those ideas from watching videos or reading books. Typically, in those forms of fiction, the hero presses the trigger and a bad guy goes down. He keeps pressing the trigger as fast as he can until he runs out of bad guys. But that's not how it works in real life.

Laser pistols are actually pretty simple in operation. There's a capacitor bank that's charged from a power pack. When the trigger is pressed, the capacitor discharges and there's a brief flash of intense light, whose duration is measured in milliseconds. What tends to get ignored is the length of time it takes to charge up the capacitor. That depends on the size of the power pack, which makes all the difference in the world.

Your typical laser pistol, the kind that real world bad guys carry around, can take ten to fifteen seconds to recharge the capacitor. One of those little laser pistols, the 15 k Joule ones that ladies buy to stick in their handbags, can take up to thirty seconds to recharge and the power pack is only good for maybe six shots before it needs to be recharged. This tends to get ignored in works of fiction.

So you're asking yourself, "What about getting a bigger power pack?" And of course, that's one possibility. The only problem is that that adds weight to the gun. The laser pistols favored by law enforcement officers tend to have bigger power packs. They also are bulky and the power packs adds about half a kilo to the mass. That's why you should never arm wrestle a cop with his gun hand. Some military small arms even use a belt mounted pack connected to the pistol by a cable. That cuts the recharge time to less than a second and you can fire the weapon all day without recharging the power pack. It's not very discrete or comfortable, though.

So why use a laser at all? Because they're simple, they're easy to use, and they have a range that is about as far as you can see. You point the weapon in the direction you want and press the button. Unless you're shooting in close proximity to a black hole or a neutron star the beam goes in a straight line, and let's face it, if you are that close to a black hole you've got other problems. Some models even have a neat aiming device that shines a low power laser beam when you press the trigger halfway. You line it up with what you want to hit and press the trigger all the way home. What could be simpler?

Another odd notion is about power. Laser pistols come in all sizes and power ranges from a 5 k Joule flea-flicker to a 75 k Joule Kunstler. Now it's true that a higher power laser will make a bigger hole, but even a ladies' gun will kill you dead if it hits a vital organ or a blood vessel. And higher power requires a bigger power pack and a longer recharge time. That's why most lasers you meet on the street are only between 25 and 50 k Joules. That's partly because those are the sizes that are easy to conceal, but also because they recharge faster. It all comes back to that— how fast can I fire the second shot?

So, what about alternatives? Well, blasters and disrupters are mostly prohibited for civilian use on the civilized worlds. They tend to be dangerous and indiscriminate. They also are bulky and take a lot of power. Almost all of them have longer recycle times between shots than lasers.

So what about needle guns? Needle guns have a lot going for them. They are small and quiet. They fire a tiny sliver of metal at very high speeds using an electro-magnetic coil. Needles can be fired as quickly as the user can press the trigger. Some models can even be set to fire two or even three needles in quick succession for one pull. Most of them have a clip that carry fifty or so of the needles and the clips can be changed out in a matter of seconds. The needle flies straight until it enters flesh. Then it starts to tumble and tear things up.

So what's the down side? First, they have limited range. The needle starts to lose velocity after ten meters or so. After twenty, they've slowed to the point where they don't do much damage. Second, it takes a real expert to use one effectively. Hit a target in a vital spot like the heart or an eye socket and they're dead almost immediately. Hit somebody in the shoulder area at ten meters and you've got someone who's just real angry. Even with a good shot to the body you can be unlucky enough to hit the sternum which will stop a needle at five meters. All this is not to say that needlers don't have their fans, like assassins. They love needlers because they're so quiet. They can slip away before any bystanders even know someone has been killed. But needle guns are definitely not for amateurs.

But didn't they used to have chemically powered weapons back in the old days? What about them? Well, first you got to find one and then you've got to find the ammunition to go with it. They do have lots of stopping power if you can hit what you're aiming at. The rate of fire is as good as a needle gun, but the magazine size is small, six to ten shots in something you can slip into your pocket. They make a hell of a noise, too. I know that from experience.

So your average street tough tends to favor laser pistols despite the recharge time issue. That's what it comes down to, the time between your first and second shot, and that's the point of this story.

The story starts at the Blue Moon, the bar across the street from my apartment. It was 1100 and I was nursing a tumbler of brown on the rocks. I don't normally drink that early, but the night before I'd met someone from my misspent youth. One thing led to another and too many brown and sodas and shots of clear had left me with a pounding headache which I was trying to mute with a touch of the dog of the hare that bit me.

I've never really understood that old saying. I know that a hare was some kind of animal that lived on old Terra, but I'd always heard that it was some sort of herbivore. I've never read that they kept dogs, either.

Anyway, I was nursing my drink. The place was dim and empty at that hour which is the way I like it. The only other person in the joint was the barkeep and he had had the decency to stand at the other end of the bar reading the racing form.

The pain behind my eyes was starting to subside when my comm announced an incoming call. I checked the ID and it read Sgt. Latimer. That was never a good sign.

"Sladek here. What can I do for you, Latimer?"

"You can get your butt over here right away. That's what you can do," the voice on the comm crackled.

"Where's here? And what's this about?"

"Just get here. Now," Latimer answered in a tone that said he meant business. He rattled off an address just to the south of New Minglewood and broke the connection.

Latimer is a detective on Star City's serious crime squad. As cops go he is reasonably honest. Somehow our paths keep crossing, but so far we've never butted heads, though there has been a lot of posturing. There wasn't any point in ignoring him. If he really wanted me, he could have me picked up within an hour. The fact that he had called first meant that he was giving me a chance to cooperate.

The address he gave me was close enough to walk to. I slammed what was left of my drink and headed out. As I walked, skirting the boundaries of New Minglewood, I tried to think which of my current activities could have drawn Latimer's interest, but all I did was draw a blank. Things had been slow for a bit and there was nothing that I was involved in that should have raised a flag.

The place, when I arrived, proved to be a cheap apartment building, five floors of small rooms with bath alcoves and no cooking arrangements, the sort of place catering to two-bit grifters who still had enough coin to rise above a flop in New Minglewood, though there was a good chance that that would be the ultimate destination of most of the residents. Those that didn't end up as corpses.

That fate seemed to have met one of the inhabitants, though. There were a couple of prowl cars parked out front blocking the street as well as the meat wagon. There was a uniform manning the door. He must have recognized me because all he did was hook his thumb towards the inside and let me pass. Rossetti, Latimer's partner, was on the next floor with another uniform questioning a broad with a cheap haircut and a bad dye job in her late forties. She was standing in the doorway dressed in a dirty robe with a joy stick parked in the corner of her mouth. Every once in awhile she'd glance nervously up the stairs.

"Rossetti. What's up?"

"Latimer's waiting. Top floor," he answered with a smirk. Rossetti and I don't get along.

Did I mention that the place didn't have a working elevator? Mankind can build ships that travel between the stars, but to get to the top floor I had to walk up five flights of rickety stairs.

I didn't need to ask which apartment. Latimer was standing in the doorway jawing with someone from the medical examiner's office. He told me to park it in the corridor while he finished with the M.E. From what I could overhear there was someone seriously dead inside.

Latimer finished his conversation and turned to me. "Take a look at the guy inside."

I stepped past him into the room. It was about three meters by four, furnished with a bed along one side and a table with two chairs. A shallow closet, built in set of drawers, a sink and a toilet lined the other side. In the middle of the floor was the lodger. Whoever he was, I didn't know him from Adam.

It was easy enough to see what had killed him. There was a hole burned into the center of his forehead. A laser pistol, probably at close range. High energy, 50, maybe even a 75 kilojoule. He was an ordinary looking guy, thinning hair, a little flabby with a bit of a paunch. There was no sign that the guy lying on the floor had been armed. He was dressed only in his shorts and a grimy undershirt. There was no place to hide a weapon.

"Who is he?" Latimer asked in a tone that said he expected answers.

"Search me. I've never seen him before in my life."

"Maybe you can explain, then, what your name was doing in the address list of his communicator? It was the only name on the list."

"I don't know, Latimer. My name floats around. I'm in business. It pays to advertise." Actually it doesn't. Not in my racket. Mostly I get by with word of mouth. You need something found? See Sladek.

"Yeah. I've heard that before," Latimer spit out sarcastically. I could tell he was in a bad mood.

"Seriously, Latimer. I've never seen the stiff before. Who is he?"

Latimer looked me in the eye. He must have believed me. That's the difference between him and his partner. Rossetti would have taken me down to the station and tried to beat an answer out of me.

"His I.D. says his name was Herman Jacobsen. From Duluth." Duluth is one of those backwater planets that don't get much tourist trade. The climate is mostly snow and ice when it isn't raining. Hard to know why anyone bothered to settle there. Easy enough to understand their leaving though, even for a cheap room on the edge of New Minglewood. "It doesn't give any current employment. The lab boys haven't told me yet if the I.D. is a fake." Half the I.D.s on Star City are fakes of some sort.

"Anything on him?"

Latimer must have figured he'd get more out of me by being cooperative rather than a hard guy. "Not much. A suit in the closet, local manufacture. A change of underwear and a couple of pairs of socks in the drawer. A wallet with the I.D. and a credit stick with five thousand dollars Crockett. I raised an eyebrow at that. Five Gs wasn't a fortune, but it meant that Jacobsen could have afforded a lot better than the cheap room we were in which probably went for fifteen a week.

"That's traveling kind of light. Nothing else?"

"Not that the crime scene boys have been able to find."

"Quite a puzzle you've got on your hands, Latimer. Sorry I wasn't able to help."

"I've got to ask, Frank. Are you packing?"

"You know me better than that, Latimer. I never carry a weapon unless I think I might need it. You start carrying a gun and somebody might get shot. Like me." I opened my jacket to show I didn't have a shoulder holster underneath. He patted me down anyway, but he was almost apologetic about it. He didn't find anything because there was nothing to find.

"What time was he shot?" I asked.

"M.E. says between an hour and ninety minutes ago. No one in this place will admit to have seen or heard anything."

"I've got an alibi, then. I was at the Blue Moon nursing a brown on the rocks. Ask Louie the barman. He should be there until 1800."

"I'll do that," Latimer said in a tone that meant he didn't think it would prove anything. It probably wouldn't.

"Can I go now? Or do you still crave the pleasure of my company?"

"Beat it, Frank. But if you find out anything, be sure to let me know."

"Sure thing." I headed down the stairs. Rossetti had worked his way up to the third floor where he was trying to get answers out of a blueskin whose command of Terran was sketchy. Rossetti gave me the evil eye but let me pass.

As I walked back to my apartment I wondered what it had all been about.

I grabbed a quick meal at the diner on the corner and then headed back to my apartment in the Aldeberon Arms, that faded relic of earlier times when New Minglewood was scheduled to be a large park rather than the slum it had degenerated into. The Aldeberon had been designed as upscale residences for Star City's technocrats, but after the plans for the park had fallen through maintenance had become sketchy and rents had fallen, a situation that had accelerated when undesirables had started to move in, myself included in that latter group. I liked it for its illusion of elegance, spaciousness and the view of the sign for the Blue Moon that I could get from the tiny balcony off the living-room.

The sight of death is never pleasant. I'd never met Jacobsen, but that didn't really matter. I poured myself a stiff drink from a bottle of real Crockett whiskey and set the music system to playing some soft jive samba. After a while, I finished the drink. Having nothing better to do, I went to bed.

The comm unit on the nightstand was beeping. A quick glance out of the bedroom window showed that the glow tubes that run down the center of Star City were still dark indicating it was the middle of the station's artificial night. A call at that hour wasn't that unusual; in my business the clients operate on a twenty-four hour schedule. I picked up the comm and read the display:

"0130 – Millicent Bundy – New Dublin"

I didn't know a Ms. Bundy and I had only a vague notion of where New Dublin was—some fifty light years more or less that-a-way.

"Sladek here," I answered sleepily.

"Sladek, I want it." Naming conventions vary from star system to star system but it didn't sound like the mental image of Ms. Bundy that had formed in my mind. It was a decidedly masculine voice of someone around a hundred kilos. Probably with large, hairy knuckles and a thick eyebrow extending unbroken across the bridge of the nose.

"You want what?"

"Don't play cute with me, Sladek—what Jacobsen had you find for him."

"I never talked to Jacobsen, and now I never will. He was found with hole in his head from a heavy laser. You wouldn't know anything about that, would you?"

"Look, Sladek. I want it. You get it for me or you might end up like Jacobsen. Understand?"

"No, I don't understand. I don't know what *it* is and I never talked with Jacobsen."

"Then you better figure it out, Sladek. If you don't have it next time I call you'll get yours." The connection was broken.

Great, I thought. Some homicidal type is calling me in the middle of the night about who knows what and threatening to kill me if I can't produce it. I tossed the comm back on the nightstand and tried to get back to sleep.

I didn't let the call keep me from getting my beauty sleep, but in the morning after a cup of joe had washed away the whiskey fog of the night before I decided I needed to do something about it, so I called Latimer.

"What is it, Sladek?" the detective answered. He was sounding out of sorts, but that could easily be due as much to a bad cup of Joe or Rossetti as me.

"You said to call you if I found anything out. So I'm calling."

There was a pause. Finally Latimer said, "So what is it, Frank?" He still sounded out of sorts, but the fact that he was using my given name meant he was trying to be nice.

"I got a call from a Millicent Bundy, only I'm pretty sure it wasn't her." I detailed the gist of the conversation.

"What was that name again?"

"Millicent Bundy. New Dublin."

I could hear the sounds of Latimer trying to work the computer on his desk. A few seconds later he reads, "Millicent Bundy, en route to Fenwick Park. On Star City for five days. Departed three days ago."

Neither one of us was surprised. Passengers in transit could buy a short term communicator unit to use while waiting for their connection. They cost twenty credits and were good for two weeks. Shills for brokers wait at embarkation to buy them back, usually for a half credit for each day remaining on the activation contract. The brokers then resell them to people who don't want their calls traced for whatever they can get. None of this is strictly legal, but not much of an effort is made to stop the practice.

"So what is it, Frank?"

"What is what?"

"This thing the guy who isn't Millicent Bundy wants."

"I haven't got a clue. I keep telling everybody that Jacobsen never got in touch with me."

"That's too bad, Frank. Sounds like you've got a problem. Maybe you'd better find out what it is before this guy calls back."

"And how am I supposed to do that?"

"You're the one in the business of finding things, Frank. But let me know when you do." The comm tootled to let me know the connection was broken.

I knew what Latimer was doing. He was using me as bait to catch a murderer. Of course no one cares what happens to bait after it's served its purpose.

It seemed to me that I didn't have a lot of choices open to me. Jacobsen had been trying to get his hands on something. He'd been planning on hiring me to do it for him. Now Bundy, or whoever he was, wanted it and he seemed to think I had it or could get it. I could either hole up and wait for him to come for me, or I could go out and do what I do best, find things. The one advantage I had was that Star City was my city, not his. I was born here and know its streets and alleys in a way that a non-native never can.

But where to start? If Latimer and the forensic squad hadn't found anything in Jacobsen's room, chances were I wouldn't either. That's the kind of thing the techs are good at. What they aren't so good at are asking questions; and getting good answers. That's where being a private investigator is an advantage.

The place to begin, in fact the only place, was with Jacobsen's building. I needed to talk to whoever had rented the room to him. But first there was something I had to take care of first.

As I said earlier, I don't usually go around packing a gun. Usually it's not necessary and guns can just lead to misunderstandings, bad ones. But Bundy was certainly carrying and had shown his willingness to use it. As long as he was out there looking for me I knew had better be prepared.

There's a small safe in the back of my closet where I keep my weaponry. It doesn't have to be big because I'm not one of those guys with a whole armory. I just have a few pieces for different occasions, a tool for every job, so to speak. There's a needle gun which is nice and quiet for short range work, a stunner, and a standard 50 kilojoule laser pistol like the police use. I even have an antique chemical propellant ballistic automatic. It fires a hunk of lead that measures .45 caliber in some ancient system and makes enough noise to stop most bad guys even if the slug doesn't. It's expensive to fire, but it's hard to beat for shock value. Subtle, it isn't, though. What I wanted was something discrete.

I know a guy who knows a weapons tech who does custom work. The pistol I grabbed from the safe was one of his creations. Essentially, it is a 25 kilojoule laser married to a the power pack of 75 kilojoule pistol. The result is a laser that lacks in stopping power but has a much shorter recharge time, down to three seconds between the first and second shot. The down side is that to get the capacitor to fit in the housing he'd had had to use a smaller battery which meant it is only good for about a dozen shots before the battery needs to be replaced or recharged. It's a tradeoff I could accept as it meant I could get off those dozen shots before my opponent could get off three. As a bonus it slides into a shoulder holster that barely makes a bulge under my jacket. As an afterthought, I slipped the needle gun into my pocket as insurance before slamming the safe door shut.

When I got to Jacobsen's building I knocked on the door labeled "Manager." It was off the first floor landing at the back of the building. Other than the sign on the door there was nothing to mark the apartment as any different than any of the other shabby rooms in the joint.

I could hear the sound of someone heavy moving around inside. A moment later the door opened a crack to reveal the doughy face of a middle-aged woman with thinning hair that had once been brown. I noted the chain that kept the door from opening any further. We were, after all, just over the border from New Minglewood. I could hear what sounded like a viewer playing in the background.

"What do you want?" she asked, more disinterested than suspicious.

"I'm interested in a room. I hear you might have a vacancy."

She gave me the once over. I guess I looked too upscale which is hard to believe. With a snort she answered, "You don't want no room. Not here at least. What's your game, mister? I already talked to the cops." At least she didn't do me the disservice of thinking I was a bull.

"All right. I'm not a cop. But I am looking for information about your late tenant. Give me something good and I'll make it worth your while."

"Show me the money, pretty boy."

We both laughed at that. I waved a Crockett double saw-buck across the door opening. For a moment I thought I'd hypnotized her.

The door shut and I could hear the rattle of the chain being undone. Then the door opened again.

"Come in handsome. Take a seat."

I picked my way through the apartment. Clothes and other pieces of junk were scattered everywhere. I took a seat in a beat up plastic chair that looked like it might just hold my weight. The manager eased her bulk into an arm chair with broken springs and torn upholstery. It protested but held. She played with a remote to mute the viewer.

"Want some hooch?" she asked waving a bottle of clear in my direction.

"No thank you, ma'am. It's a bit early in the day for me." We both knew that wasn't strictly true, but she let it slide.

"Such manners. Money first, answers later."

I placed the twenty on the table next to her where I could grab it if she was just playing games with me.

"What do you want to know, handsome?" she leered.

"How long was Jacobsen here, for a start?"

"He moved in three week ago. Answered an ad and took the place right away. Paid for two months up front. Cash, Crockett dollars."

Star City credits are the official currency, but there aren't many places in human space where Crockett dollars aren't accepted. It wouldn't be that unusual for someone from out of town to be carrying them.

"Did he say where he was from?"

"Do I look like I'd ask? People in this kind of place don't appreciate questions."

"I just thought he might have mentioned it, that's all."

"People don't usually volunteer, either."

"No, I guess not. Did he have any luggage?"

The manager took a slug from the bottle. "Just a valise sized thing. But that's more than some of our guests."

"No package?"

"What's that about? The detectives asked the same thing."

"Just curiosity, ma'am. Did he have any visitors while he was here?"

"Just the one, I guess." We both knew she was referring to the killer.

"I don't suppose you got a look at him?"

She laughed at that. "I don't get up out of this chair often. It's better that way."

I took that as a no. "Did he go out much?"

"No. Just for food as far as I could tell. There's a place on the corner that won't poison you."

"If you don't get up from the chair, how could you tell?"

She pointed up to a corner of the room next to the door. There was a screen with a camera feed of the building's entrance. "He wasn't gone long enough for him to go anywhere else."

It looked like Jacobsen had been waiting for something. That was the only reason I could think of for him to have sat in that crappy room for three weeks.

"So he never went anywhere but the diner for three weeks?"

"I didn't say that, handsome."

"What did you say?"

"Nothing, yet." We both knew what she was implying. I reached in for a ten spot to place on top of the twenty.

"You're a real gentleman, sport. Not like that weaselly cop that questioned me. I don't know if he went there or not, but yesterday, before he got killed he asked me where Carmody and 47th was. I told him and he went out."

Carmody is a street running up and down the length of Star City about a third of the way around from where we were. 47th is a circumferential street that intersected it about a third of the way down from the head end. The location was in a commercial district.

"Know anything else?"

"I wish I did, handsome. I could use the cash. But that's all I know."

She reached out for the money on the table but I placed a hand on it. She looked up in alarm.

"There's just one more thing, ma'am. I'm wondering how it is that you knew when Jacobsen went to eat, but you didn't see the killer."

"I was taking a nap. I always take a nap in the afternoon." She had answered with such a hurt tone that I thought it just might be the truth. I lifted my hand from the bills.

"Thank you for your help, ma'am. I'll let myself out."

As I walked to the entrance I could hear the chain being fastened behind me.

I might be out thirty dollars, but at least I had the next step in my investigation. It took me twenty minutes to get to Carmody and 47th. Once there I stood on the corner trying to decide which building had been Jacobsen's destination.

Across the intersection from me were the offices of a spaceliner insurance company. That didn't seem promising. The building on the corner where I stood seemed to be small offices, mostly medical from the directory. That had possibilities, but I had no way of knowing which of several dozen doctors and dentists Jacobsen might have visited. Even if he had, chances were it would be a dead end. The corner to my right seemed to be taken up with a retail establishment for women's apparel. I could probably rule that out, too. That left the corner to my left. It was another office building, but the ground floor right on the corner was occupied by a small shop that seemed to sell candy and snack items from various planets.

It seemed the most likely destination for Jacobsen. If nothing else, it would be the easiest to check out. I crossed the street and stepped through the door. The shop seemed empty, but there was a doorway behind the counter leading into what looked like a storeroom.

"Hullo? Anyone here?" I didn't get any reply, just the sort of dead echo you get from an empty room. I tried again with the same results.

I was about to leave when my curiosity got the better of me. I've got to work on that. One of these days it will get me killed. I stepped behind the counter, my fingers instinctively wrapping themselves around the grip of the needler in my pocket. I needn't have worried. The shopkeeper wasn't going to give me or anyone else trouble ever again. He was lying behind the counter, a laser burn in the center of his forehead, just like Jacobsen.

I was standing outside on the corner when Latimer arrived. He took a quick look inside before joining me. The detective had seen enough death that it didn't affect him, at least not outwardly.

"So, Frank, did you kill him?"

I glanced at him in disgust. "Would I have called you if I had?"

He leaned against the side of the building, probing his gum line with a toothpick for the remains of a "meat" sandwich. "Maybe. Sometimes you're too smart for your own good, Frank."

"I talked to the manager at Jacobsen's building. She said he had asked for directions to this intersection. I didn't even know this was the place he was interested in until I found the dead guy."

Latimer thought that over for a second, then asked, "You packing, Frank?"

"Yeah. I hear there's someone going around ventilating brain cases." I pulled back my jacket to show the pistol in its holster.

Latimer reached in and grabbed it with his thumb and forefinger. I didn't mention the needle gun in my pocket as I didn't think it was relevant.

"Cute toy," the detective said examining the laser. "25 kilojoule?"

"Yeah."

"Kind of lightweight, Frank. Good thing in this case. The laser used on the shopkeeper was a fifty at least." He handed the pistol back to me.

"Yeah. Same as the one used on Jacobsen."

"So, you think they're related?"

"Makes sense. Jacobsen talks to this guy. They both end up dead. Same laser. Unless you've got another killer running around."

"So what is this thing he's looking for, Frank?"

"I still haven't a clue, Latimer. Not a clue. But I don't think he's got it."

"Why do you think that, Frank?"

"Jacobsen asked directions to this guy yesterday, early. He's only fifteen, twenty minutes away, so he probably saw him then. Jacobsen is killed that afternoon. If he'd picked it up, whatever it is, then Bundy would have got his hands on it. He wouldn't have had a reason to call me last night and he wouldn't have had any reason to pay a visit here, either."

"So he's still looking?"

"That's the way I've got it figured."

"And he still thinks you have it or can get it?"

"Probably. In any case, I may be his only lead now that he's killed Jacobsen and this guy."

"So what you going to do, Frank?"

"Me? I'm going to have a drink. Care to join me?"

"I've got work to do. Take care, Frank."

It was early enough that the Blue Moon was still quiet. There were two guys at the other end of the bar drinking liners of yellow and talking about nothing in particular. The bartender was using a dirty rag to spread a fresh coat of grease on a succession of glassware. And there was me, staring at a tumbler of brown as the ice cubes slowly melted.

I was trying to figure a way out of this mess. Bundy, for want of a better name, thought I had the thing, whatever it was. Sooner or later he'd probably come gunning for me. I didn't know what it was he wanted and I didn't know what he looked like. The worst of it was I'd been dragged into this business just because Jacobsen had had my name on him. I wasn't even making any money. In fact, I was out the thirty bucks I'd paid the manager.

I'd just drained the last of my drink when my comm vibrated to alert me to a call. It was Latimer.

"Sladek."

"So you're still alive?"

"For the moment. What's up?"

"We had a bit of luck. The insurance company across the intersection, they have a security imager pointed at the shop. It caught a man entering it about an hour before you got there. He came out about two minutes later."

"What's he look like?"

"Average height and build, coloring kind of neutral."

"Great. So I don't have to worry about two meter midgets or a bearded lady. You sure it's him?"

"No, but the M.E. says the shopkeeper was killed about that time. The imager didn't record anyone else entering the shop until you showed up. Do you want to see the image?"

"Sure. Why not?"

A low-res, slightly out of focus image appeared on my comm. A guy coming from the right entered the shop. Latimer was right. The guy was of average build and dressed in the same suit half the men on the street were wearing. Nothing much happened for two minutes, and then the same guy came out and walked briskly to the left. His head was down and turned towards the building so you couldn't get a good look at his face, but the front of his jacket fanned just long enough to show a shoulder holster with the butt end of a heavy laser pistol sticking out.

"Thanks, Latimer," I said when the image was done.

"Sorry, but it was the best we could do, Frank." When I didn't say anything, he broke the connection.

After that I didn't feel like another drink. I grabbed a carton of take-away from the noodle joint next to my building and went up to sit in my apartment.

It was just after the glow tubes outside dimmed for the night that the call came. It was the same voice as before, but this time the I.D. read Lester Schwanck.

"I want it, Sladek. Give it to me or you get what Jacobsen got."

It was obvious that denying I had it wasn't going to do any good. I was getting mad about that, mad about the whole thing. Mad enough to do something about it.

"OK. I've got it. You can have it, but it will cost you."

"How much?"

"A grand. Crockett." I had no idea what the thing was worth, but I figured a thousand would be a good take for a middleman.

"Alright. But I need it tonight."

"Fine by me. But not here." I gave him an address down city, a place where most of the surrounding buildings were empty.

"In two hours?"

"Make it one." The connection broke.

I should have called Latimer then. It would have been the smart thing to do. But like I said, I was mad. I didn't like the idea of being dragged into something without having any say in it. Well, now I was going to get my say.

I didn't have any idea of what it was I was supposed to be handing over to Bundy, or even how big it was, but my guess was that it wasn't too big. I had an old bag, the kind rich guys put there smelly clothes in after exercising. In my imagination the thing would fit in there. I stuffed some old towels into it to give it a little bulk and heft and hoped that would be convincing enough.

Star City, like any living city, is in a perpetual state of renewal. Sections grow old, become abandoned and finally get torn down and built over with new buildings to begin the cycle anew. The address I had given Bundy was one of those areas in the abandoned stage, a block of buildings scheduled to be torn down for some sort of shopping complex. At that hour of the night there wouldn't be anyone hanging around. I didn't want any innocent bystanders getting shot and I didn't want any witnesses.

The site of the meet was an alley that ran down the middle of the block. The only illumination was what filtered in from the streets at either end. It wasn't pitch black inside, but there were plenty of shadows. I arrived ten minutes early and parked myself in one of the shadows.

I'll say this for Bundy, he was punctual, arriving right on time. He had entered the alley from the other end. He walked down the center of the alley, his right arm loose at his side holding something in his hand, a laser pistol, the one that had killed Jacobsen and the shopkeeper.

As he reached the middle of the block he called out, "Sladek. You here?"

I could have killed him then, but I didn't. I've killed men, but I'm not a killer. Instead I stepped out of the shadows, the bag in my left hand, the needle gun in my right. We were a little less than ten meters apart.

"Do you have it, Sladek?"

"Do you have the grand?"

Bundy coughed a short laugh. "We both know there is no grand, Sladek."

"The jokes on you, then. There's no whatever it is, either. Jacobsen never contacted me. I was just a name in his comm. Maybe he intended to talk to me, maybe he didn't, but it never happened. All I know is that you killed him and the shopkeeper and you mean to kill me."

"If you didn't talk with Jacobsen, how'd you know about the shop on Carmody?"

"Jacobsen asked his landlady directions to the intersection. I went into the shop and—well, you know the rest."

"That's too bad, Sladek. Too bad for you."

Bundy was fast, I'll give him that. I hardly had time to react as his gun hand came up. I dove to the side, the needle gun getting off a three needle burst that went wide. Bundy had missed, too, but as I landed, the needle gun was knocked out of my hand.

I kept rolling, reaching for the laser in my holster and counting off the seconds while Bundy's weapon recharged. We were both moving in the shadows at the sides of the alley. We fired at nearly the same time, both missing, but the flare of the lasers as they struck the bricks gave away our positions.

Bundy must have figured from the flash that the pistol was just a standard 25 kilojoule laser with a ten or fifteen second recharge time. The pistol he was carrying was a 60 with a heavy duty power pack and a shorter recharge. He took a step out of the shadows, his laser pointed straight at my heart. I could see him mentally counting down until he could fire again.

I shot first, catching him in the face. His knees started to fold just as the ready light on his pistol went green. When he hit the ground it came loose from his hand and skittered across the pavement.

I didn't move for quite awhile. Bundy, or whatever his name was, had been good. A real killer. I was lucky to be alive.

After I called Latimer I hung around. There was no reason not to. He and Rossetti showed up along with the M.E.'s squad and some uniforms that blocked both ends of the alley. Latimer looked around while Rossetti kicked the body as if making sure he was dead.

Noticing the bag lying where I had dropped it he asked, "Is that the thing he was after?"

"That? No, that's just some dirty laundry."

"OK, Frank. If that's the way you want to play it. No skin off me. I've got a dead killer and two cases solved."

"Check for yourself, Latimer. Jacobsen never contacted me. I don't know what they were after and I don't care."

Latimer picked up the bag, stuck his hairy paw inside and handed it back to me.

Rossetti, who had been looking over the M.E.'s shoulder turned around and said, "Nice shooting, Sladek."

"Not so nice. I missed the first time. So did he."

"So how did it play out, Frank?" Latimer asked. "This guy was good. That should have been you lying on the ground."

"You know better than that, Latimer. It's not how fast you can get off the first shot; it's how quick you are with the second."

THE
SUN NEVER
RISES

THE SUN NEVER RISES

Star City is in the middle of nowhere, a tiny little hollowed out rock orbiting a failed sun light years from any inhabited planet. It also, because it serves as the major transit point for that region of space known as the sphere of human settlement, is in the center of everything. Because of this fact, Star City has become a magnet for all sorts of people. Not only does it draw more than its share of con-men, grifters and charlatans, it also draws a fair number of artists, poets and writers, though sometimes it is difficult to tell them apart.

Many of the latter tend to congregate in a district of Star City known as "the Souk." Originally, it had served as an unofficial ghetto for those non-humans who weren't wealthy enough to be welcome in polite society. What distinguished the Souk from the more notorious New Minglewood was that most of the residents made a more or less honest living. It was the Souk's combination of low rents, cheap eateries and all night drinking establishments that first attracted the artists as they worked on their masterpiece. Later, it was the district's reputation that proved the draw as it became almost obligatory for aspiring artists and would be writers to spend time, if only briefly within its confines. But mostly it was the parties.

I first met Marcus Fitzroy in the Blue Moon. Of course, this was before he had become a famous author. The Blue Moon is a bar on the edge of New Minglewood, a slum that is the home for the dregs of Star City. The Blue Moon is also across the street from the apartment building where I live, which is convenient. It was the middle of the day, and as I was between jobs I was there for a lack of anything better to do. In the middle of the day, the Blue Moon tends to be quiet, and there were only two customers in the place, myself, and a tall, thin man who looked to be in his late twenties occupying a seat a few meters down the length of the bar that ran along one side of the place, two mugs in a dark bar staring at the drinks in front of them and studiously avoiding contact with anyone except the bartender, and then only that which was necessary to keep the glass in front of them full.

At that time, Fitzroy hadn't yet achieved the genial corpulence which was to become his trademark. He had the lean, hungry look of someone who wasn't eating enough and who was drinking too much. He also had that hollow look of someone who was abusing drugs, most likely blank, though he didn't look as though he had yet slipped into addiction.

He made a response to some random comment of the bartender's. I made the mistake of looking up and making eye contact, if only for a second. With that, our fates were sealed.

He moved several seats closer to me, bringing his drink with him.

"Why do they call this stuff 'brown,' anyway?" he asked, gesturing at the drink in front of him. He had an accent I couldn't place, a faint broadening of his 'A's that would have marked him as not a local if that hadn't been obvious already.

"They call it brown because they're too honest to call it whiskey," I answered, almost by reflex.

"And 'clear?'"

"Depending on whether it has any flavor or not, clear is either not gin or not vodka. Take your choice. It all comes out of the same vat before they add the artificial flavors and coloring. The only thing authentic about the booze on Star City is the alcohol content."

"Thanks for the philosophy. My name is Marcus Fitzroy, by the way."

I felt forced to respond, "Frank Sladek."

"What's your line, Frank? What's your business?"

"This and that. Mostly I find things for people," I replied. My answer was mostly true.

"Find things? What kind of things?"

"Missing items, money, wives. Whatever clients want to get back."

"Wives? Where can they go on this rock?"

"You'd be surprised at how many places there are to hide on the inside of a cylinder fifteen kilometers long and three in diameter," I replied with a shrug.

"Interesting. So you're some kind of private detective, then?"

"Some people call me that. I've been called worse," I said starting to be annoyed. Out of self defense I asked, "So what's your line, Marcus? I take it you're not from around here."

"You've got me there, Frank. I can see that you're good at your job." He then proceeded to tell me his life story. I listened because I didn't have anything better to do. I even paid attention to bits of it.

I gathered that he had been working as a journalist during the recent civil war on Nordholm. Though not involved personally, he had been covering the story mostly from the rebels' side. When they finally lost, he, along with a lot of other people, had found himself persona non grata and been forced to take the first starship he could arrange passage on. That's how he had ended up on Star City. He claimed that he was working free lance as a stringer for one of the interstellar news agencies and working on a novel about his experiences in the civil war. The latter was, at least, true. You might have heard of it if you do anything as anachronistic as read novels. *A Farewell to Holm* was the book that was to make Fitzroy's reputation after he left Star City.

But that was later. He wasn't working on it then or much of anything else. Mostly he was just drinking and partying.

By the time he had finished his tale, it was late afternoon and the after work crowd was starting to file in. I bid my adieu claiming pressing business, figuring I'd never see Fitzroy again. My pressing business was picking up a meat sandwich at the diner on the corner. Like the booze, protein on Star City comes from a vat in two flavors, brown and white. I had the brown with "gravy." It wasn't half bad.

I was wrong about not seeing Fitzroy again. He started dropping in at the Blue Moon occasionally. I use the place as sort of an office, so I'm there often enough that our paths were bound to cross. He offered to buy me a drink. I accepted. I don't know where he was getting his money from, but he always seemed to have enough to pay for drinks.

He seemed to have a fixation about my being a private detective. He started to pump me about my "cases." I spun him some yarns about half of which were true. I also let him buy me another drink. He claimed that he was gathering material for a book he was going to write. Turns out that eventually he did, though I've never read it. I've been told by someone who is into that kind of stuff that *Some Have, Some Haven't* was not one of his better works.

After that, I was running into him every few days. I thought of finding another watering hole, but the Blue Moon was just too convenient. He kept pumping me for stories and talking about the civil war. I got the impression that a lot of the stories he told had happened to other guys and not himself. I know some of my yarns were second hand. What can I say, it was entertainment over drinks. Who expects honesty?

He was also trying to get me to go to parties in the Souk. It seemed there was always a party going on somewhere if you just knew the right people. Marcus seemed to know everyone, so he was never short of invites. I kept begging off because of business, which was partially true. By its nature, a lot of what I do is done in the evening and the wee hours of the morning. He kept asking, though, and one night, out of boredom, I took him up on the invite.

The Souk is within easy walking distance from the Blue Moon, so we strolled on over. The party was being held in a big upstairs apartment that had been converted into some kind of art studio/gallery. It was a typical party. The booze was free, but no better than at the Blue Moon. The food, which had been catered by the restaurant on the ground floor, had a lot of strange spices. A sound system was playing the Jive Samba loud enough to make it hard to talk. Some of the women weren't bad looking, though.

Most of the artists were posers younger than Marcus. It turns out that very few of the "artists" in the Souk really do much work. They mostly spend a few months or a year on Star City before heading home to work in daddy's store. It's probably just as well. I didn't see much hanging on the walls of the gallery that was worth looking at. Marcus introduced me to a couple of people before we went in search of the bar. I got us a couple of browns with ice and soda.

A fat guy seemed to be holding court in the corner. Marcus told me that it was Jack Feldman. Feldman had written a turgid novel that had been all the rage in half a dozen systems fifteen or so years earlier. As far as I knew he hadn't written a thing since and had become a more or less permanent resident of the Souk where he lived off his previous fame. Since arriving on Star City, his body had become as corpulent as his prose had been bloated. None of which seemed to prevent the pretty young things from hanging on his every word.

Marcus was dragged off by a willowy blonde, leaving me to stare at the appetizers trying to decide which of them might be edible. I found myself explaining to a matronly woman that no, I wasn't an artist and I wasn't a poet. After fifteen minutes in which she finally decided I wasn't even a writer, she wandered off into the crowd. I looked around to see if I could spot Marcus, but he seemed to have disappeared. The willowy blonde was talking to some geek with a scraggly beard. I was getting a headache from the music, the last appetizer I had had was starting an argument with my stomach. I decided to call it a night and head home.

I'd almost made it to the door when a short brunette in a paint stained shirt forced a glass containing something red into my hand.

"Marcus says that you're a private detective."

"Marcus says a lot of things," I responded, taking a closer look at my benefactor. Unlike most of the women in the room, she seemed almost cheerful, with none of the typical fashionable gloom. She was also, I realized, quite attractive. "Some of them may even be true."

"Well, you aren't an artist, are you?"

"No. That's one thing I'm not."

"By the way, my names Lucinda."

"Frank Sladek."

"I've heard of you," she said, her expression suddenly going serious for a moment. I decided that she was a little drunk, but only a little.

"It's too noisy in here. Would you like to see my paintings? My studio is only a block away."

"Sure, why not." I figured it would be a graceful way to exit the party.

We walked the block to her studio which was on the top floor of a four story building. There was no elevator. Oddly enough, she did want to show me her paintings. Surprisingly, they were actually quite good in their own way. They were mostly weird landscapes seen under alien suns. I'm not sure if they were meant to be realistic. I hope not, but I wouldn't know. I've never been farther than the Promenade in one direction and the freight docks in the other. Whether real or not, they had a vibrancy that had been missing in the works hanging in the gallery. Later, Lucinda gave me one, my favorite, to hang at the foot of my bed. A year or so later she left for Crockett where I hear she became quite successful. Yes, she was *that* Lucinda. We didn't go back to the party.

In the morning, Lucinda made breakfast for me. In addition to her talents as a painter, she proved to be a reasonably good cook. That probably went a long way towards explaining her well fed look.

As she set the plate in front of me she remarked, "I'm concerned about your friend Marcus."

"He's more of an acquaintance," I interjected.

Ignoring my comment, she continued, "You know he does blank, don't you?"

"I've suspected that," I admitted. Blank was a relatively new drug, at least on Star City. It had the affect of suppressing memories. In the short term, its affects were relatively harmless, possibly even therapeutic. Long term use, however, basically left nothing remaining of the personality. "Perhaps he's trying to forget his experiences in the civil war."

"Forgetting isn't good for a writer, Frank. Or any artist, for that matter. All we are are memories. Talk to him, please. He looks up to you."

This was news to me. I'm not used to having people respect me. It comes with the profession. Being underestimated is even an asset at times. I was also wondering if Lucinda's latching on to me at the party had been as much of an accident as it had seemed. Not that I was complaining.

I mumbled some sort of agreement around a fork full of omelet. Something about the look in Lucinda's eyes made me think that she wouldn't let it rest until I did.

"How'd you end up on Star City, anyway?" I said trying to change the subject.

"I guess like most people. I was heading from someplace to someplace else. I knew a few people here, so I dropped in to see them for a bit. I just haven't moved on yet. For the work I do, one place is as good as another. You were born here, weren't you? That must be weird."

"I don't know. Living with nothing above your head but sky seems kind of bizarre to me."

She laughed at that. She had a good laugh. After breakfast she pushed me out saying she had to work.

I started hanging around the Souk, meeting up with Lucinda when she was available. Unlike most of the artists, Lucinda actually seemed to work at her art, painting most days from early in the morning to the late afternoon. While she was working, she didn't like to be disturbed. This wasn't a problem as most of the expatriate crowd spent those hours sleeping it off or nursing hangovers in preparation for the next night's parties. I had my own business to attend to, as well, but we hooked up often enough to keep it interesting.

It was about that time that the refugee ship from Nordholm arrived. They'd had a rough time of it. Halfway through their trip they'd had a drive malfunction that popped them back into real space travelling at better than nine tenths the speed of light. It had taken the crew more than a month subjective time to fix the ship. The result was one of those Lorentz Contraction kind of things you read about, but which rarely happen in real life. Though subjectively the passengers and crew had only experienced three months of travel, it had been over a year and a half of since they'd left the planet.

Knowing Marcus had a background in the civil war, the local bureau chief for *Interstellar Press* gave him the assignment of covering the docking. Marcus asked me to come along. Because they were refugees and not paying passengers the ship had been ordered to dock at the freight ring instead of the passenger end of Star City. I think Marcus was a little afraid of going down there. I wasn't doing anything, and I admit I was a little curious about the whole business.

We were in position at the docking bay when they opened the hatch. The seven hundred or so passengers that filed out were a pretty sorry looking lot. They were mostly women and children, the last ship to escape from the last rebel position just before it fell to the loyalist forces. They'd taken off with short rations as it was, not planning on an extra two months voyage due to the drive malfunction. The ones that could still walk were pretty emaciated, especially the kids. After the ambulatory had debarked the stretcher crews went to work. Marcus and I watched as a seemingly endless stream of them came out of the hatch. The last hundred or so had their faces covered. They hadn't survived.

I could see it was affecting Marcus, all the horrors of the civil war coming back to him. I suggested we leave, but he insisted on staying until the last stretcher had emerged. I read his piece on the newsfeed later. It was good, damned good, even after the editor had cut it down by a half.

After that, Marcus was changed. He wasn't drinking as much, at least during the day. I'm pretty sure he had stopped using blank as well. He said he was writing again. He let me read the first chapter of what was to become *A Farewell to Holm*. It was good stuff. The writing was crisp, verging on terse, yet you could almost feel the loyalists' heavy weapons shattering a village.

Jack Feldman had thrown a little party at his apartment. Not a big one, only twenty or thirty people, mostly older writers who'd actually done something once and a few of the new ones. For some reason, Lucinda and I were invited, or at least that's what Marcus had said. Once we got inside, it was so crowded you couldn't tell who was there. At least no one threw us out.

Feldman had settled himself in a big stuffed chair in the corner of the living room. He was surrounded by the usual sycophants and bimbos. Feldman was praising the piece Marcus had done on the refugee ship, saying it was "decent for a work of journalism." Lucinda and I gravitated to the kitchen in search of free booze. After a while Marcus joined us.

"What a load of crap Jack can throw," he shouted. There were so many people talking it was hard to hear. He had a tall, athletic blond on his arm. She didn't look like an artist or poet. More like a rich girl slumming. In an interval where she went to powder her nose, Marcus confided that that was the case. She was on a layover waiting for a connecting ship and had wanted to find something more "authentic" than the shows and casinos up at the top of Star City.

A little after midnight Lucinda and I left the party and headed back to my place. Lucinda had decided my apartment was better for sex because it didn't smell of paint and turpentine.

It must have been after three when a pounding came on the door. Lucinda pulled a pillow over her head. I got up and, pulling on a pair of pants that was laying on the floor, I went to see about the source of the commotion.

Turning on the door camera I could see that it was Marcus. He knew where I lived because a few weeks earlier we'd adjourned to my apartment from a session at the Blue Moon when it had gotten too crowded. I was regretting the lapse in judgment.

"Marcus, it's late," I said into the intercom.

"Frank, you've got to help me."

"This is really an inconvenient time, Marcus. Can't it wait till morning?"

"No it can't. I'm serious. You've got to help me. I think someone is trying to kill me."

He sounded like he was serious, not just drunk. I remembered that one of the side effects of withdrawal from blank was paranoia.

From behind me came a voice, "Let him in, Frank, before he wakes the neighbors." It was Lucinda. She was unselfconsciously wearing one of my T-shirts and nothing else. I looked at her for a moment and then opened the door with regret.

Marcus insisted that I lock the door behind him. I got him to sit down in a chair in the living room while Lucinda mixed him a brown and soda.

"Okay, Marcus, what's this all about?" Lucinda had mixed a drink for me as well. I noticed that she hadn't made one for herself.

"I'm being followed. Two men. I think they want to kill me."

"Why would anyone want to kill you, Marcus?"

"Because of things I know. From the civil war."

While he was explaining, I glanced out the front window. There was a guy I didn't recognize walking down the street. He wasn't doing anything suspicious, but as close as we were to New Minglewood, it wasn't the neighborhood for a casual late night stroll.

"What kind of things?"

"It was a civil war, Frank. There were a lot of people who were playing both sides waiting to see how it all came out. I know some of them, some that are high up in the Loyalist government. Their contacts with the rebels aren't known. But I know things; dates, places, stuff that could be a major embarrassment to some people if it got out."

"Is this stuff going to show up in the book you're writing, Marcus?"

"Maybe, Some of it. I don't know, I haven't written it yet," he said in exasperation.

While he was talking, I kept an eye on the street. The stroller had disappeared around the corner. I was starting to think that Marcus was imagining it all when I noticed another stroller coming from the other direction. I got a good look at him as he passed under one of the rare streetlights. He was tall and lean, dressed conservatively. There was a bulge under his jacket. It might have been a gun. It could just as well have been a fifth of booze tucked in his pocket.

"Just who knows what you know, Marcus? And who knows that you're writing a book?"

"Hell, Frank, just about everyone knows I'm writing the damn book. It's not like I've been making it a secret. I've told everybody I've met in the last half year that I'm writing the book."

"But who cares, Marcus? Who on Star City cares about what happened on Nordholm?"

I had kept looking out the window. The first stroller was back walking down the other side of the street in the other direction. As he passed, he looked up at the apartment building for just a second. It had all been very casual. And very professional.

"Keep talking, Marcus," I said as I got up and went into the bedroom. I retrieved the needle gun I keep in my nightstand, checked the clip, and stuck it in the waistband of my pants.

Lucinda had watched my actions with interest. "You really are a private eye, Frank, aren't you? I thought that was just a line."

I took up my seat again where I could look out the window.

"Go on, Marcus. Who might want you dead? Either here or on Nordholm."

"I don't know. Lots of people, maybe. I got around quite a bit during the war."

"There must be some likely suspects. Star City may not be that big on law and order, but it does take its neutrality pretty seriously. You don't send hired muscle in unless you're damned serious."

The first stroller has disappeared again, but the second was coming back. As he looked up when he passed I caught his eye and waved. I also took an image with my communicator. That must have caught him by surprise because he missed a step before walking on. After that, I didn't see either one of them again. I didn't know whether that was a good sign or bad. The

Aldeberon Arms didn't have much in the way of security, and it did have a back door into the alley behind.

After a half hour or so, I figured that they had given up, at least for the night. They might or might not know who I was, but breaking in on someone who was expecting you might prove to be too messy for their employers.

"Look, Marcus. You can sleep on the couch tonight. I'll see what I can do about your shadows in the morning."

Lucinda and I retired to the bedroom. Her eyes were still wide when I placed the needler on the nightstand where I could get it quick. That didn't slow her down any, though.

In the morning, while Lucinda was foraging in my kitchen for the makings for breakfast for three, I tried to figure what to do about Marcus's situation. Problem was I didn't know who I was up against, and Marcus wasn't proving to be of much help in that department. But an inspiration hit me while I was getting dressed.

After breakfast I went and unlocked the steel cabinet that sits in the back of my closet. I drew out two items and relocked the case. One was a pocket stunner, the other a 25 kilojoule laser pistol.

Returning to the living room I announced, "I have to go out for a bit. I want you to stay here, Marcus. Lucinda, I want you to watch him. Take this, just in case," I said handing the laser to Marcus.

"What's that?" he said, recoiling from the pistol as if it was radioactive.

"It's a laser pistol."

"Yeah, I know, but I've never used one before. I've never shot any kind of gun."

"I thought you were in the civil war."

"I was a journalist, Frank. A reporter. I didn't carry a weapon. I might have been shot if I had. Besides, you know, the pen is mightier than the sword and all that."

"Tell that to the two guys that were parading outside last night," I said in disgust.

"I have." That was Lucinda.

"Have what?"

"Shot a gun before," she stated quietly.

"OK," I handed the laser to her. She held it like she knew what it was.

"Marcus, take this. It's a stunner. It won't kill anyone, so you don't have to worry about making a mistake. If anyone besides me tries to come through that door, point it at them and press the button. Understand?"

Marcus took the stunner. At least he was holding it with the business end pointing away from him.

"Lucinda, back Marcus up, but don't shoot unless you have to."

She nodded in agreement. "Frank, how long are you going to be gone?"

"I don't know. An hour, maybe two." I grabbed my hat and walked out the door.

There was one guy I knew that might be able to help me. The problem was, we weren't necessarily on the best of terms. That was kind of natural, he was a cop.

I had a good idea where to find him at that hour of the morning. Around the corner from the security services building is a diner. The food may not be great, but it is hot, greasy and plentiful. The joe is high in caffeine. Most of the patrons are cops of one flavor or another.

As I had hoped, Latimer was there, a pastry and a mug of joe on the counter in front of him. Latimer is a detective sergeant. He's also mostly honest which on Star City is saying something. We've had a number of confrontations over the years, but mostly we tolerate each other. His partner, Rossetti, was sitting next to him. Rossetti hates my guts on general principles. The feeling is mutual. I took the stool on the other side of Latimer.

"Well, look what the cat drug in, Latimer," Rossetti said, "Our least favorite shamus."

"Top of the morning to you, flat-foot."

"Will you two can it," Latimer objected. "I'm trying to eat my breakfast." To make his point he took a big bite out of his pastry and washed it down with a slurp of joe.

"Was there something you wanted, Sladek," he finally said, turning to me, "or did you just want to aggravate Rossetti so my day is miserable?"

"I came in here as a concerned citizen, Latimer. There's something I heard that I thought you should know."

"And what might that be, Frank?" The fact that he had changed to my first name might or might not be a good thing.

"The word on the street is that there is some hired muscle from out of town." On Star City everything in the rest of the universe qualifies as "out of town." "Two guys, good chance they're from Nordholm. Probably arrived in the last few days."

"Nordholm?" Latimer queried, suddenly paying attention. "Anything to do with that refugee ship?" The ship was still berthed at the freight docking ring and the passengers were being held in "quarantine" while the powers that be decided what to do with them.

"Not that I know of," I replied truthfully. "But there are enough other people from Nordholm passing through." I didn't want to name Marcus unless I absolutely had to.

"So, if you don't mind my asking, Frank, just how did you discover this pair?"

"I happen to look out my living room window last night, and saw these two parading back and forth in front of the Blue Moon like they were casing the place." Latimer knew that I lived just across the street from the bar. "It looked to me like they might have been carrying weapons." Latimer glanced at me, his practiced eye noting the bulge under my left arm. He raised an eyebrow. I don't normally carry a gun unless I have to. He also knew I had a permit.

"OK, Frank. Your information is duly noted. Anything else, or can I finish my breakfast in peace?"

"I got an image of one of them," I said, matter-of-factly.

"So you just happen to have had a camera handy?"

"I was calling my mother. My communicator has got an imager." I pulled out my comm. and brought up the image of assassin number two. Latimer showed no sign of recognition, but he whipped out his own comm, and touched it to mine to download the image. He diddled with the screen. A few seconds later he read out:

"Johann Krieger. Malmo, Nordholm. His entry form says he's a sales rep for Kock Industies."

"Never heard of him," I said, "or Kock Industries."

"Me neither. The form says he was traveling with a guy named Julius Schmidt. They're listed as staying at the Rigel Royal." There was nothing exceptional in that. The Royal is a nice respectable mid-level hotel favored by businessmen with expense accounts on layovers waiting for connecting flights. It's big with lots of turnover of residents. Perfect for anyone trying to stay anonymous without being obvious about it.

"These two have anything to do with you, Frank? Or one of your clients?"

"Not that I know of. I've never been to Nordholm. Or anywhere else, for that matter. And I'm kind of between clients at the moment."

"Yeah," Latimer said with a shrug. He seemed uncertain how to deal with the situation. "Well, thanks for the info. I'll be in touch if there's anything you need to know about."

"You know where to find me. So long, Rossetti," I said in parting. The latter just glared at me.

One of the engineering marvels of Star City is the remarkably efficient tram system, probably because it was part of the original design and not an afterthought of what passes for local government. Four lines arbitrarily labeled north, south, east and west run down the length of the cylinder that makes up the living space of Star City with perpendicular cross routes located every couple of kilometers making endless loops around the circumference. The automated trams run every five minutes, which means that no two locations are more than a brief tram ride and a couple of short walks from each other. As the trams are free, only the really rich bother with any sort of personal transport. Deliveries and services are mostly handled by battery powered vehicles of various descriptions.

Of course, the apartment where I live is located almost exactly in the center of one of the squares carved out by the tram tracks. This leaves me with two more or less equal length paths from a tram stop. However, as one passes through the middle of New Minglewood, I usually take the other, which just happens to cut through a corner of the Souk. It was this path that I took back from my visit with Latimer.

As I passed through the Souk I was hailed by Jack Feldman. He was sitting at a table of an outdoor café looking distinctly worse for wear. His right eye was sporting an impressive shiner and his face was marked with other abrasions. As I answered his wave I was feeling glad that I had left the party when I had, though in my previous experiences with that crowd I had only witnessed verbal abuse.

"Mr. Sladek. Good Morning. Could I have a minute of your time?"

I wanted to get back to check on Marcus and Lucinda, but some sixth sense told me that it might pay to find out what Feldman wanted.

"Sure, Jack. I could use a shot of joe." I had barely seated myself at Feldman's table when the blueskin waiter brought out a small cup brewed in the manner of the Souk, which is even stronger than on the rest of Star City.

After the waiter had departed Feldman asked, "Have you seen Marcus, my dear boy?" There was an unusual note of urgency in his voice.

"Not since I left your party last night," I lied. "Why?"

"Well," he continued almost breathlessly, "after nearly everyone had left, around midnight or maybe a little later, two brutes crashed the party looking for him. He was gone by then, of course, with that blonde beauty he'd been chatting up. When I told them that I didn't know where he was, they threatened me. I asked them to leave, but they got physical. They did this to me," he said, pointing to his eye. "And other things. Well, I really didn't know where he was, but they wouldn't accept that answer. I finally told them where he's been staying, but they still weren't satisfied. I'm afraid that I had to tell them about his association with you to make them leave. I do hope they didn't burst in on you last night."

"No, but they did parade back and forth in front of my building until I waved at them and snapped an image of one of them. Did they say anything about what they wanted with Marcus?"

"No, just that they were from Nordholm and wanted to look him up for a mutual friend. Some chap named Walker or something. Quite frankly, Mr. Sladek, I didn't like the look of the pair. I don't think their intentions towards dear Marcus are at all friendly."

"I think it's quite likely you are right about that, Jack."

"I do hope the boy is all right, Mr. Sladek."

"So do I," I responded. "Well, I have to run. Thanks for the conversation."

I got up and left thinking that Feldman might not be much of a writer anymore, but he had probably handled the situation as well as possible.

I knocked on my door, posing for the door cam. I didn't want to be stunned or worse is a case of mistaken identity. Lucinda let me in, looking relieved.

Briefly, I related Feldman's story. Lucinda uttered a "poor dear" when I mentioned the black eye. Marcus seemed indifferent to Feldman's health, but I could see that he was worried, probably about his own skin.

"There's something you're not telling me, Marcus," I said.

"What do you mean, Frank?"

"Like, why are these two goons after you, for starters?"

"I told you, I don't know why they are after me."

"OK. Do you know who this guy Walker is?"

"No. Well, maybe," he hesitated.

"Spill it, Marcus." I was using my working voice. I don't think Marcus had heard it before.   Even Lucinda seemed uncomfortable.

"There was this incident. It happened early in the civil war when it still looked like the rebels might actually win. I might have seen something—"

"Go on, Marcus," I encouraged.

"I was hanging around the headquarters of General Garcia. He was leading the rebel Third Army at the time, perhaps their best force. I had been writing dispatches for the news services on the fighting. I'd been with them some time and they had gotten used to me just hanging around in the background. Things hadn't been going so well. The rebels were running low on supplies and didn't have any money to buy them.

"One day I could tell they were expecting something big. This guy shows up. He was kind of a weaselly looking guy wearing this crisp, pressed safari suit. Introduced himself as 'Walker.' He and Garcia have a private meeting, but I was kind of in the back of the tent being quiet. Anyway, Walker hands Garcia this suitcase. The general pops it open, reaches in and takes out a sheaf of brand new one hundred Crockett dollar notes. The case must have contained a million or more dollars Crockett. Then Walker disappears. But after that suddenly the rebels don't have any supply problems for a while."

"So you think this General Garcia actually used the money on the war rather than pocketing it for himself?"

"Yeah. He was an honest man. Completely committed to the rebel cause. He died in battle later that year. That's when things started going South for the rebels."

"So, do you have any idea who this Walker guy is and where the money came from?" I asked, getting to the heart of the matter.

"I never saw him again while I was on Nordholm. But later, I saw I guy looked a lot like him in a news vid. He was some kind of aide to the Kocks. They own one of the big industrial combines on Nordholm. They are also big supporters of the loyalist government."

"Interesting. The two toughs that beat up Feldman and are after you are traveling with papers saying they're sales reps with Kock Industries. But I don't get it. If the Kocks are in with the government, why were they bankrolling the rebels?"

"Like I said, Frank, early in the civil war it wasn't clear who was going to win. There were a lot of people playing both sides of the fence so they'd come out on top no matter what the outcome was. But now, well, it might prove a big embarrassment. The rebels are all dead or in exile. The loyalist party pretty much has the run of things. If it became public knowledge that the Kocks had been backing the rebels they could lose everything, including their lives. The loyalists play rough."

"And this Walker?"

"Walker was the go-between. He might end up the scapegoat. Or he might not. Given his position, he might end up squealing on the Kocks. There are a lot of people in the loyalist party who wouldn't mind seeing them take a fall, especially if they could pick up the pieces personally."

"So where do you figure in all this, Marcus?"

"I don't think anyone noticed me at the time the money was handed over, but I did mention the incident in some of my dispatches without giving any names or anything of course. I didn't want to burn my bridges with the rebels."

"So this Walker and probably the Kocks know that you witnessed the handing over of the money and can identify Walker as the agent?"

"Yeah. Probably."

"Marcus, by any chance were you planning to put this incident in your book?"

He looked puzzled for a moment. "I don't know, Frank. I haven't decided yet. Maybe. It depends on how the plot plays out." That's why Marcus was such a good writer. His life is on the line and he's worrying about plot details.

"It doesn't matter, I guess," I said. "Walker and probably his bosses will figure that as long as you are alive, you are a threat."

"So what can I do, Frank?" Marcus said, sounding like a little boy again.

"I don't know. But I'm pretty sure you can't stay on Star City any longer. Even if we deal with Krieger and his pal, there will just be another guy taking his place."

The news hit Marcus hard.

"Look, you can stay here for a couple of days until we get things sorted out," I said, trying to cheer him up. "It should be safe."

"Thanks, Frank. I'll just go home to pick up a few things."

"I don't think that would be a good idea, Marcus. Krieger and Schmidt might be waiting for you."

"But I don't even have a toothbrush," he protested.

"Give me your key. I'll go grab enough of your things to last a few days. Lucinda, can you stick around until I get back?"

She looked dubious. "I can stay a while, Frank, but don't make it too long. I've got work to do."

That was Lucinda, willing to face hired assassins, but only if it didn't interfere with her painting schedule.

Marcus was staying in a one room apartment on the top floor of a building in the middle of the Souk. Not much of a place, but then it was the Souk. I'd been there a few times to share a drink with Marcus.

If the building had ever had a working elevator, it had ceased to function years earlier. I caught my breath at the top of the last flight of stairs. The hallway was quiet, but then it was still mid-morning. The artists were still sleeping it off and the honest people were already at work. As a precaution, I pulled my needler from its holster.

I fished Marcus's key out and was about to insert it in the door when I noticed it wasn't latched. Cautiously I pushed it open. The place was empty. It had also been tossed. They hadn't bothered to be particularly neat about it, either. The sheets had been pulled off the bed and clothes were scattered everywhere. The table where Marcus did his writing had been tipped over and his computer was missing. It didn't look like they had taken anything else. It was hard to tell. It had been several weeks since I had been up to the room, and I'd never paid that much attention.

I stuffed some of the loose clothes into a case and grabbed a toothbrush and a few other articles from the bathroom. There didn't seem to be much else to do.

I was back at my place in less than a half hour. Lucinda, impatient to get back to her painting, said good-bye and promised to return when she was done. I kissed her at the door, and then locked it behind her.

Surprisingly, Marcus didn't seem to be that upset about his apartment.

"Do you think I'm an idiot, Frank?" he asked with a smile. "I learned long ago that nothing's permanent. And I certainly wasn't going to leave anything important lying around where just anyone could check it out. It's all here," he said pulling out a chain that hung around his neck. A memory stick dangled from it.

I admit that I hadn't expected so much foresight on Marcus's part. "What if they had grabbed you?" I asked.

"I've got a backup of everything important in the data vault at the Bank of Star City." The Bank of Star City had a well-earned reputation as the one local institution that was both honest and competent. This isn't quite correct; I know a shoe-shine boy that you can trust to give a good polish for a buck.

"So what now, Frank?"

"Now we get some sleep. I didn't get that much last night, and I don't expect to get much tonight, either."

I waited until Lucinda returned in the late afternoon. She had brought some take-out from a café in the Souk. I ate a few forkfuls, and then repeating my instructions not to let anyone in, I left. It was time to see if I could find out a little more about Krieger and Schmidt.

I knew the head of security at the Rigel Royal from having helped him out once. I had helped the hotel avoid a certain amount of embarrassment when one of their guests had proved to be pulling a major con. Ever since, he would call me in when something discrete was needed that he didn't feel he could handle himself. It worked both ways, with me getting the occasional favor.

Gustav Deutsch's title is head of security, but the fact is he's what they used to call a "house dick." Gus is a beefy guy with enough muscle to handle a drunken guest, enough manners to smooth ruffled feathers, and enough smarts to know when to use which. The Royal is a very respectable mid-level hotel and Gus works hard to keep it that way. The cleaning staff don't steal, the working girls don't roll their clients, and the guests end their stays at the hotel happy.

I found Gus in his usual post, sitting in one of the comfortable chairs in the hotel lobby. It was no coincidence that he had picked the one chair where he had an almost unobstructed view of the broad room. I took a seat in the chair next to him and spent a few moments enjoying the view while Gus pretended not to notice me.

Finally he said, "Haven't seen you in a while, Frank. What have you been up to?"

"Nothing much. A little of this, a little of that."

"Does it pay well, the this and that?"

"Well enough, I guess. I'm still eating."

There was a pause while Gus eyed a guy making his way across the lobby. By local standards, he was dressed like a tramp, but with a clientele drawn from every human occupied planet in the galaxy, it was never safe to judge just by appearances. Styles and customs vary tremendously. Gus lost interest when the tramp approached the reception desk and checked in.

"So, Frank. Is there something I can do for you, or are you just here for the buffet?"

"I'm fishing for a little info on two of your guests. Krieger and Schmidt. From Nordholm. They've expressed interest in a client of mine."

Gus raised an eyebrow at the mention of Nordholm. I guess it was on everyone's mind since the refugee ship had come in. He pulled out his comm, spoke the names into it and waited a few seconds.

"They checked in three days ago, open ended stay, paid with a Bank of Crockett Gold Card. Arrived on the Nordholm Star. No departure listed. Nordholm passports, occupations salesmen. Anything else you want to know, Frank?"

"You wouldn't happen to have a room number, would you?" I asked.

"Just what is this about?" Gus asked suspiciously.

"I don't want to alarm you, Gus, but Krieger and Schmidt may not be innocent salesman, Gus."

Gus gave me another raised eyebrow. "What leads you to think that, Frank?"

"They tossed my client's place. I also think they're packing heat. I don't think their intentions are necessarily peaceful."

Gus poked around his comm a little more, and then stood. "Let's take a little walk, Frank."

He led me around the corner of the lobby to where the lift tubes were. Stepping inside he said "twelve" and disappeared upward. I followed him, repeated the number and rose after him. Gus was waiting in the hallway when I stepped out of the tube on the twelfth floor.

"It so happens that Mr. Krieger and Mr. Schmidt are not in their room at present," Gus said. "I thought you might like to see the view from 1217."

"Lead the way."

I followed Gus down the hallway. He stopped in front of a door, and after looking both ways brought up his comm and pressed the screen. The door popped open and we went inside.

I think the rooms at the Rigel Royal look like hotel rooms across human space. Two beds along one wall, a dresser along another, video unit on the wall that displayed some scenic landscape from an unnamed planet. There was a bathroom next to the entrance and a window along the wall opposite the door. Krieger and Schmidt were, neat, almost too neat. Their clothes had been placed in the drawers of the dresser in military precision. In the bathroom, toilette articles had been placed neatly, one set on either side of the sink. There was a bottle of imported booze, but it was only missing about three fingers.

There was nothing to mark Krieger and Schmidt as anything except a pair of compulsively neat salesmen. Gus raised his eyebrow again as we gave the place the once over. Gus has very expressive eyebrows.

There was an oversized suitcase sitting on a stand next to the dresser. It looked like a salesman's sample case. It was locked. Gus pretended not to look while I fiddled with it. It was an old-fashioned mechanical lock, a lot harder to pick than an electronic one, and much more than you'd expect on a case of sample ladies underwear or whatever.

I finally got the lock opened and dropped the front of the case. My whistle got Gus's attention. The case contained the pieces of a military grade sniper laser, all snug in form fitting foam. With the scope and target finder it probably had an effective range of three kilometers. On Star City that means you could lay down on a roof somewhere and shoot up at someone on the other side of the cylinder with a good probability of hitting them.

It's wasn't an amateur's sort of weapon. Not a hunter's, either. They have lousy rates of fire because of the time needed to recharge the capacitors, but that shouldn't matter because anyone who knew how to use it would only need one shot.

Star City has a somewhat lax stand on weaponry, but we do tend to draw the line at heavy stuff and military grade. Neutrality is the cornerstone of the foreign policy, and the powers that be frown on anyone outgunning them.

"Just what are these guys up to, Frank?" Gus asked. He had a worried expression on his face.

"Do you really want to know?"

"Just what I have to."

"I think these guys are on Star City to kill someone. He's a friend of mine. I don't know the details, but it has something to do with the Nordholm civil war."

Gus grunted. "So what do we do about it?"

"I'd like to handle it quietly. I'm sure the Royal would appreciate that. Maybe you could voice your suspicions to the police."

"That the way you want to play it, Frank?"

I nodded. "You might mention it to Latimer."

"Yeah. I think we better get going, Frank. Can you button that thing up?"

I snapped the case closed and we left.

Gus called me later that night. The police had taken Krieger and Schmidt into custody as "undesirables." They were to be placed on the next ship for Nordholm. Somehow, though, I didn't think our troubles were over.

Marcus, on the other hand, was of a different opinion. He felt relieved and wanted to resume his old life as if nothing had happened. Nothing I said caused him to change his mind. He went back to his old apartment, but called me later that day.

"I feel like celebrating, Frank," he said in his old charming manner. "I think we should go out to dinner. Do it up big time. You, Lucinda, Jocelyn and me. Someplace special."

"Who's Jocelyn?" I asked. I'd never heard the name in connection with Marcus before.

"Jocelyn? That's right, you haven't really been introduced. Remember the tall blonde I was with at Feldman's party."

"Vaguely," I replied. I hadn't thought much about it at the time. Marcus had a habit of picking up one good looking woman or another. None ever seemed to hang around for long.

"Anyway, about dinner. It was Jocelyn's idea, by the way. Said she wanted to cheer me up. She suggested the Café Stellar."

"That's a bit out of my league, Marcus," I said non-committally. The Café Stellar was the restaurant on top of the Casino. It's prices were reputed to be as astronomical as its name. The food was supposed to be worth it though, if you could afford it.

"Don't worry about it, Frank. Jocelyn said she'd pick up the tab. Her daddy's filthy rich. Owns a quarter of some planet I've never heard of. We've got reservations tonight at 20:00."

"I'll check with Lucinda."

"Don't bother. I've already talked to her."

"I guess it's settled then. Dinner at 20:00."

Jocelyn had arranged for a cab to pick us up. I couldn't remember the last time I'd ridden in a cab rather than take a tram. The only car I seem to ride in much is the back seat of Latimer's prowler when he drags me in for questioning.

Jocelyn was already in the car with Marcus, but we had to pick up Lucinda at her studio in the Souk. She was waiting outside on the curb. I'd seen a lot of Lucinda the last month or so, but I'd never seen her dressed in anything except the clothes she painted in. As I took in the view as we pulled up, I decided that that had been a mistake. She was wearing a dress, something shimmery and slinky and just long enough to look classy, the kind of dress that only comes custom tailored and only with lots of cash. I knew Lucinda came from money, but it wasn't the kind of subject we talked about.

I jumped out of the cab to hold the door for her. As she stepped in, she gave me a smile that made the effort worthwhile.

We probably could have gotten to the Casino quicker taking the tram, but that wasn't the point, I guess. We pulled up at the VIP entrance. A real live doorman opened the cab's door and helped the ladies out. As he held Jocelyn's hand he nodded his head and said, "Miss Jocelyn." She replied with a very polished "Thank you, Chester." I wondered how rich you had to be to be on a first name basis with the doorman at the Casino.

An elevator whipped us up to the top of the Casino where the Café Stellar was located. Along the way I had noticed a couple of strategically placed security men giving me the evil eye. I had the urge to open my jacket to show them I wasn't packing a weapon, but I figured that wasn't necessary. They had known that the moment I'd stepped through the front door. If there was one place we'd be safe, it was the Casino.

Dinner was fantastic. I don't know what half of what I ate was, but it was all delicious. It also seemed that there was something more to wine than just red or white. I found myself watching the others to make sure I was using the right utensil. Jocelyn did all the ordering though she consulted with Lucinda on some of the choices. Even Marcus seemed more at home than I was.

After we'd finished we sat around talking. The management seemed in no hurry to kick us out. We were drinking something called coffee. It was like nothing I'd ever had before. It certainly didn't bear any resemblance to joe.

"I'd like to thank you, Frank, for taking care of Marcus's situation," Jocelyn said. I couldn't quite place her accent, but I'd heard it before. All during dinner she'd politely deflected any inquiries that Lucinda or I had made about her background.

"It was nothing," I replied.

"You're too modest, Frank. I think you handled those two thugs very adroitly. You must be very good at your job."

"There's one thing I still don't understand, though," I said.

"What's that?" Jocelyn said more alertly than was warranted.

"How Marcus spotted those two as being after him?"

"Actually it was Jocelyn that spotted them," Marcus chimed in.

"Oh?" I asked.

"It was just a suspicion I had, really," Jocelyn answered. "We were walking to the tram station from the party. I thought we were being followed. When I got a good look at the face of one of them I remembered that I'd been seeing the same face for the last week or so hanging around the Souk."

"But why did you assume they were after Marcus? They might have been after you."

"Don't be silly, Frank. Why would they be after me. Marcus is the famous one." I thought that odd. Marcus hadn't made a name for himself at that time. He was at best a free-lance journalist with an occasional by-line on one of the news services.

There was a lull in the conversation after that which was broken when Lucinda said she was going to powder her nose. In one of those unfathomable feminine rituals Jocelyn got up and accompanied her.

"Well, what do you think, Frank?"

"Of Jocelyn?"

"Of course, you ass."

"She's certainly charming, if a bit—I don't know, mysterious."

"That's part of the appeal, I think," he responded. "Frank, I've got a favor to ask?"

"What?"

"I want you to take this, keep it safe," he reached into his inside jacket pocket and pulled out a memory stick, placing it on the table in front of me.

I palmed it in a magician's move and stuffed it in a hidden pocket in my own jacket. "You sure, Marcus?"

"It's a duplicate. All my notes and everything I've written so far of *A Farewell to Holm*. Just in case something should happen to me."

I looked at him quizzically.

"Despite what you think, I'm not an idiot, Frank. I know they might send someone else after me. I just want some insurance."

"You know, Marcus, don't you, that someone might already be here?"

"Yeah, I've thought about that."

The conversation didn't go any farther as Jocelyn and Lucinda returned from powdering their noses or whatever it was they had done. Dinner broke up shortly after that. The cab took us home. After dropping Lucinda and me off in front of my apartment, Lucinda said as she watched the receding cab:

"You know, I just don't trust her." I didn't think she was just being catty.

"Neither do I, Lucinda, neither do I."

The next few days were pretty uneventful, and I didn't see much of Marcus. He was busy working on *A Farewell to Holm* most of that time. Jocelyn was busy doing whatever rich girls did. During the day Lucinda was busy painting. She was working on a new series of images. They were disturbing, even violent, but somehow strangely beautiful. Me, I was doing a little of this, a little of that and mostly spending my afternoons in the Blue Moon. At night Lucinda and I, well, there's no need to get into that as it's not part of this story.

I was surprised, then, when Marcus came pounding on my door one morning after Lucinda had left for her studio. When I let him in I could see that he was agitated in a way that I hadn't seen before.

"What is it, Marcus?" I asked. "Is someone after you again?"

"It's gone!" was all he could reply.

"What's gone, Marcus? Slow down and tell me all about it."

"My memory stick! It's missing!"

"When was the last time you saw it?"

"Last night. I took it off when Jocelyn and I—." For a writer Marcus could be remarkably reticent about certain things. "She says it gets in the way—" he said sheepishly by way of explanation.

"I get the idea, Marcus. You took it off last night—"

"And it wasn't there this morning."

"Where's Jocelyn?"

"You can't think she took it, can you Frank?" he responded as if the idea had never occurred to him.

"Was anyone else in your place between the time you took it off and when you noticed it missing?"

"No—but Jocelyn? Why would she want it?"

"That's a good question, Marcus," I answered. Ever since the dinner, something had been bothering me about Jocelyn, but I hadn't been able to pin it down. Now, listening to Marcus, things were dropping into place.

The first thing was her accent. I'd been trying to place it without much luck. Now it came to me. She sounded a lot like Marcus. Not so much on the surface, but in the inflections, the way she pronounced certain words, the specific words that she used for some things. Humans have spread out to dozens of worlds, but on most of these worlds they speak a common language derived more or less from American back on Earth. But each planet has its own little quirks, special vocabulary and phrases. Jocelyn worked hard to cover it up, but in the little unconscious details she sounded a lot like Marcus, like someone who had been born on Nordholm. And she had never mentioned where she was from, which was odd. Usually people are only too happy to talk about their homeworld.

"Where's Jocelyn from, Marcus?" I asked straight out.

"I don't know. Some agricultural planet out towards the fringe I think."

"Not Nordholm?" I asked.

"No. Why would you think that, Frank?"

"The accent, for one," I responded.

"What accent?" Marcus said, puzzled. "Jocelyn doesn't have an accent."

"She doesn't have an accent to you, Marcus. That's because you both grew up on Nordholm. To me she has a noticeable accent and she sounds a lot like you."

"That's ridiculous, Frank. If she was from Nordholm, she would have mentioned it."

"Yes, she would have, considering how much that Nordholm has been in the news since the refugee ship. And seeing as you are from Nordholm. Usually, when two people meet who are from the same place, they compare notes; see if they know any of the same people or same places. Jocelyn hasn't done that, has she, Marcus? Maybe that's because she doesn't want you to know."

"That's crazy, Frank. Why would she not want me to know she was from Nordholm?"

"Maybe it's because she wanted to get close to you without arousing your suspicions. Maybe it's because she wanted to find out where you kept all your notes from the war."

Marcus started to protest, but stopped, just standing there with his mouth open. I could see in his eyes the pieces of the puzzle dropping into place in his mind.

"There's another thing, Marcus, that's been bothering me, except I didn't know what it was. Jocelyn said that night at dinner that she had noticed Krieger and Schmidt hanging around for a week, which was why she was suspicious of them. But Krieger and Schmidt hadn't been on Star City for a week. Their ship had only docked three days earlier."

"If, as you seem to be suggesting, Frank, that Jocelyn is some sort of spy for the Nordholm government, why would she alert me to Krieger and Schmidt?"

"Marcus, if there's one thing I've learned in my line of work on Star City is that there are never just two sides. Think about it. Who wants the information you have? We know the loyalist government wants it, but the Kocks want it, too, to keep it out of the hands of the loyalists. And those are just the two players that we know about. There could be others, as well, who are afraid of what you know, or what they think you might know."

It was starting to make sense to Marcus. I could see the panic building in his eyes. "What am I going to do, Frank?"

"What you should probably have done when you first spotted Krieger. I don't think you can stay on Star City and be safe, Marcus. It's time to move on. You should go to Crockett or someplace else where they actually believe in law and order."

"But won't they be expecting that, Frank? Won't they be watching all the liners leaving Star City?"

"Oh, they'll be watching the liners, all right, Marcus. But there are other ships besides the liners, ships where you'll be safe once they undock."

"How can I do that? I don't know anything about freighters."

"Leave that to me, Marcus. I have some contacts. How much cash can you come up with?"

"I don't know. Maybe five thousand."

"That should be enough," I said. "What you have to do, Marcus, is act like nothing has happened until I can arrange things. That may take a few days. But Jocelyn and whoever else may be after you can't be sure that you haven't stashed a duplicate of the data someplace."

"But I have, Frank. You've got a copy and there's another in the data vault at the bank."

"See. That's why we've got some time. They'll wait until they can get their hands on the duplicates. All you have to do is act like you don't know it."

"Easy for you to say, Frank."

It took a few days to arrange passage for Marcus. While I had connections and connections who had connections, I wanted to work with someone who I trusted and to do it all quietly. That meant working with the limited number of tramp freighter captains that were reliable. The problem with tramps is that they don't run on nice regular schedules or travel the most popular routes.

I spent a lot of time looking at the arrivals and departure listings, but I finally found something promising, The Serengeti bound for Montego. I'd helped the captain out a few years back when one of his crewmen went missing, so he owed me a favor. His destination, Montego, was a planet in a system less than five years from Crockett, close enough that Marcus would be able to make a connection without much problem should he so wish. Montego was a largely water world that had been settled mostly from the over-populated Caribbean islands in the first mad wave of colonization out of Earth. Most of what land there was was spread out amongst thousands of islands with relatively small populations. The good thing about that was that strangers, particularly from someplace like Nordholm, would stand out like a sore thumb, making it hard for would be assassins to go unnoticed.

I gave the captain a call and arranged for a meeting at a gin joint near the freight docking ring. He was willing enough to carry a passenger off the books. We haggled about the price, settled on a fare half of what he had asked and twice what I had offered, and drank a shot of brown to settle the deal. Marcus was to show up at the docking port a few hours before the scheduled departure. The time was the middle of the day which is the best time to do something if you don't want it noticed. With any luck Jocelyn would be busy pretending to shop.

When I told Marcus he seemed less than pleased.

"Frank, do you really think this is necessary?"

"Only if you want to keep breathing. You've already dodged one pair of killers, and my guess is Jocelyn is just waiting to get her hands on the rest of the copies of your notes before she sticks a knife in your back. And those are only the players that we've identified."

"But this Montego, Frank. I've never even heard of it."

"It's a lovely world, Marcus. Lots of nice tropical weather, beautiful beaches, lovely oceans. I hear the fishing is great. You'll love it." I was going from what the Serengeti's captain had told me. I'd never been there, myself, of course. I've never been off of Star City. I had to admit that the idea of all that water and open sky scared the crap out of me, but I was trying to do a sell job to Marcus. "Besides, it's only a short hop from Montego to Crockett. There's a weekly liner from the spaceport. You'll be in the fleshpots of Crockett before you know it drinking real booze and eating real food."

"You sound like a bloody travel agent, Frank. I'm a writer, not a tourist."

"You can write anywhere, Marcus. But only if you're still breathing."

"I guess you're right," he agreed reluctantly. "I'm going to miss, you, though."

"Send me a postcard from Montego."

I had agreed to escort Marcus to the ship. I didn't really have any reason to expect trouble, but that little sixth sense at the back of my brain was feeling uneasy. Over the years, I've learned to listen to that feeling. It wouldn't hurt to take a few precautions.

I'd gotten up before Lucinda, showered and dressed. Looking at my reflection in the bedroom mirror I could see Lucinda stretching with a yawn before jumping off the bed and heading for the bathroom. I was convinced that main reason she had been spending so many nights at my place was that it had a shower which her studio lacked.

While she took her turn in the shower I opened up the safe in the back of my closet where I keep most of my weapons trying to decide what would be appropriate. I finally decided on a Kunstler 50 kilojoule laser with a military style power pack. It was a little heavy, but the extra punch and shorter recycling time was worth it in a serious fire fight. I was strapping on the shoulder holster when Lucinda popped out of the bathroom wrapped in nothing but a towel. A troubled look crossed her face when she saw the pistol.

"That's a pretty big gun, Frank," she commented. "What's happening?" Despite the incident with Krieger and Schmidt, I don't think she had ever really fully understood what it was I did for a living.

"I've made arrangements to get Marcus off of Star City. I'm taking him to the ship."

"You never mentioned anything about this before," she said, her voice tightening. "Didn't you trust me to keep a secret?"

"I didn't make the final arrangements until yesterday. It just didn't come up last night," I finished lamely.

"But you think you might need some heavy firepower." Lucinda knew enough about weapons to recognize the Kunstler as something more than the little needle gun I'd been carrying around in my pocket since the night Marcus had showed up with his story about people being out to get him. "Were you going to tell me anything?"

"Lucinda, I didn't want you to worry."

"What makes you think I'd worry, Frank?" She threw the towel on the bed and began to dress.

I wasn't sure whether she was mad because I might be going into danger or because I hadn't trusted her enough to tell her. I shrugged. As an afterthought I slipped a little pocket laser in my boot top. My needle gun was already in the side pocket of my jacket. Putting the jacket on, I checked myself in the mirror to make sure nothing was too obvious.

"Will you be here tonight, Frank?" Lucinda asked uncertainly.

"Of course, I'm just walking Marcus to the ship. It should only take a couple of hours."

"Well, I've got work to do, then," Lucinda said and walked out the door.

I went over the place that Marcus was staying at. He'd moved since his old place had been tossed by Krieger and

Schmidt, but he was still in the Souk. He had all his possessions packed into two carry-on bags. He was still traveling light in those days. I didn't offer to help him with the bags. I wanted to keep my hands free. Marcus didn't seem to notice.

"You didn't tell anyone you were leaving, did you?" I asked.

"No, of course not, Frank. I'm not an idiot." He seemed insulted by the question.

"Did you see Jocelyn last night?"

"We had dinner," he replied. "We had sex, too, afterwards, if you must know, Frank, but I didn't say anything about leaving. I left this morning before she woke up."

I let it drop. We took a tram down towards the freight end of Star City getting off a stop before the entry check point for the lower docking ring. Access to the docking ring is restricted, more to control theft and smuggling than for security purposes. You need a boarding pass, ship's ID or some other sort of credential to get past the check point.

Neither of us had a pass, of course, but I had made arrangements to get access. About half way around the ring there was a door for maintenance access. A couple of fifty credit notes had convinced a guy I know to lend me his ID card and that of a co-worker for the day. I was supposed to get them to him by 1700 so he could work the evening shift.

The door was unmarked and down the length of a narrow corridor under the theory that obscurity is sometimes the best defense. There was a card slot next to the lock. I knew the door scanner would flag security if more than one person entered at a time, so I sent Marcus through first. After the door had shut behind him, I inserted the ID card, waited for the door to open, and walked through. On the other side of the door was the docking ring itself, a hundred meters wide and curving up in the distance in either direction.

Marcus was standing just the other side of the door, his hands raised. Jocelyn was standing there, a laser pistol pointed at his chest.

"Nice to see you again, Frank," Jocelyn said in her rich girl voice. "Please remove the weapon from your holster and put it on the floor. Carefully, Frank. We wouldn't want any accidents, now, would we?"

I withdrew the Kunstler using only my thumb and forefinger and placed it on the deck in front of me.

"Good, Frank. I'm glad you're being reasonable. Now kick it over to me."

I did as she asked. She picked it up in her left hand.

"What's this all about, Jocelyn?" Marcus asked innocently. I don't think anyone could be as naïve as he sounded.

"Oh, I think you know, Marcus. But it's a little too public here. Why don't we move over that way?" Most cargo is moved by robots, but there were a few people off in the distance. Her laser pistol pointed in the direction of a pair of shipping containers waiting to be loaded onto a ship. The containers were each about ten meters long and three high. The space between them would be pretty well shielded from the view of anyone not directly in line with the gap. We did as she asked.

"I'll take the memory stick you wear around your neck now, Marcus," she ordered once we were between the two containers.

"Just who are you, Jocelyn? Who do you work for?" Marcus asked.

"The complete journalist to the end, aren't you, Marcus," Jocelyn replied. "I would have thought you'd have guessed. I'm sure Frank has figured it out." In point of fact, I hadn't. All I knew was that there was more than one side in this game.

"For the record, then, I work for Nordholm State Security, Marcus. We're very interested in what's on the memory stick. Who we can trust, and who we can blackmail. The Kocks for example."

"You know about Walker, then?"

"Walker is dead, Marcus. I shot him myself. But he was just a little weasel doing dirty work for the real money."

All this time, the laser in Jocelyn's right hand was pointed at the middle of Marcus's chest. But her eyes were locked on me.

"Why don't you just kill the Kocks? The NSS doesn't really need evidence, does it?" Marcus asked.

"No, but their deaths might make people uneasy. Besides, it may well be more advantageous to have a threat to hold over the Kocks than to just eliminate them. But enough chatter. Just hand over the memory stick. Do it without any fuss and I promise I'll make it quick, Marcus. If you make me work for it I can make your death both slow and painful."

"You know I've got another copy in a data vault of the Bank of Star City, Jocelyn, don't you?"

"Of course, Marcus. But if you disappear, it will just stay there until they erase it when the rent isn't paid. We can live with that. Now hand it over."

Marcus glanced over at me, hoping that I had something planned to get us out of it. I just shrugged.

He reached inside his shirt and pulled the chain holding the memory stick up over his head. He reached out with it dangling from his fingers, but as Jocelyn extended her left hand to grab it a look of surprise swept across her face. At the same instant a red spot blossomed between her two breasts. She had been shot from behind by a high powered laser.

"Dive, Marcus," I yelled hoping the cycle time of the laser would prevent whoever had shot Jocelyn from picking us off.

My hopes must have been answered, because we both had reached cover behind the ends of the shipping containers, one on each side of the gap. I noticed that Marcus still had the memory stick clutched in his hand. I pulled the needler out of my pocket and poked my head around the corner of the container and whipped a couple of needles down the length of the gap. I wasn't expecting to hit anything, I just wanted to keep them honest and give us time to judge the situation. It seemed to have had the right effect, because I saw boots dragging across the gap as somebody scurried to hide behind the other end of the shipping container.

So far it had been a surprisingly quiet gun battle, as neither lasers nor needle guns make much noise. Someone could have been fifty meters away and not have heard a thing.

Marcus was sitting with his back against the container on his side, his face white as a sheet. Reaching into my boot top and pulled out the laser pistol I had stashed there. It was a little thing, 15 kilo joules, and the power pack was probably only good for a dozen shots, but it might give us an advantage. I'm a pretty good shot with a needle gun, but ten meters was getting close to the effective range.

I tossed the pistol to Marcus. He bobbled the catch, but recovered and held it in his hand staring at it as if wondering what it was. I've always marveled at his later reputation as a hunter of big game.

"What am I suppose to do with this, Frank?"

"The little button on the side turns it on. You point it and pull the trigger. It takes fifteen seconds to cycle before you can fire another shot. It only has enough power for about a dozen shots, so use them wisely. I don't expect you to hit anything with it, Marcus, just keep their heads down when I tell you to. Got it?"

"I think so." He didn't sound all that certain.

I poked my head around the corner of the container again. I pulled it back quick and a laser pulse struck the edge just where my head had been. I'd seen enough, though. There were two of them. Like Marcus and me, there was one hiding behind the end of each container. I also had noticed that the Kunstler was lying on the deck next to Jocelyn's body. I didn't think that the gunmen at the other end could see it.

"Who are these guys, Frank?"

"Damned if I know. Probably back up for Krieger and Schmidt. Maybe the plan all along was for those two to act as decoys while this pair just waited for the right moment."

"So they work for the Kocks?"

"Is there anyone else on that memory stick of yours?"

"A few," Marcus answered. I could see him doing some mental calculus matching names and motives.

"We can worry about that later, Marcus. Let's just try to stay alive now."

"So what do we do?"

That was a good question. At the moment it was a standoff, both sides hiding at opposite ends of the two containers. There was nothing else on the ring within fifty meters that would provide cover. I knew that the two facing us couldn't wait indefinitely. Sooner or later somebody was bound to wander by that might ask questions. Marcus and I could afford to sit, but they would have to act, and act soon.

I kept thinking about the Kunstler lying in the gap. If I could reach it, it would change the balance of power, but with two guns covering the gap it might as well be on Earth. I could hear them talking it over on the other end, too, but I couldn't make out the words.

They stopped talking. I could hear the sound of footsteps on metal. Somehow one of them had managed to get on top of the container. There must be a step or ladder or something on that end. On our end, the container was smooth. There was no chance to get up. I could hear the footsteps approaching cautiously.

"Marcus, I'm going to fire a shot down the gap, and then I'm going to try and reach the Kunstler. If the guy on the other end pokes his head out shoot at him. And try not to hit me. Ready?"

I didn't wait for his reply, just let a flight of needles whiz down the gap before I dove for the Kunster trying to keep Jocelyn's body between me and the gunman. It worked, sort of. I reached the body, but the Kunstler was just out of reach. Lying behind Jocelyn I saw him poke his head out to fire. I snapped a quick burst from the needle gun. There was a scream of pain that was cut short. I had hit him in the eye and the needle had torn through his brain killing him.

His friend had moved, though and as I looked up I saw his laser pointing down at me from on top of the container. As if in slow motion I could see his finger tightening around the trigger, then he toppled forward, falling off the container onto the deck below. Marcus had shot him through the heart.

I stood up shakily. "I thought you couldn't shoot. You got him right in the heart."

Marcus's face had gone even whiter. "I was aiming at his head," he admitted sheepishly. He came up next to me and stared down at the body. For a moment I thought he was going to be sick.

"What do we do now?" Marcus asked.

"You've still got a ship to catch."

"What about Jocelyn? And these others?"

I checked the bodies. They were all dead. "We can't leave them here. Too many questions. It's probably best if they just disappear."

I got Marcus to the Serengeti and with the help of a couple of the crewmen we dragged the bodies to the Serengeti's cargo hatch. I got the captain to agree to dump them someplace en route to Montego. It took another thousand dollars, but fortunately, Jocelyn had had that much on her.

Marcus and I said our good-byes, shook hands, and then he walked through the Serengeti's hatch. After the hatch closed behind him, I realized that I would probably never see him again.

I waited on the docking ring until the Serengeti unberthed and then headed home. It was before noon when I got there.

Over the next few weeks Latimer came around several times and asked a few questions about the missing, but I could sense he wasn't really interested in the answers. Off world assassins were bad for business. The story was finally let out that Marcus had booked passage on a freighter to gather material for an article. This seemed to satisfy everyone. Jocelyn and the unnamed gunmen were quietly forgotten.

Marcus made it to Montego without incident, but didn't book passage to Crockett until some six months later. He spent the intervening time finishing *A Farewell to Holm*, the book that made his reputation. While on Montego Marcus also took up deep sea fishing, writing a couple of articles on the subject that circulated widely in the galactic press and were the beginning of his reputation as an outdoorsman. He still goes back there for a month or so every year to fish and drink. The local ministry of tourism loves him. Marcus has created quite an image for himself these days hunting large creatures on one planet or another and writing about it. Some people get into that sort of thing, mostly accountants who have never shot a gun. Me, I don't see the sport. I did read *The Old Man's Fish*, which wasn't half bad.

I've read *A Farewell to Holm* and thought it was good. I also read *The Sun Never Rises*, which is a sort of fictionalized account of his time on Star City, but I didn't like it as well. Jack Feldman threatened to sue over what he perceived was an unflattering depiction of himself, but secretly I think he was pleased by the attention he received because of it. They even briefly reissued his one book because of it. There's also a character in *The Sun Never Rises* that is supposed to be loosely based on me, but personally, I didn't see the resemblance.

Marcus kept his word and sent me a postcard from Montego along with an autographed first edition of *A Farewell to Holm*. He's done the same with each of his subsequent books, even the ones I can't bring myself to read. I keep them on a shelf in my apartment. They've appreciated in value quite a bit since they were issued. I think of it as my retirement plan.

After Marcus left, Lucinda started spending fewer nights at my place, finally stopping all together. I was never quite able to figure out what bothered her the most, the sometimes violent reality of my life, or the fact that I hadn't trusted her enough to tell her about Marcus's departure. She finally moved on to Crockett where, as I've mentioned, she became quite famous. In addition to the painting I hang over my bed, she gave me another painting as a parting gift the day she left. It was wrapped in paper and she told me not to open it until after her ship had departed. When I unwrapped it I discovered it was a portrait, one of the very few that she's ever done. The subject is very disturbing and appears not quite human. A few years later a guy I know who knows about such things told me I could probably sell it at auction on Crockett for several hundred thousand. I'll have to think about it. Meanwhile it hangs in the entry of my apartment where people can't read that Lucinda had written on the back "Portrait of Frank Sladek."

I still run across Jack Feldman occasionally. We nod politely and move on. Most of the rest of that crowd has moved on as well, to be replaced by a fresh hoard of want to be artists and poets more interested in drinking and sex than work. I try to avoid the Souk if I can.

And Frank Sladek? What happened to him? He's back sitting at the bar of the Blue Moon and making a living finding things for people. When *Some Have, Some Haven't* came out, he had a few minutes of fame because Marcus supposedly based the main character on him, but that died away when people realized the book wasn't as good as some of Marcus's earlier ones. It's just as well; fame is not an asset in my line of work.

Lizardmen Carry Two Guns

LIZARDMEN CARRY TWO GUNS

It was the middle of the afternoon and I was in the Blue Moon having a drink when I got the call. I'd been doing that a lot since Lucinda had left for Crockett, having a drink in the Blue Moon in the middle of the afternoon, that is, not getting a call. Not that I was drunk. I wasn't that far gone. But I was kind of at loose ends, with no girl and no current clients.

The call was on the link I use for business, which meant it might be a job. I don't have an office, it has always seemed like an unnecessary expense, and given the nature of my business, keeping the overhead low is a good thing. Most of my clients contact me over the comm or meet me at someplace like the Blue Moon, which is a nice quiet saloon on the edge of New Minglewood, where the clientele know enough to mind their own business. I like it that way and so do most of the people who hire me.

Some people call me a private detective. I've got a license that says the same thing. But mostly I find things for people— things that have gone missing. Sometimes I act as a go between, which often amounts to the same thing.

Anyway, I wasn't drunk, but I had been drinking when the call came in. Which might explain why I took the job. Otherwise, I probably would have never touched it. Not that I'm a bigot or anything, but I just don't like working for lizardmen.

The fact was, I also needed something to occupy my time. I'd kind of been neglecting the business end of things for a while, but with Lucinda gone, I figured that it was time to get back to work.

The comm said the caller was a "Mr. Smith." The Thessarine language is hard for humans to pronounce correctly, something about getting the sibilants right, so lizardmen tend to use nicknames when dealing with humans. That, and they just don't like giving out their true names. It works both ways. Lizardmen can never quite master the vowels in human languages, they just don't come out sounding, well, human.

I know that there are some people who claim they can recognize the individual patterns of mottling on the faces of lizardmen, but to me they all look alike. Not that I've seen that many. They tend to be fairly rare in what is referred to as the human sphere of influence, that irregular blotch of space where the sons and daughters of Terra have settled. Those that do show up rarely get farther than Star City. There is a certain amount of trade in commodities between the two species, but relations tend to be distant. As far as I knew, I'd never seen Mr. Smith before, but that was just a guess.

"Sladek here. You wanted to talk business?"

"Mr. Sladek. Are you available for employment?" As I said, the vowels weren't quite right, but otherwise Mr. Smith's Terran was quite fluent.

This is where I made my first mistake. "I might be if the job is right."

"I understand that on occasion you act as an intermediary in certain commercial transactions. Is this correct?"

As I said earlier, I sometimes act as a go-between when the two parties don't really trust each other. I've got something of a reputation for being relatively honest, which on Star City is saying something. I replied, "On occasion."

"I would prefer not to make arrangements over the comm. Would it be possible for you to meet me at Ssassaire's, in, say, an hour to discuss the matter further? I am prepared to pay all your usual contingencies."

"Sure, I can make it. Ssassaire's you say?"

"Yess, Ssassaires's in the Souk. I'm sure you will recognize me. If not, I am aware of you appearance, Mr. Sladek." That should have been another tip off, but I was really not in the mood to be cautious.

"I'll be there. In an hour." I hung up the comm.

The edge of the Souk is only a ten minute walk from the Blue Moon, so I ordered another shot of brown from the bartender.

Out of the two million or so inhabitants of Star City, only about fifty thousand or so are non-human. Most of those live in a part of the station known as the Souk. It's not really a ghetto, and there are a fair number of humans who live there too, mostly because the rents are cheap. It's very popular with the artsy crowd at the moments. There are a lot of small restaurants on the ground floors of the buildings serving variations of the local cuisines of dozens of planets and nearly as many species. Walking the streets of the Souk is to be assaulted by the scents and odors of a mélange of exotic spices. Some are quite pleasant, some will turn your stomach if you get to big a whiff.

I'd never been in Ssassaire's before, though I'd passed by it walking dozens of times. It catered to the few Thessarine on Star City, who liked to keep to themselves and discouraged outsiders. Besides Thessarine food doesn't have the cross cultural appeal of say Somany or even blue-man cuisine.

Outside on the street, the glow tubes that run down the center of Star City were still bright, but as I stood in the doorway looking inside it was quite dim. It was also artificially humid with the smell of lush vegetation, evoking the Thessarine home world, I assumed. I let my eyes adjust a moment before stepping fully inside.

The place was nearly empty. Off along one side there was a bar of sorts with a lizard barman using a rag to wipe a glass. Another lizardman stood idly at the doorway to the kitchen. Sitting at a table in a rear corner was a third lizardman. I guessed that this was Mr. Smith. Oddly enough there was a human woman sitting at the table with him.

Walking over to the table I asked, "Mr. Smith?"

"You are prompt, Mr. Sladek. Have a seat."

I sat. Mr. Smith was a typical lizardman, but then, to most humans, they all look alike. Thessarines are bipedal, usually a little under two meters in height, and have slightly scaly skin that is mottled in an intricate pattern of greens, tans and blacks that must have been great camouflage in the primordial jungle. They had two large, black eyes set over something that isn't quite a nose and a wide, toothy mouth set in a weak chin. The best way to describe one is to imagine what might have happened on Earth if a giant rock hadn't wiped out the dinosaurs seventy odd million years ago and the fast smart ones had kept evolving without competition from little furry things. They might well have ended up something like the Thessarines. In lizardman fashion, Mr. Smith was dressed in garments that weren't quite a shirt and pants. It occurred to me that they could quite easily conceal a laser pistol or a needle gun. He motioned to the woman sitting next to him.

"This is Karissa. She assists me when it is convenient to have a human intermediary."

I nodded to the woman. She was slender and of medium height with hair cut short. It was a bleached blonde that looked as if it was the result of sunlight rather than chemicals. She was dressed unusually, but with Star City serving as a transit point for dozens of planets one learns to accept quirky fashions. She wasn't particularly attractive in a conventional sense, but there was a certain brittle presence to her that drew you in.

"You have a reputation of being discrete. Is that correct Mr. Sladek?"

"I tend not to get complaints in that department."

"Then we understand each other. There is a certain transaction I wish to make and I wish to avoid unnecessary attention. I would like you to act as my agent for this transaction."

"And the nature of this transaction?"

"A certain object of no great intrinsic value but of symbolic significance is arriving on Star City in a few days. I have made arrangements to purchase this object. You will carry the currency for the transaction, exchange it, and return with the object. I am prepared to pay substantially if you are successful and can carry out the transfer with a minimum of as you say—fuss."

"Sounds simple enough. What's the catch?" I'd learned long ago that when people set up deals in dark public rooms there is always a catch.

"Ah. Yess. Astute of you, Mr. Sladek. I see your reputation is justified. There are, as you surmised, other parties who for their own purposes are interested in obtaining the object. They might make a counter offer to the human bringing it in. It is possible they might even use unscrupulous means."

Thessarines have a reputation for being highly ethical between themselves even when they are of opposing families, clans, nations. This ethical behavior does not necessarily extend to other species.

"Would these unscrupulous means extend to the use of force?"

"Possibly."

"I see," I said. "Just how much is this—object—worth?"

"It has no price, Mr. Sladek. However, I have agreed to pay one million dollars Crockett for possession of the object."

"So when you say no price, you mean priceless," I replied. Mr. Smith only nodded. "And, not to be too sordid, what would my—commission be for handling this transaction?"

"Five thousand dollars Crockett. I will give you one thousand, as you say, up front, and the balance upon completion. I will also cover any legitimate expenses."

"Expenses?"

"It may be necessary to pay a few small bribes in the case of unforeseen eventualities."

"I see. Will you be needing an itemized list of—expenses?"

"I will rely on your honesty, Mr. Sladek."

"Do I have your assurance that possession of this object violates no laws on Star City?" I asked. Not that there were many laws on Star City, but those in power did tend to frown on certain classes of extremely deadly weapons or mind damaging pharmaceuticals.

"The object in question is neither a weapon or a drug and was obtained lawfully, at least by he who currently possesses it."

"I think, then, we have a deal, Mr. Smith."

"Good. Karissa?"

The woman reached into her purse and withdrew a roll of bills that would have choked a horse, supposing I knew what a horse was. She began to count them out. They were $20 Crockett bills which is unusual. Most people only use the $100s for convenience. Fifty of them made quite a pile. I picked them up and stuffed the wad into my inside jacket pocket.

"When and where do I make the exchange?"

"The details are indeterminate at this point, but within a few days. The object will be arriving on a freighter. I will have Karrisa contact you when they are confirmed and she will give you the currency for the transaction at that time."

"I'll be waiting," I said.

There was an awkward moment of silence. Finally Mr. Smith said, "There is nothing here requiring your further attention, Mr. Sladek."

I took my cue and departed.

I didn't know it then, but my meeting with Mr. Smith was the first move in a complex multi-player chess game in which I was just one of the pieces. But was I a knight or a rook? I couldn't see myself as a bishop, or was I just to be a pawn? More importantly, at least to me, was I intended to be a sacrificial pawn?

The wad of Crockett double sawbucks in my pocket was making me nervous. Funny thing about that. Most of my business tends to be in cash. I often found myself walking around with five or ten hundred dollar notes and never thinking twice about it, but the pile of fifty twenties seemed to weigh my jacket down like they were made of lead. I also felt like the bulge they created in my jacket was acting like a target for every bravo walking the street. I decided to ditch them at my apartment before doing anything else.

My apartment is just across from the Blue Moon. Yeah, I know, convenient. Only a short ten minute walk through a neighborhood on the edge of New Minglewood. There was really no reason I should feel uneasy. It was still early evening, and there was still plenty of traffic moving around. The glow tubes a kilometer and a half above on the spine that runs down the center of Star City were just beginning to dim for the night. It would be an hour before they went out.

I'd gone maybe two blocks when I realized I had a tail. He wasn't very good at it, either. It took another block for me to spot him, but then he stood out like a sore toe. He wasn't a local, I could tell that from the way he was dressed and the way he moved, like the pseudo-gravity due to the spin on the city wasn't what he was used to. That, in and of itself, wasn't that out of the ordinary. With Star City being the prime transit point for human space, it tends to attract every con-man, grifter, and two bit hood on the make from just about every planet humans have settled on. But this guy was a recent arrival, and hadn't taken any pains to conceal the fact. Either he was an amateur or he was confident enough in himself not to care.

Now, follow the leader is a game you get a lot of practice in in my line of work. I could have lost him in three blocks if I had wanted to. But I didn't see the advantage in that. I've always found that the ones you can see are a lot less dangerous than the ones you don't. Instead I decided to play him and find out his racket.

I took the next street on the left and then waited at the next right for him to round the corner. I disappeared from his view just as he caught sight of me. Halfway down the block was an alley, I ducked into it and stepped into the first doorway. My shadow must have been afraid that he'd lost me because he turned into the alley almost jogging. He didn't even bother to look into the doorway as he went by.

I snuck up behind him and shoved the big knuckle of my first finger into his back and let his imagination do the rest. I know it's a dodge as old as Grock the first caveman, but it's surprising how often it works.

"I don't want no trouble, Mr. Sladek," my shadow said. He was medium height but with broad shoulders and big thighs, like he'd grown up on some planet where the gravity was more than Terran normal. The sides of his head were shaved, leaving only a strip of blonde hair running down the middle to the nape of his neck where it hung long. He spoke with an accent I couldn't place, but then there are so many planets it's hard to keep them straight. My guess was it was some backwater that had been settled a long time ago in the first wave of human settlement. "Look, I just want to talk."

It bothered me a little that he knew my name. Not that I don't have something of a reputation, but for a new arrival to have found it out meant it wasn't just casual.

"You could have called and made an appointment. My business hours are between 1300 and 1700."

"It wasn't until you met with Smith that I knew you were involved."

"Involved? Involved in what?" I gave him a little nudge with my finger. Let him guess whether it was a laser or a needler.

"The Egg. Or didn't Mr. Smith tell you what it was he wanted you to fetch for him?"

This guy seemed to know more about my business than I did. "What goes on between me and a client tends to be confidential. What goes on with guys in dark alleys not so much. What's this egg? And give me the straight before I decide to fry a kidney." I'd decided in my own mind that my fake gun was a laser pistol. Details like that are important in putting over a bluff.

"So he didn't tell you? It's the Iridium Egg."

That was the first I'd heard of it. "Iridium Egg? What kind of dingus is that?"

"It's a sculpture made out of iridium. It's shaped like a lizardman's egg. It's got a ring around the middle of what look like pebbles. They're uncut diamonds. It has some sort of religious or philosophical importance to the lizardmen. No one knows how old it is, maybe thousands of years, but it's been lost for at least the last five hundred. The rumor was that it was buried somewhere on a planet just over the boundary with human space during the last big holy war amongst the lizardmen."

"So? What's this egg got to do with me?"

"The rumor is that it was dug up by some prospector out on Belladona. Your Mr. Smith is trying to buy it. You're the middleman."

"So what's it to you? And why were you tailing me?"

"There's more than one party looking to acquire the Egg. Different clans or families or whatever they are of lizardmen. They're willing to pay plenty. I'm just trying to get a piece of the action. I'm willing to offer you twice what Smith is offering you if you put it in my hands rather than his."

"Sorry. I don't work that way." I didn't like the implication that I could be bought. At least so cheaply. I was starting to wish that I really did have a laser in my mitt.

"I'll make it three times. Four. What did Smith promise you? Three grand? Five?"

I lied. "Ten."

"See, the lizards are willing to pay plenty for the Egg. Name your price."

"Like I said, I don't work that way." Pushing him against the wall of the alley, I patted him down. I found a little 25 kilojoule laser in his right jacket pocket. Not much more than a toy, but better than a knuckle. Other than that he seemed clean.

"Beat it before I change my mind. And stop sticking your nose in my business."

He must have decided that I meant it because he took off down the alley and didn't look back.

The laser wasn't much of a weapon, but I felt better on the walk back to my apartment. If anyone else was tailing me, they were too good for me to spot. I stashed the wad of currency into the safe built into the back wall of my closet behind my dress shirts. I was tempted to stop at the Blue Moon for a drink, but at that hour it gets crowded and noisy. Instead I decided that I needed something to make me forget the smell of lizardmen. The diner on the corner would take care of that.

They were serving brown stew. It's called that not because of the color but because of the vat they pull what passes for meat from that makes up the protein. Most people who weren't born on Star City would find it disgusting, but it reminds me of home cooking. Real comfort food. Just like momma made before she took off with some con-man who said he was from Terra. She never came back. Actually her stew was never that good, either.

It turns out my efforts to expunge the scent of lizardman were wasted. As I left the diner I found myself face to face with another scaly face. I said earlier that I can't tell one from another, but that wasn't strictly true. This one was a little taller, his garments were a little more garish and the mottling of his scales wasn't quite the same as Mr. Smith. I could see that he was packing a pistol, too. It looked like a 75 kilojoule with a heavy duty power pack. It made the piece I had left in my pocket look like a toy.

"Meester Sladek?" His terran wasn't as good as Mr. Smith's. He had more trouble with the vowels.

"That's me."

"You've been contacted by Mr. Smith, I believe."

"Maybe."

"No matter. I am Mr. Jones. I will pay you for the Egg. More than Smith."

"The only eggs I have are in my refrigerator."

"Do not attempt amusement, Sladek. You will have the Egg. I want it. I will have it. One way or the other."

"I already told one guy that I don't work that way. I've made a deal with Mr. Smith. I intend on keeping it."

"As you wish, Sladek. You've been warned." He walked past me giving me a bump with his shoulder as he did. It was a cheap shot. He didn't look back as he reached the corner and disappeared out of sight.

"Great," I said to myself. "What more can happen to me?" I have a feeling I shouldn't have asked that question, because a few seconds later an unmarked prowl car pulled up to the curb next to me. Inside were two of my least favorite flatfoots, Detective Sergeant Latimer and his flunky partner Detective Rossetti.

"Get in back, Sladek. We're going for a little ride."

The door popped open and I got in the back seat. There was no point in resisting. I figured I was safe. Latimer was in the passenger seat. He never lets Rossetti drive unless he wants to talk. Rossetti pulled away from the curb and drove off.

I won't say that Latimer is my favorite cop, but over the years we've come to a sort of understanding. He's what passes for an honest cop on Star City. Rossetti I'm not so sure about, but Latimer usually manages to keep him on a short leash.

"Since when have you taken to hanging around lizardmen, Sladek?" the detective asked. He wasn't exactly being belligerent, but there was an edge to the tone of his voice.

"Who told you that?"

"You were seen meeting with one that goes by the name of 'Mr. Smith.' We've been keeping an eye on him. A little bit later you were approached by another. 'Mr. Jones.' So what's the deal, Frank?"

"Just business. Mr. Smith had a job for me. He wants to make an exchange while keeping a low profile. Probably because of the hostile attitude towards aliens on the part of the police. As far as I can tell, it's strictly legitimate."

"That's a laugh, Sladek," Rossetti chimed in.

"Keep your eyes on the road," Latimer countered. I get the impression sometimes that he hates Rossetti more than I do.

"So what's this exchange, Frank?"

"Usual. Some guy is bringing in a package on a freighter. I meet him; give him a bag of money in exchange for the package."

"So what's in the package?" Latimer asked with the patience of a career flatfoot.

"Smith didn't say," I replied.

Latimer turned around and gave me his best cop stare. "You can do better than that, can't you, Frank?"

"Smith didn't say. The one goes by Jones seemed to think it was some dingus called the 'Egg.' So did some other guy, for that matter, though he called it an 'Iridium Egg.' He was human, by the way. From some fringe world by the way he talked."

"Yeah, we know about him. He's a two-bit hood named Kreskin. Might be from Belladonna. Might be from somewhere beyond that."

"Why the interest, Latimer? What's the deal with this egg dingus?"

"Christ, Frank. Do your homework," Latimer said in disgust.

"The first I heard about this 'Egg' was when Kreskin came up to me suggesting I double-cross Smith. What the hell is it?"

"It's some sort of religious artifact. Or political totem. Or whatever excites a lizard. But in any case there are at least two factions on the lizard home world who have been fighting for millennia over the thing. It disappeared about five centuries ago, but they still have kept at it, though without the same intensity. If the Egg resurfaces all hell could break loose. I just don't want it to happen on Star City. Now do you understand. Frank?"

"I take it the Smith and Jones aren't on the same side in this thing?"

"That about sums it up, Frank. Jones will try anything to intercept the Egg."

"And Kreskin?"

"He's just a hood trying to make a dishonest dollar. He figures if he can grab the Egg he can sell it to the highest bidder."

"He didn't seem like he had the beans to pull something like that off."

"Probably doesn't," Latimer agreed. "By himself. But we think he's working with some out of town muscle." 'Out of town' is Star City slang for anyone not from this little hollowed out asteroid circling a brown dwarf that we call home.

"Thanks for the info, Latimer. I'll remember to keep my head down when the photons start flying."

"You do that, Frank. But I'd like to keep it from coming to that if I can."

"What's to keep you from just kicking Smith and Jones off Star City? Let it be someone else's problem."

"That probably wouldn't solve anything. The Egg is going to be arriving sometime in the next few days. If not Smith and Jones, it would be someone else. Either other lizardmen or their proxies. At least Smith and Jones we know. Besides, relations with the lizards are kind of touchy right now, and the Smith and Jones factions carry diplomatic weight. If we deported them without good cause it would cause all sorts of problems."

I stared at the back of Rossetti's head for a moment. I could sympathize with Latimer's position. His job was to keep people from making waves on Star City, and whichever way this Egg business went looked to be a tsunami.

"A thought occurred to me, Latimer."

"Yeah?" I could tell he was taking things serious when he passed up the chance for a snappy comeback.

"The Egg thing. What are the chances it's the real deal? I mean, could it be a fake?"

"Figure it out for yourself, Frank. The thing has been lost for five hundred years. There aren't any realistic pictures of it, just icons and vague descriptions. Suddenly it surfaces on a back water planet on the fringes of human space like Belladonna where it's supposed to have been dug up by some farmer. I'd say that the chances are slim to none that it's authentic. But it doesn't matter what I think, Frank. It's what the lizards think, and they aren't going to take a chance that the other side might get the real Egg. Even if it is a fake, they're going to be out for blood or whatever it is that flows through their veins."

"OK. So you've got yourself the makings of an interstellar mess on your hands. Just what do you want me to do, Latimer? I already took a grand from Smith to do the job."

"Oh, go ahead and make the exchange, Frank. The quicker you do it the quicker the Egg is off of Star City where it's not my problem anymore. It's just that if things start going bad, I want you to let me know before they get worse. Got it, Frank?"

"Sure thing. Anything for you, Latimer, and for the good of Star City." I was trying to sound like a tough guy but both of us knew I kind of meant it.

"Yeah. Joke about it Frank. Just remember to watch your back and keep your head down."

"Is there any other way to live in this rock?"

"This is your stop, Frank. Get out," Latimer said. Somehow, after driving around we'd ended up in front of the Aldeberon Arms, my apartment building. The door of the prowl car popped open. I took the hint. "Remember to keep in touch."

Rossetti turned to give me a leer. "Have a nice day, Frank." With that the cruiser drove off.

There's not much to say about the next few days. Nothing really happened except that every time I left the apartment I was followed. One of the tails I recognized as one of Latimer's men. I think he was being visible intentionally. But there were others I didn't know, guys that knew their business. I'm pretty certain there were some that I missed, too.

There wasn't much I could do about it. I wasn't sure I wanted to, either. I was probably pretty safe as long as everyone had their eyes on me.

It wasn't until the afternoon of the third day that things started moving. I was sitting in my apartment nursing a whiskey and soda and listening to some jive samba while I stared out at the building across the street, which isn't all that bad a way to waste an afternoon. Then the buzzer announced someone at the door.

I got up and looked at what the hall camera showed. It was Karissa. She must have been shopping because the shapeless bag she'd been wearing the first time I saw her had been replaced by a high-necked sleeveless sheathe in white. She was wearing white boots that came up to mid-calf as well. Not exactly the height of fashion, but a big improvement, nonetheless. If only she'd chosen some color other than white which only served to make her complexion look more pale. She was toting a shoulder bag that was much too large to be a purse even by current standards. I unlocked the door and let her in.

"The ship will be arriving late tonight," she explained without preamble. "The exchange will take place tomorrow morning." She gave an address that would make sense only to one of the robotic freight movers in the warehouse district down by the lower end of Star City. I had a pretty good idea of where it was.

"This bag contains the currency," she said as she let it slide from her shoulder to the floor.

I undid the seam and looked inside. In a concession to practicality, Mr. Smith had chosen to use fifties rather than twenties. It's surprising how much space a million dollars takes up when it is in fifty dollar bills. I resealed the bag and picked it up. Karissa was stronger than she looked. The bag wouldn't fit in my safe so I just tucked it in the back of the closet in my bedroom.

"Is that it?" I asked. "No additional instructions?"

"I'm to stay with you until you have the package. Once the exchange is made I will call Mr. Smith. He will tell me where to go with the package."

"I see," I said. I guess that I couldn't blame Mr. Smith. If I was trusting someone with a million dollars Crockett I'd probably include a chaperone, too. It's just that my apartment isn't equipped with a guest room.

A bright idea struck me. "Have you had dinner, yet?"

Karissa looked at me as if I was crazy, but I could see the yearning in her eyes. Not for me, for the food. "No. But what about the money?"

"It'll be safe. There are people watching the apartment. I know for a fact that the guy on the corner who's been reading the newssheet for the last three hours is a police detective. Besides, no one is going to touch us until we get our hands on the Egg."

Karissa looked at me in alarm. "You're not supposed to know about the Egg."

"Why? Everybody else seems to."

She didn't seem to know how to answer that. Instead, she just looked down at the carpet.

"Could I use your restroom before we go?"

"Sure, right through there," I said, pointing at the door to my bedroom.

Karissa disappeared for a while. I had time to finish my drink as I waited. I was thinking of making another when she reappeared.

She hadn't been wearing any cosmetics before. Now she had applied some lipstick in a light rose shade. It didn't look as if she'd done anything else, but her cheeks had lost some of their pallor. She hadn't been carrying a purse other than the moneybag, but there had been some stuff in the bathroom. What can I say? Women just have a habit of leaving things behind. Obviously Karissa had put them to good use.

The restaurant I took her to was on the edge of the Souk. It was quiet, particularly that early, but the food is good. The menu seemed to confuse her so I ordered for us both. I ordered a carafe of red wine, as well. Not that it had ever seen the slopes of a vineyard. Or grapes for that matter, but it was the product of one of the better vats and had been aged for at least a week.

We didn't talk much during the meal. Mostly I just watched Karissa put it away. It was like she hadn't eaten for a month. Whatever Mr. Smith had been feeding her wasn't much. Which might explain why she was so skinny.

She slowed some down over dessert. She was still on her first glass of wine, but the carafe was nearly empty. Which might explain my next question:

"How did you end up working for Mr. Smith?"

"You mean, how did I end up working for a lizardman?"

"OK. Yes. That's what I meant."

"Simple. I needed a job." She was completely unself-conscious in her reply. "There aren't many employment opportunities for women where I come from. Not if you don't want to be a farm wife or a whore. I saw an ad in the paper. Assistant. It paid what seemed like a fortune at the time. I was surprised when I found out it was a lizardman, but I was desperate. I took it."

"How long ago was that?"

"Oh. Two years ago, I guess."

"Just how old are you, if you don't mind my asking?"

"Eight. Almost nine." That's the problem with so many planets circling so many suns. There's no such thing as a standard year or day. A lot of planets don't even have the right satellites for the concept of a month to mean anything. Star City keeps pretty much to the conventions of old Terra, but it has the advantage of being a completely artificial environment. Looking at her, she could be anywhere from sixteen to twenty-six.

"So how's it working out for you? Working for Mr. Smith, I mean."

"It's alright. We travel a lot. Back and forth across the border between human and lizard space. Mostly arranging the exchange of commodities. I go long times without seeing a human. But Mr. Smith treats me decently. It's just that he doesn't always understand what a human needs."

"So why don't you quit?"

"And do what? Find a nice guy and settle down? I don't have much chance of that, do I?"

"No. I suppose you don't." I finished the last of the wine. "Did you want anything else?"

"No. I'm full. I can't remember the last time I ate this much."

I settled up the bill and we left. It was a nice night, but then it always is on Star City. We walked for a bit, Karissa drinking in the sights of so many people. She seemed to enjoy that, but I sensed it frightened her a little, too. Finally we ended up back at my apartment.

"I don't have a guest room, but the sofa is pretty comfortable," I said.

"That's alright. I don't mind sleeping with you. I don't get many chances to be with a man."

Put that way, how could I refuse? It wasn't her first time, that's for sure, but it must have been awhile since her last. She was a ferocious lover in a way different than any other woman I'd been with. Finally I just let her have her way with me.

When I woke Karissa wasn't in the bed. I could hear the shower running in the bathroom. Ten minutes later, it was still running. When she finally came out of the bathroom she was dressed only in the old bathrobe I keep on a hook on the inside of the bathroom door. There was a strange expression on her face that I had never seen her show before. I think it was meant to be a smile.

"We've got plenty of time. Would you like some breakfast?"

That seemed to require some deep thought. Finally she answered, "Yes. That would be nice."

I know that some of the backwater planets are pretty primitive and their inhabitants are lacking in the social graces, but I was starting to wonder just how much contact Karissa had had with humans the last few years.

I'm not much of a cook, but I whipped up a couple of omelets. They were nothing fancy and certainly didn't look pretty, but Karissa dug into hers as if it had been prepared by a three star chef. The cup of Joe I gave her she barely touched, but then I can't blame her. It's kind of an acquired taste.

After she had cleaned her plate and polished off the third piece of toast I asked, "So what's the plan?"

"Plan?

"I know I'm supposed to make the meet and exchange the bag of currency for the Egg. Where am I supposed to meet you afterwards?"

"I'm going with you to the meeting. I thought you understood that."

"I guess I'm a little vague on just why I'm involved at all."

"You know Star City. I don't. You know how to get around without attracting attention. From your reputation Mr. Smith assumed that you would be armed in case of trouble."

"Is he expecting trouble?"

"There are others who want the Egg. And not just lizardmen."

"OK. I escort you to the meet. I bring a gun in case of trouble. We make the exchange. What then?"

"I have a short term comm. When we have the Egg I call Mr. Smith. He has made arrangements to leave Star City."

That actually made some kind of sense. A short term comm. was a communicator that people in transit could buy for use on the local net. They were relatively cheap, usually twenty credits and normally came with a two week contract. If you were on Star City for less than that length of time, and most people in transit were, there were dealers at departure who would buy the units back for maybe five credits. They'd then resell the comms to locals who didn't necessarily want their calls traced. They'd only be good for a few days, but most people who were interested would have dumped the units after they had been used once or twice, anyway.

I went into the bedroom to get dressed. While I was at it, I opened the case tucked into the back where I keep my store of weapons. Normally, I don't go around armed on the philosophy that if you start walking around with a gun people get shot, maybe you. However, this seemed like an occasion to break the rule. The question was, which weapon to take? I had a couple of laser pistols of different sizes including one that I could hide in a shoulder holster without it being too visible. I had a needle gun, too. It was small and quiet, but only good for short range. Unable to choose, I split the difference and slipped the laser into the shoulder holster. The needle gun I tucked into my pocket. As an afterthought, I grabbed the little laser pistol I had taken off of Kreskin.

Karissa only took a few minutes to dress. She hadn't bothered to put on make-up.

I asked her, "Do you have a weapon?"

"No."

"Can you shoot one?"

"Yes."

I handed her the laser pistol. The way she took it made me think she knew what she was doing. It also turns out her dress had a couple of nearly invisible pockets. The pistol disappeared into one of them.

I checked the time. It would take us a while to get to the meet.

"Ready?"

She answered in a flat voice, "Yes." I couldn't tell if she wasn't worried or was just too nervous to show it.

Normally lugging around a bag with a million dollars Crockett would put me on edge, but this time I figured we were pretty safe. Everyone involved seemed like they were willing to wait until after the exchange was made. Besides, I knew that Latimer had his eyes on us. The man on the corner who had been reading the news had gone off shift, but I recognized the guy who kept glancing at his comm every few minutes as his replacement. He studiously avoided eye contact as we walked by. I suppressed the urge to say, "Give my regards to Latimer."

Star City was built in a hollowed out asteroid circling a brown dwarf. It's basically a cylinder about fifteen kilometers long and three kilometers in diameter. We all live on the hollowed out inside. The cylinder has docking rings for starships at each end.

The "head" end is where the starliners deposit and pick up their passengers. It's also where all the amenities are like hotels and casinos. Freighters dock at the other end. That's where all the warehouses, recycling facilities and food vats are. That was where we were headed.

One nice thing about Star City is that it has a decent public transport system. Four tram tracks run the length with connecting links running circumferentially every so often. The trams run fairly frequently. The result is that no location is very far from a tram stop. The best thing is that the trams are free. It was a short walk to the closest station where we hopped on to a "down" car. I assumed that one of Latimer's men was on the same tram or would be reporting down the line to someone to keep an eye out for us.

It wasn't surprising that the meet had been set for the warehouse district. There are very few people around to notice what goes on. Most of the freight is moved by robotic cargo handlers. It's quite possible for a piece of freight to be off-loaded from one ship, put in storage for a week, a month, or a year, and then to be loaded onto another ship without ever having been seen or touched by a human being. Robots don't need much in the way of illumination, either, which means that there were plenty of dark corners to hide in.

The address Karissa had given me was that of a yard where cargo containers were stacked three deep. The only movements were of the handling system that stashed, sorted, and retrieved the pods in response to some computer system down at the docking ring. Number codes for each location had been painted on the ground in luminous paint, but those were only there for the convenience of the rare human.

It didn't take long to find the number we were looking for. I glanced around looking for Latimer's men, but I couldn't spot them. I wasn't worried. I figured that Latimer was using his most experienced officers.

We only had to stand around for a few moments before our contact stepped out of the shadows between containers. We gave each other the once over. He was a typical spacer, fit, artificially tanned, and with something of an attitude. He had a small bag slung over one shoulder. I don't know what he thought of me.

"You from Mr. Smith?"

"Yes."

"You got the money."

"Yep."

"Show it to me."

I unsealed the bag. "You can count it if you want."

"I ain't got all day. I'll trust Mr. Smith." The implication was that he didn't trust me. I didn't take offense. I wouldn't have, either.

"You got the Egg?"

"In the bag."

"Mind if we take a peek?"

He unzipped the bag. "You can look but don't touch."

I have to say, it didn't look like that much. It was an ovoid shaped piece of metal with an odd color to it. For all I knew, it might be iridium. It was about fifteen centimeters long and maybe ten wide. Around the shorter diameter a ring of irregularly shaped pebbles had been inset. Were they uncut diamonds? How should I know?

Karissa seemed to study it intently. Finally getting impatient I asked, "Well, is it the real dingus?"

"It matches the description Mr. Smith gave me. But he's never seen it before. No lizardman alive has."

"OK. So do we make the deal?"

"Yes."

I resealed the bag of money. The spaceman did the same with his bag. He held out his bag by the strap. I mirrored his move. There was a pause while we waited to see who would let go first, but we must have gotten impatient at the same time, for he was left holding the money and I had the Egg.

"I've got a ship to catch. Dasvidaniya." I didn't recognize the lingo, but a moment later the spacer had disappeared back into the shadows.

"I guess you can call Mr. Smith now," I said, glancing around nervously. My sixth sense told me things were about to get interesting.

Karissa pulled out the comm unit a placed the call to Mr. Smith. There was a short conversation, mostly on the lizardman's side which I couldn't hear. The girl hung up, dropped the comm and kicked it under the nearest container. We wouldn't be needing it again, and it couldn't be used to trace us.

"What next?" I asked.

"We're to meet Mr. Smith," Karissa replied and gave me an address. "He'll be waiting."

Our destination was in another part of the warehouse district about halfway around the circumference of Star City, maybe five kilometers if we walked it, fifteen minutes if we took the nearest circumferential tram.

"Might as well get going. Do you want me to carry the Egg?"

"No," Karissa said. "You need to keep your hands free." It seemed she was expecting more trouble than I was.

Our location was about halfway between tram lines, about half a kilometer in either direction. The one downwards was the last one in that direction, just outside the docking ring. It would have the most traffic. It made more sense to me to head upward. When I explained my reasoning, Karissa agreed. We headed up.

Except for a couple of robots moving around, the streets were deserted. That made it easy for me to spot our tail. He was being discrete, hanging back a couple of blocks. He wasn't trying to conceal himself exactly, but he was keeping to the shadows as much as possible. At that distance it was impossible for me to recognize him, but I assumed he was one of Latimer's.

We were in sight of the tram line when my sixth sense kicked in. I could see someone hanging around the tram stop, illuminated by the lights of the stop. Him I could get a good look at. He didn't look like a cop. The guy behind us had closed up by a block.

I said softly to Karissa, "When I give the word head down the cross street to the left. Don't slow down and don't wait for me."

She glanced at me nervously, but I could see she understood. We were almost to the cross street when I saw the guy at the tram stop reach into his jacket. He might have been reaching for his comm. He might just as easily be reaching for a pistol.

"Now!"

I reached into my jacket and pulled out the laser pistol. I didn't bother to look to make sure that Karissa was headed to the cross street, but I could hear the sound of her boots on the pavement. The guy at the stop had produced a laser pistol. I glanced back at the tail. He was running forward, a laser in his hand. He was bringing it up to fire. It was aimed at me.

I turned the corner into the cross street and pressed myself into the wall of the building on the corner. A chip of brick spattered out from where the laser had hit the corner, but other than that, the only sound was of Karissa's boots, running now. I ducked around the corner, fired a snap shot and ducked back into cover. I didn't think that I had hit him, but the shot would slow him down.

I had fifteen seconds before the laser would be recharged for another shot. I didn't wait, but headed down the street, keeping to the shadows on the side, following the sound of Karissa's boots. Fifty meters down the street there was a doorway set into the façade. I ducked into it just as our two pursuers turned into the end of the street. I got off another shot, one that hit home this time, not lethally, but enough to put him out of action. He shouted something in a language I didn't recognize. His partner got off a shot, but he rushed it and it went high, hitting the far side of the doorway a few centimeters above my head.

I took the advantage of the moment, and ran down the street, knowing that he couldn't fire another shot until his laser recharged. Of course, not knowing what kind of weapon he had, I didn't know how long that would be. I went another fifty meters and then turned to fire. So did he, but we both missed.

We went four or five blocks that way, trading shots every fifteen seconds or so, neither one of us doing damage to anything other than the brickwork of the building facades. This kept me so busy that I didn't realize at first that I couldn't hear the sound of

Karissa's boot's anymore. She'd probably taken a turning or gone to ground. I didn't blame her. It was the smart thing to do.

As I reached the next intersection I fired another shot. This time my opponent didn't fire his, but slowed his pace, knowing that my laser couldn't fire for another fifteen seconds. As he approached for the kill shot I fumbled for the needle gun in my pocket. He stop, raised his pistol, the targeting beam on and working its way up my torso. He was close enough that I could see his arm tense as he got ready to fire. The needle gun was clear of the pocket, but I wasn't going to be able to get a shot off in time.

Suddenly he crumpled to the ground. Karissa stepped out of the shadows, the little laser pistol that I had taken from Kreskin in her hand. A weapon like that is rarely lethal unless it hit something vital. Karissa's shot had taken him in the left eye socket. She looked even paler than usual, but I could tell that she wasn't in shock.

"We better keep going," I said.

"Do you think there are others?"

"I think we have to make that assumption. There was supposed to be a cop trailing us. Neither of these thugs were cops."

"Police?" Following us? You knew about that?"

"Yeah. I arranged it with a local bull named Latimer. To keep anything from happening. I guess it didn't work. Look, we better keep moving if we're going to meet Mr. Smith. We've got a bit of a hike. I don't think it's safe to take the tram. Not now."

We still had nearly four kilometers to go to the meeting place. I kept us at a brisk pace, but not so fast that we couldn't hear if we were being followed. If we were, they were holding back, because I couldn't spot anyone.

By the third kilometer both of us were dragging. Karissa was plodding along, wincing at each step. Those boots of hers hadn't been made for hiking. I wasn't doing much better and I was breathing hard. I'd been spending too much time lately doing arm curls in the Blue Moon.

Finally, we reached the address Mr. Smith had given for the meet. It was a warehouse of some sort. The only sign was in machine readable form for use by robots. We paused in the doorway to catch our breath. I gave a look up and down the street, but it was empty.

"Ready?" I asked.

Karissa only nodded. I tried the door and found it unlocked.

Mr. Smith was standing in the middle of the space, an overhead light illuminating the mottled skin of his face. I could sense that something was wrong. His hands were empty, held out from his body. A laser pistol was lying on the ground maybe five meters from his feet.

As we approached him a voice came from the darkness, a voice heavy on sibilants. It was Mr. Jones, holding a heavy laser pistol in his hand as he stepped out of the darkness from where he had been hiding, shielded from view by a stack of shipping boxes.

"Mr. Sladek. We meet again. Do nothing foolish and you may live. The female, too, if you like. Place your weapon on the ground and kick it away. The woman's, too."

I placed the laser on the pavement and gave it a kick. It slid across the slick surface. Karissa did the same.

"Good. The Egg? Do you have it?" Mr. Jones asked excitedly. Mr. Smith was eyeing him, looking as if he wanted to sink his fangs into Jones' neck.

Karissa nodded.

"Show me," Mr. Jones commanded.

Karissa unsealed the bag, reached in for the Egg and held it in the palm of her hand. There was a sharp intake of breath on the part of both lizardmen. It didn't matter if the dingus was real or not, both of the lizards believed it was.

"Put it back in the bag, place it on the floor, and step away," Mr. Jones said. Karissa did as he asked. "Good, now move together so I can see you all at once." Karissa and I moved towards Mr. Smith. I'm no expert on alien facial expressions, but I could sense that the lizardman was just waiting his chance.

Mr. Jones moved forward towards the bag, keeping his laser pointed at Mr. Smith. It was an alien weapon, probably of lizard manufacture judging by how well it fit Mr. Jones' three fingered hand. I found myself wondering how quickly it cycled. It looked like it had a heavy duty power pack.

The lizardman was bending to pick up the bag when Kreskin's voice came out of the darkness. "I'll take that." Kreskin wasn't alone, there were three others, each holding pistols and looking like they could use them. Mr. Jones didn't wait to judge the situation, but turned and fired. Kreskin went down. I could tell he was dead. It didn't do Mr. Jones any good as one of Kreskin's henchmen fired, burning off half his head. What was left of the lizardman slid to the ground.

I grabbed Karissa and was reaching for the needle gun in my pocket. It's not a long range weapon, but its higher rate of fire might make up for it. The three toughs weren't quite sure what to do. Mr. Smith took care of that for them. From somewhere he had managed to produce another laser pistol. He got of one shot off before getting hit himself. Both shots went home.

I got the needler up and got off three quick shots before I felt a burning along my right forearm. The needle gun dropped and skittered across the pavement. The man I had aimed for dropped as well, one of the needles had hit his torso and penetrated to the heart.

That left one attacker standing. Of course he still had a laser pistol in his hand. Mr. Jones and Mr. Smith were both dead. So were Kreskin and two of his men. I was unarmed and my right hand hung uselessly at my side. The guy with the gun just smiled as he approached me, the laser pointed right between my eyes.

If he had fired right away, he might have pulled it off, but he had a touch of the sadist in him, and he wanted to draw things out. Unfortunately for him, he had forgotten Karissa. She was edging towards the body of Mr. Jones. The gunman didn't notice her until too late. She reached into the lizardman's shirt and came up with another laser pistol. The gunman was just turning when the beam caught him just in front of the ear. It came out the other side of his head.

Karissa was still holding the laser when she came over to me.

"How'd you know Jones had another weapon?" I asked rather stupidly.

She just looked at me. There was no concern or pity in her eyes. "I thought you knew, Frank. Lizardmen always carry two guns."

I gave a little laugh, then a wince as pain shot through my arm. "So what now?"

"Now? Now I take the Egg. I know who Mr. Smith was working for. He's got a ship waiting on the docks. If I deliver the Egg I can get enough currency that I never have to see another lizardman as long as I live."

"That makes sense," I said. "What about me?"

"You, Frank? I won't forget you." She walked over to where Mr. Smith's body lay. She reached into a pouch on his belt and pulled out a roll of twenty dollar bills. Slowly, as she walked back to me she counted out forty of them, thought about it, and then counted out ten more. The rest she stuffed in the bag with the Egg.

"Here, Frank. Here's what Mr. Smith promised you. And a bonus. I said I wouldn't forget you. "

"Thanks, Karissa. I won't be forgetting you any time soon, either."

"I'd better go, Frank, before anyone shows up."

"Look me up the next time you're in Star City."

"I'll do that," she said as she turned and walked away.

I sat there for awhile just looking at the shadows she had disappeared into, then I pulled myself together and found something to wrap around the burn on my arm. I was in no hurry. Everyone else in the warehouse was dead. I picked up the needle gun and slipped it into my pocket. The laser went back in the holster. When enough time had passed that I figured Karissa had gotten to Smith's ship I called Latimer.

He showed up with a tactical squad and a dozen uniforms. As if they were needed. They all stood around looking foolish as Latimer counted the bodies.

"Sheesh, Sladek," Rossetti said, "What is it with you and corpses. It seems every time you give us a call the joint is full of dead people. And lizards this time."

"So what happened, Latimer?" I asked ignoring him. "I thought you had a tail on me?"

"We did. They got him with a neural sap. It wasn't until he didn't check in that we knew anything was wrong and by then we'd lost track of you. Where's the girl and the Egg?"

"Gone. Mr. Smith had a ship waiting on the docking ring. She's taking the Egg back to the lizards."

"Well good riddance. I'm glad it's out of my hair."

"Won't having two dead lizards on your hands cause you grief?"

"I'll just put in my report that they killed each other. That should satisfy the diplomats. That is what happened, isn't it, Frank?"

"If it's in your report, it must be true. Who am I to argue with the police?"

"Good. You need the police surgeon to look at that arm?"

"No. I can take care of it."

If Karissa ever made it back to Star City, she didn't try to get in touch. That's the way things go. But I did learn one thing I'll never forget. Lizardmen always carry two guns.

FEAR

OF

FALLING

FEAR OF FALLING

How do you know when you're in love? I suppose people have been asking that question since they stopped living in caves, maybe earlier. I'm no expert on the subject, that's for sure. Over the years I've had various flings and affairs with women. Some lasted weeks, even months, most barely lasted the night, but only once did it amount to what I assume was love. And that ended badly.

I was in the Blue Moon doing not much of anything when the call came in. It was the middle of the afternoon and I was staring at a half-empty glass of brown in front of me while trying to ignore the argument between two loud drunks at the other end of the bar. I thumbed the screen of my comm to see who it was. The screen lit up to display the name Miss Hohenberg.

I didn't recognize the name. My mind formed an image of an aging spinster with a face like sauerkraut. It didn't matter. The number she had called was the one listed in the directory for professional purposes. A new client would come in handy. Business had been sporadic recently and my cash reserves were dwindling. I told the two drunks to shut up and answered the call.

"Frank Sladek."

"You are the private investigator?" The voice didn't match the name. The image my mind had formed dissolved to be replaced by one much younger and slinkier, clothing optional. So I have a dirty mind.

My license says I'm a private investigator. But that is more of a bureaucratic label than anything else. I don't do divorce work or insurance fraud. The reality is mostly I find things for people. Things being lost wives, missing money, stolen property. Still, the P.I. label is something that most people find easier to wrap their heads around.

"Yes, I'm that Frank Sladek," I responded trying to sound encouraging without sounding desperate.

"Would you be able to meet this evening to discuss a—" she hesitated a moment as if trying to think of the proper term, "—a commission?" The voice might conjure up sultry images, but the diction spoke of education and precision.

"I think my schedule is free to allow me to meet with you, Miss Hohenberg," I answered.

"Actually the meeting is to be with my employer, Mr. Kaminski-Jones."

"That's too bad," I said. "I was looking forward to seeing you in person, Miss Hohenberg."

I think she took that the wrong way. The voice turned frosty. "Oh, I'll be there, Mr. Sladek, but Mr. Kaminski-Jones is the one who will be engaging your services. Tonight at 1900?"

"I'll be there."

She gave me the address and added, "Mr. Kaminski-Jones expects promptness," before breaking the connection.

The name Kaminski-Jones sounded familiar, but I couldn't quite place it. The address, on the other hand, was on the Hill.

The Hill is really more of a bump, a low ridge that runs around the circumference of Star City about a third of the way down from the high rent end where the passenger liners dock. At its highest point it's only thirty meters or so above the more or less uniform surface of the cylinder that takes up the inside of the hollowed out asteroid that is Star City, but as it's the only real bit of relief in that surface it has long been a prime bit of real estate where the wealthy and the powerful make their homes. Some tech had once explained to me that it owes its existence to a geological anomaly in the rock that would have been too expensive to eliminate without disrupting the structural integrity of the Star City. I hadn't understood a word of it. What I did understand was that anyone who lived on that ridge had money, whether new, old or undefined.

Out of curiosity I used my comm to do a search on Kaminski-Jones. There was a lot of information, mostly about the family which had operated a fleet of starliners for generations as a sort of feudal empire with the captains all coming from within the ranks of the family. The system seemed to have worked, because as a collective entity, the family Kaminski-Jones was incredibly wealthy.

The particular Kaminski-Jones that lived on Star City was something of a hero. He had been captain of a liner that had suffered a rare malfunction of the system that drove the ship through tachyon space. The ship had been left intact, but with a broken drive system that was dangerously radioactive. Kaminski-Jones had personally led the repair crew which had restored the drive and saved the ship. Most of that crew had perished in the effort. Kaminski-Jones had survived, but had suffered neurological damage in the process so severe that regeneration could not reverse the effects. Unsubstantiated rumors hinted that the damage had extended beyond the physical to his mental functions. Unable to resume his duties as captain, he had been hailed as a hero and pensioned off with a generous allowance from the family. Having spent his entire life aboard his family's great starliners he had decided to settle on Star City in his retirement, the artificial space station being the closest thing to a ship he could find. He had bought a mansion on the Hill and lived as a semi-recluse. At least that was what I was able to learn from the comm.

It was just turning twilight as I walked up the Hill from the tram station. The giant glow tubes that run the length of the spar that forms the central axis of Star City had been dimmed to provide a simulated night to the residents of the hollowed out asteroid that formed the giant space station. The original design team of Star City had determined that providing a diurnal cycle keyed to that of Earth would be beneficial to the physiological and psychological well-being of its inhabitants. As a bonus, there was also a variation in the length of daylight to provide artificial seasons based on a 365 day cycle (no leap year). The temperature, however, was maintained at a more or less constant twenty-two degrees Celsius year round, thus avoiding the necessity of seasonal wardrobes for the less affluent citizens. It also made life easier for passengers in transit, who, after all, were the reason for Star City's existence in the first place.

Kaminski-Jones's residence occupied a place on the top of the Hill. Living in a part of Star City with a spotty maintenance program, I climb enough stairs that I arrived at the front gate without being noticeably winded. As with most of the houses on the Hill, the estate was surrounded by a high wall that blocked a view of the interior. The fact that anyone with a decent set of binoculars could get an excellent view of the grounds just by going a third of the way around the cylinder that formed Star City and looking up, seemed not to have been considered.

I pushed the button marked "Guests" next to the gate and stood patiently in the view of the security camera. A few moments later a male voice announced "Mr. Sladek, you are expected. Please follow the path to the front door of the house." This was followed by a click as the gate swung open.

I don't usually get invited to places on the Hill, but I've been to enough that the scene that greeted me wasn't totally unexpected. A brick path just wide enough for two people to walk side by side wound through a garden landscape of various types of foliage. On a cylinder with a surface area of roughly one-hundred and fifty square kilometers with a population of several million, even the extremely wealthy can only afford a limited number of square meters of surface area. But clever landscaping and the avoidance of long sight lines can create the illusion of vast spaces. Though the linear distance between the gate and the front door was probably less than twenty meters, I was forced to walk five times that far, cross a small ornamental bridge and climb several short stone staircases. Not that it wasn't a pleasant stroll. Considering the effort and expense that had gone into the design it should be.

It was almost exactly 1900 when I reached the house. At least I would get points for punctuality. The entry consisted of a double door two meters wide and three tall. Though I assumed there was some sort of automatic announcement system, there was also a mechanical knocker attached to one of the bronze doors. I lifted it and knocked three times. You don't get many chances to do that kind of thing on Star City.

As expected, the door pulled back, opened by an older man in a dark suit. This was not, I presumed, Kaminski-Jones. I was proved right when he said, "Mr. Kaminski-Jones will see you in the library in a few moments. If you will follow me, Mr. Sladek?"

With a limited number of job opportunities, human servants aren't unknown on Star City, but it had been a while since I had run across such a paragon of a butler. He ushered me into a library which proved worthy of the name. A tall room about the size of my apartment, it was lined with shelves tall enough that a sliding ladder arrangement was required to reach the upper shelves. The shelves were full of books, real ones, printed on paper.

I did a quick estimate in my head and came to fifteen thousand volumes give or take a grand or two. While I waited, I amused myself by reading titles. Some I recognized, most I didn't. A few I couldn't even guess the language they were written in. Most were old. Some very old. I'm no expert in such matters, but in my business being able to judge an object's value is an asset. I calculated the collection probably was worth several million dollars Crockett, at least.

A door at the far end opened to reveal Kaminski-Jones. He was a tall, thin man with short white hair. He looked to be twenty or thirty years older than me, but that's always hard to judge. By his slightly jerky movements and the faint mechanical click that came with each step I could tell he was wearing an exoskeleton underneath his impeccably tailored suit. The injuries he had suffered in the accident must have been really bad for him to still require such an aid decades after the incident.

"I see you've been studying my collection, Mr. Sladek. Excellent. I seem to have found the right man for the job. Allow me to introduce myself, Captain Kaminski-Jones."

I took his offered hand and said, "Frank Sladek."

"Exactly. Tell me, Mr. Sladek, you can read, can't you?"

The question wasn't that surprising, or even insulting. With most books available in digital format and the ability to vocalize them built into every comm unit, actual reading was something of a dying art. But in my line of work, any skill might prove to be an advantage, and being able to read was no exception. Still, there is something about holding a printed book.

"Yes, I can read, Mr. Kaminski-Jones. I even have a few books of my own. Not as many as you—" I finished waving my hand around the room.

"Few people do, Mr. Sladek. Few do," he said with a dry chuckle.

"Miss Hohenberg mentioned that you might have a commission for me?"

"Ah, right to the point, Mr. Sladek. I can appreciate that. You have a reputation for finding things. Is that correct?"

"That's what I do." I qualified that with, "mostly."

"I'd like you to find something for me. Something that was stolen from me."

"Let me guess. A book?"

"I see you are a man of wit as well as learning, Mr. Sladek. But yes, a book. Have you ever heard of *Dante's Divine Comedy*, Mr. Sladek?"

"Yes, I've read parts of it. A translation, of course, not in the original Italian. Too many fart jokes for me, I'm afraid."

"You amuse me, Mr. Sladek. You are aware then, that it was originally written long before man took to space."

"I knew it was a long time ago."

"Do you have any idea how valuable a first edition of the Divine Comedy would be?"

"No, but I can imagine it would be quite a bit."

"You are correct, Mr. Sladek. As you put it, quite a bit. And do you have any idea just how many copies of the first edition are known to be in existence?"

His manner was starting to wear on me, but as they say the customer is always right. I would play his game if that was what he wanted. "I would have to say very few, Mr. Kaminski-Jones."

"Exactly one, Mr. Sladek. And even of that I was in doubt until a month ago. From time to time, I purchase collections from other individuals, either from their estates, or if they are forced to liquidate due to financial difficulties. These are often poorly cataloged. Such was the case when I purchased a collection on

New Virginia recently. The original owner is irrelevant. As I usually do, I sent Miss Hohenberg to catalog the collection and arrange for shipping. As is typical, this lot had a few gems and a lot of dross. However, one item proved to be a surprise, a very pleasant surprise."

"I take it a copy of the *Divine Comedy*?"

"Exactly, Mr. Sladek. It's doubtful the previous owner had any idea what he had. It had been packed away in a box of other books in foreign languages. Miss Hohenberg, however, is very thorough and has an excellent command of ancient languages. She recognized the item for what it was and contacted me immediately. Such a find, of course, would be the pinnacle of my collection. She arranged transport of the book along with the rest of the collection. Unfortunately, somewhere in transit the book disappeared. When the shipment was examined upon arrival it was gone, though the other volumes in the shipment all arrived safely."

"Excuse me, Mr. Kaminski-Jones, but with an item this valuable, weren't special precautions taken? I would have thought, particularly with your family connections, security could have been arranged that would have made a theft unlikely."

"Ordinarily, yes. However, this particular item presented certain difficulties. You see there is something of a cloud on the title. Not that I don't have a completely legitimate claim to it. But I wished to avoid attracting attention. Once it was in my possession here on Star City, well, as they say, possession is nine tenths of the law."

"I'm not sure they really say that, but your point is taken. Just what kind of clouds are we talking about?" I was getting a little suspicious of Kaminski-Jones. Even the rich, especially the rich, have been known to bend the law at times.

"We'll have to go back into the history of the item, quite far back. Originally, it was part of the collection of the Vatican Library. When the Catholic Church went bankrupt in the twenty-fifth century, they were forced to liquidate the library. At that time much of the library was acquired by the Italian National Library. At some point during the political instabilities of the twenty-eighth century the volume in question disappears from the records of that institution. You understand there was quite a bit of corruption on Earth in general at that time."

"So I've heard." Not at all like modern times, I thought to myself.

"Rumors placed it on various planets over the next few centuries, but nothing definite. As far as I've been able to discover from the records of the collection that I bought, it was bought and sold a number of times by people who didn't have the slightest idea of what the book really was. Until I bought it quite legitimately."

"I take it various other parties might see it otherwise?"

"Yes. The Reconstituted Catholic Church for one. There is, of course, no Italian government anymore, but Earth might make a claim. Possibly even the government on New Virginia. I would probably win any legal case, especially if it was held here on Star City, but such a case might drag on for years. You can understand why I might want to avoid undue attention, Mr. Sladek, I'm sure?"

I could, of course. If I had been advising him, I probably would have suggested doing the same thing.

"Do you have any idea when or where the item was stolen? If it disappeared before it reached Star City, I'm afraid I'm not the man for the job."

"I appreciate you candor, Mr. Sladek, but I am, in fact, confident that the item is someplace on Star City. I'm not a complete fool. I had Miss Hohenberg place a passive tracking disk in the binding of the book. When the tracker is activated in proximity to the book, there is a signal which can be detected. And that's where you come in, Mr. Sladek. I'd rather not go to the authorities for the reasons we have discussed previously. I wish instead for you to recover the item."

"That does seem to be within my line of business, Captain."

"Yes, that's what my sources tell me."

"Not to seem too mercenary, just what would this commission pay?"

"I am prepared to offer you five thousand credits to undertake the recovery with another ten thousand upon the successful completion of your task provided undue attention is avoided."

"Plus expenses?"

"Of course, Mr. Sladek. Are we in agreement?"

"Oh, I think you can count on that."

"Good. I will arrange for the funds right now. Cash will be acceptable?"

"Cash is always acceptable."

"If you will give me a few moments. In the meantime, I will have Miss Hohenberg go over the details of the shipment and the tracking disk."

He must have pressed some hidden signal button. Either that or Miss Hohenberg had been listening to our conversation waiting for her cue. The door through which Kaminski-Jones had entered opened again and a woman walked through. Something about her grabbed my attention, though I couldn't say just what.

She looked to be in her late twenties, but she might have been older. She was slightly above middle height and neither heavy-set or rail thin, trim without being overtly athletic. Her dark brown hair was pulled back and braided in a rather severe style. She was wearing a loose fitting dress that reached her knees of a pale grey material that draped her body without clinging to or concealing the curves. She wore sensible shoes.

In other words, she looked like the popular image of what a personal assistant to a wealthy man should look like, all business and no show, attractive but not distracting, classy rather than gaudy.

"Miss Hohenberg, Mr. Sladek," Kaminski-Jones said by way of introduction.

"We spoke on the comm," she replied tersely. I smiled. She didn't, though she did incline her head.

"I will leave you two to discuss the technical details," Kaminski-Jones said before withdrawing.

There was a period of awkward silence as I waited for her to begin. I took advantage of it to look her over. I decided that I liked what I saw. She gave me the once over, too. I didn't think she approved.

"I believe that Captain Kaminski-Jones gave you a synopsis of the history of the book—" She had been listening in. I decided that I liked the way she said "synopsis." That not something you can say of every dame.

"The book is about this big," she said, using her hands to give the approximate dimensions. I hadn't noticed her hands before. They were lovely; smooth and expressive with long slender fingers. She continued, "It's bound in calf-skin. For shipment it had been sealed in an opaque padded envelope which was in turn placed inside a metal box with appropriate padding. I managed these details myself, Mr. Sladek, so I know they were intact when I handed over the book to the purser of The Delta-Epsilon-Iota. That liner is part of the Kaminski-Jones fleet, and the purser is a junior member of the family. There is no reason to doubt his honesty."

I admit that I was letting my gaze, if not my attention wander. There was a lot to take in.

The first hint of exasperation crossed Miss Hohenberg's face. "Are you paying attention, Mr. Sladek?"

"Believe me, Miss Hohenberg, I'm paying attention." I tried to keep the leer out of my voice. It wasn't easy. "The book is approximately 18 by 10 by 3 centimeters, bound in calf-skin. It was sealed in an envelope which was placed in a metal box. You handed it to the purser of the Delta-Epsilon-Iota. There is no reason to suspect that it was mishandled before it reached Star City. Does that about sum it up, Miss Hohenberg?"

"Exactly, Mr. Sladek," she replied with just a hint of amusement.

"I was paying attention. I always do. I find that's a big asset in my profession. It's surprising how many of my colleagues don't. Of course, they tend not to last."

"To continue, then. I equipped the book with a tracking disk. This was concealed in the spine of the book and would not be visible in a casual examination. The tracking disk is of an advanced model. It is a passive device which only responds when 'pinged' with a specific code by a keyed monitoring unit. That unit can be set to either a directional or omni-directional mode and has a range of roughly a kilometer. I verified that the book was on the liner when it undocked from the New Virginia station."

"You weren't on the ship?"

"No. Mr. Sladek. We were aware that there were certain parties interested in acquiring the book. It was decided that there would be less chance of it being intercepted if I were to act as a decoy. I arranged passage on another starliner, this one taking a direct jump to Star City. I carried with me a package exactly similar to the one containing the book with the exception of the volume enclosed."

"And that was?"

The question seemed to distract her for a second. "I don't see that it matters, Mr. Sladek."

Seeing as how my question had flustered her, I continued the needle. "In my business, Miss Hohenberg, I find everything matters."

"Well, if you must know, it was a copy of *The Love Songs of Suzie Wong*," she said with a flush of embarrassment. Suzie Wong was a current popular sensation on a dozen planets. Frankly, I had found it to be pornography masquerading as literature. That hadn't stopped it from being a best seller.

"I bought it in the hotel shop on New Virginia. It was chosen solely because its dimensions were nearly the same as the book."

"I'm sure, Miss Hohenberg. Continue, please."

"The Delta-Epsilon-Iota made one stop before jumping to Star City, another planet in the New Virginia system. I arrived back at Star City a day before it docked. I was on the docking ring when it arrived and monitored the hand-over from the purser to the Custom's agent. The tracking disk was present at that time."

"The book went through Customs?" I was surprised. Smuggling by passengers on starliners is something of a sport on Star City. You'd be surprised at the kinds of things that are carried in personal luggage. However, except for weapons, the authorities tend to turn a blind eye to all except the most egregious or incompetent efforts.

"Again, it was thought to be less conspicuous to do so. The package was handed over, passed inspection and was picked up by me personally. I then took it directly here."

"You didn't check the tracking disk again?"

"I didn't think it was necessary. Also I didn't want to attract attention."

"I take it that when you opened the package, the book was gone?"

"Yes. It had been replaced."

"May I ask by what?"

"A thesaurus."

"How prosaic. Did you alert the Customs authorities?"

"No. Again, we didn't want to attract attention. Even if the book had been recovered by Customs, questions of ownership might arise. The captain decided to seek your services." The way she said it made me thing she had not been agreement with the decision.

"You didn't approve, Miss Hohenberg?"

"It's not my place."

"I see."

She opened a drawer in a library table in the middle of the room and pulled out an electronic device.

"This is the monitoring unit for the tracking device. The operation is quite simple. This switch selects the mode. This button sends out a ping. The display gives an indication of signal strength and distance." She handed it over to me.

"Seems simple enough."

"Good. Are there any other questions, Mr. Sladek?"

"Would you care to have dinner with me, Miss Hohenberg?"

"No," there was just an instant of hesitation. "I don't think that would be appropriate. Hadn't you best 'get on the case,' Mr. Sladek?"

"Perhaps you are right," I said with a wry smile.

"I'll have Jenkins show you out," she said.

"That won't be necessary. I can find my own way."

"Oh, I think it is necessary, Mr. Sladek." The smile she gave me could have chilled a mug of yellow.

I'd used tracking devices before. There's nothing particularly new about the technology. This one seemed particularly sensitive, though. The principle was simple; the tracker periodically sent out a coded pulse. When a tracking disk with a matching code received the pulse it would echo it back. The beauty of the scheme was that the disk didn't have to have its own power source which made it easy to hide and hard to detect. Similar devices had been used to keep track of inventory and prevent retail theft for a thousand years. The difference was that while most systems had a range of a few meters, this one was good for nearly a kilometer and had a highly directional mode.

Still, the inside of a cylinder fifteen kilometers long and three kilometers in diameter has a surface area of roughly a hundred and fifty square kilometers. I spent the morning riding up and down the length of Star City on the tram lines trying to pin down the location. I finally narrowed it down to an apartment building in a working class neighborhood.

The place wasn't a slum, but it wasn't exactly the Taj Mahal, either. Security was about what you'd expect in such a place, which is to say nonexistent. I entered through the front door and walked up the stairs to the top floor. It was the middle of the day and only a few people were around. Most were at work. Those that worked the night shift were asleep. It made my job easy.

By roaming the corridors I pinned down the location of the tracking disk to apartment 3C. I suppose I could have barged in, gun blasting, but that only works in the vids. Instead I knocked on the door of the building supervisor.

This was opened by a heavy set woman in her late sixties. She was wearing a shapeless print dress that did nothing to conceal her figure. She eyed me suspiciously.

"What do you want? We don't allow no salesmen."

I might have been hurt by that crack, but then I'd made a point of dressing in such a way that her observation wasn't unreasonable.

"Good morning, ma'am.   I'm from the Amalgamated Insurance Company." I showed her a set of phony credentials to prove the point.

"I don't need no insurance. I don't believe in it. My late husband had insurance and look where that got me."

"I'm not in the sales department ma'am," I said, maintaining my best minor functionary pose. "I'm in risk assessment. I'm just making some routine inquiries for one of our clients about one of their employees. I was wondering if you could tell me who lives in apartment 3C?" I figured that if whoever lived in 3C had taken the book, they probably worked for somebody involved in the shipping industry.

"What have they done?"

"No ma'am. You misunderstand me. They haven't done anything. I'm just verifying the address they gave on their employment forms. It's just a matter of routine. Just to maintain their security clearance, you understand."

"You sure they're not in trouble?" she asked suspiciously.

"No ma'am."

"Well, their names are Quinley and Melbourg. They never give me no trouble; always pay their rent on time. Nice boys, really."

"Thank you ma'am. I'm glad to hear that. Well, you've given me all the information I need." As I left I said in my best insincere voice, "I hope you have a nice day." It always is a good idea to stay in character when doing an impersonation.

I didn't necessarily want to go barging in. Thinking it might be better to catch them leaving, I decided to observe the apartment for a while.

There was a small café across the street with outdoor tables. I sat at one of the tables and ordered a cup of joe and a pastry. The pastry, when it came, was about what you'd expect, gooey and too sweet, but the joe wasn't half bad. I drank it slowly while nibbling on the pastry and pretending to read a newsfeed on my comm.

Apartment 3C was in the front on the left hand corner of the building. I could see what was probably the living room window from my seat in the café, but I couldn't see any signs of life. To keep the waiter happy I ordered a sandwich after about forty-five minutes along with a second cup of joe. This seemed to satisfy him. The sandwich was meat with a slab of cheese substance that had never seen the inside of an animal. It wasn't that bad, really. The lunch crowd came and went in the café, and there was still no sign of movement across the street. I began to worry that Quinley and Melbourg might have discovered the tracking disk and removed it.

I'd been sitting at the café long enough that I was risking becoming obvious. I was also getting impatient. I attracted the waiter's attention, paid my check and left him a nice tip. The joe had been all right.

I got up, walked down the street, and turned the corner. As I suspected, the block with the apartment building had an alley running down its middle. Making sure I wasn't being observed, I entered the alley and began counting doors. I came to the one I figured belonged to the apartment building and tried the door. It was unlocked and led onto the back stairway.

I went up to the third floor until I found myself in front of 3C. I've got a little dingus that works magic with electronic door locks. Strictly illegal, of course, but this one is camouflaged to look like a little flashlight. It will even light up if you press the big red button on top. I grabbed the door handle and was about to activate it when I realized the door was unlatched.

I exchanged the dingus in my hand for the needle gun I carried in my pocket and slowly pushed the door open. I couldn't hear any sounds from within the apartment. Stepping inside, I closed the door behind me.

The apartment was typical. The door let onto a narrow hall. There was a small galley kitchen to my right, and an even smaller bathroom came next. There was only one door on the left, the bedroom. A quick glance inside revealed only one bed. At the end of the hall was the living room which ran across the front of the apartment. It wasn't a big room, maybe three meters by seven. A small table on the right formed the dining area. To the left was a sofa and a couple of stuffed chairs. Quinley and Melbourg were seated in the chairs. They were dead.

It didn't take more than a glance to determine how. Each sported a small burn mark in the center of their foreheads. Very neat shooting. I figured it must have been a high powered laser with a big energy pack. I could tell it had a quick recharge time, because both men had been caught by surprise without having time to move. Your average laser pistol like a 25 kilojoule Baretta takes ten to fifteen seconds to recharge between shots. This couldn't have taken more than a second or two. That meant a military or assassin's weapon.

I didn't see the book lying around anywhere. That wasn't surprising. I keyed the tracker. It gave back a reassuring beep. A few more pings and I narrowed it down to a little cabinet in the dining area. There was a vase on top with some plastic flowers. The tracker indicated that the disk was inside. I removed the flowers and shook the vase. I could hear a clinking sound. When I tipped the vase upside down a little disk about the size of a thumbnail fell out. I felt like a prize chump.

I felt even more of a chump when I heard a voice behind me say, "Well, if it isn't our favorite shamus, Sladek. Looks like we've finally got the goods on you this time. Double homicide. Sweet."

The voice was that of Detective Rossetti. He's a cop that hates my guts. He usually partners with a Detective Sergeant Latimer who I won't call a friend, but who at least is honest. I wasn't to be disappointed.

"Raise the hands and drop the gun," Latimer's voice came from the hallway. I did as he asked. Rossetti spun me around and slapped restraints on my wrists.

"What gives, Frank?" Latimer asked, a note of disappointment in his voice. "I thought you were above this sort of petty mayhem."

"It wasn't me, Latimer. These boys were shot by a laser. All I've got on me is a needle gun. You can search me."

"Don't worry, Frank. We'll do just that."

Rossetti gave me a pat down, being none too gentle in the process. Luckily I didn't have another gun or anything obviously illegal on me.

Latimer plucked the tracker out of my left hand where I still had it.

"What's this little gizmo, Frank?" Latimer asked with curious smirk.

"It's a tracker. I was looking for something that had been stolen from a client. I think these two were the thieves."

"So you tracked them down and shot them, eh? Just what was it that was stolen, Frank?"

"I'm not at liberty to reveal that, Latimer," I answered.

"Who's your client, then?"

"He prefers to remain anonymous."

"And I suppose you're going to tell me that you found these two like this and someone else beat you to this mysterious stolen object."

"Something like that," I admitted.

"I'm sure. Well, we can sort that out at the station. Rossetti, call the crime scene guys. Maybe they can find whatever our friend was looking for."

We hung around for the fifteen minutes until the forensics squad showed up, then Latimer and Rossetti bundled me into their cruiser for a trip to the station. It wasn't the first time I'd taken that ride. I just hoped it wouldn't be my last.

They stuck me in an interrogation room at headquarters and let me stew for a bit. That was fine with me. I hadn't killed Quinley and Melbourg, and sooner or later they'd figure that out. At least Latimer would. Rossetti I wasn't so sure about. Once he got an idea in his head it was hard for him to change his mind. That's why Latimer is the senior partner. In the meantime, I took advantage of the situation and took a nap.

It must have been two hours later when Latimer came finally came in. Rossetti wasn't with him. That told me a couple of things. The first was that Latimer had realized they didn't have any evidence pinning the killings on me. The second was that they didn't really have any evidence pointing at anyone, and Latimer was hoping I could fill in the blanks.

Latimer started out with his best "good cop" manner. "OK, Frank. Why don't you tell me what really happened?" He's really not very good at the good cop role.

"Like I told you already, Latimer, those two guys were already dead when I got there. I didn't see anyone else hanging around."

"So what were you doing there? How'd you find Quinley and Melbourg?"

"My client had a tracking disk placed in the stolen item. I used that to track the guys down. I found out they worked on the docking ring. That's probably where they nabbed the item."

"How'd you find out where they worked?"

"The landlady told me."

"Landlady?"

"Landlady, building super, whatever. Heavy-set woman lives on the first floor. I asked her about the guys in apartment 3C."

"She just spilled the information, Frank? You didn't maybe misrepresent yourself?"

"What can I say, Latimer. I guess I've got a charming personality and an honest face."

"Can the crap, Frank. What happened next?"

"I had some lunch. In the café across the street. They make a good cup of joe, by the way. I didn't see any activity in apartment 3C. After a while I decided to see if Quinley or Melbourg were home. When I knocked on the door it swung open. I went in."

"Just like that?"

"Yeah, just like that. I found Quinley and Melbourg dead. I also found the tracking disk. It was in the bottom of a vase of plastic flowers. The item was gone."

"Just what is this 'item,' Frank?"

"It's a book."

"A book? Two guys get snuffed over a book?"

"It's an old book. Valuable, I guess," I tried to sound vague. "My client is a collector."

"And just who is this client?"

"I'd rather not say."

"Is that the way you're going to play it, Frank?"

"For the moment."

That seemed to stump Latimer. It was pretty clear that the crime scene boys had told him Quinley and Melbourg had been shot by a laser pistol. I'd only had a needle gun on me, one that I had a permit for. I hadn't seen any other weapons in the apartment.

"Let's face it, Latimer. You know I didn't kill those two. You don't have any evidence to hold me. Can I go now?"

"Not just yet. There's someone wants to see you, first. I don't know what you've gotten yourself into, Frank, but you seem to be attracting attention." With that he got up and left.

I sat around stewing for another fifteen minutes before the door of the interrogation room opened again.

The newcomer looked like an action hero in some vid. He was a couple of centimeters taller than me and maybe ten kilo's heavier, all of it muscle. It didn't take the tan on his ruggedly handsome face to show that he wasn't from Star City. The cut of the wide lapels on his pink jacket told me that much. I don't follow galactic fashion that closely, but I was guessing he was from Earth. Somehow, trends always seem a little more extreme on the mother world.

He gave me the hero stare before taking the seat Latimer had abandoned. I stared back blankly. I smiled, too.

It seemed I wasn't following along with the script. After a few seconds he reached into the pocket of his jacket and pulled out a card. Using the tips of the fingers on his left hand he slid it across the table towards me like he was trying to avoid contamination.

I picked it up. It was about five centimeters by three and made of some light metal. It had a picture of a globe in one corner and the caption:

Jordan Manning – Earth Agency for Recovery of Terran Heritage

"E.A.R.T.H." I said after laying it back down on the table. "Nice touch. Must have taken a whole room full of geniuses to come up with that one."

"You don't want to mess with Earth, Mr. Sladek," he said in a steely voice. I wasn't sure whether he meant the agency or the whole planet.

"I wouldn't think of it, Manning."

"I know what you were looking for, Sladek."

"I guess that makes two of us. No, actually three if we include the guy that stole it and snuffed Quinley and Melbourg. Unless you told Latimer."

"He doesn't need to know at this point."

"I'm sure he'd be glad to hear that. You know they bug these rooms, don't you?"

"Don't play funny with me, Sladek. That book is the property of the people of Earth, and it's my duty to get it back."

"That seems to be a matter of opinion," I responded. That seemed to raise his hackles. To rub it in I added, "It seems to me that with the Human species spread out over a couple of hundred star systems, no one place has got more of a call on Earth's heritage than any other."

"That's not the way my agency sees it, Sladek."

"That and a credit will buy you a cup of joe in a cheap diner." I admit I was enjoying jerking Agent Manning around. "It doesn't matter, though. I don't have the book or the dingus, or whatever. Someone else got to it first."

"Who?"

"You got me. I didn't even know that there were extra players in this game. I thought I was just tracking down some two bit thieves working the docking rings."

"Be that as it may, Sladek, that book is the property of Earth. If you find it, I advise you to turn it over to me or you'll be in big trouble."

"That's a matter for my client to decide."

"Just who is your client, Sladek?"

"My client prefers to remain anonymous for the time being."

"We'll see about that." He glared at me for a while in silence. I gave him my best sappy grin. After a couple of minutes he reached out, palmed the card on the table and stuck it back in his pocket. He got up and left the room.

A few minutes later Latimer was back. He had a big grin on his face like someone had made his day. I realized it must have been me.

"I got to hand it to you. You sure got his goat, Frank."

"Is that guy for real?"

"Who knows. He waltzed in here after we brought you in for interrogation and flashed some fancy credentials in our faces. No way to tell if they are real or not. The Earth Consulate hadn't heard of him or his agency. It will take at least three weeks to get a message to Earth and a confirmation back."

"And in the mean time?"

"In the mean time we let him run around as long as he doesn't get himself in trouble."

I grunted. "Am I free to go now, Latimer? Or do you have more clowns to talk to me."

"I'll tell you what you can do, Frank. You can get out of my hair. That's what you can do. And try and not find any more dead bodies for a while if at all possible. It's getting to be a bad habit of yours."

"It's not my fault people seem to get themselves snuffed in my vicinity. What about my gun? You know it wasn't the one that was used on Quinley and Melbourg."

"Pick it up at the checkout desk. I assume you remember where that is?"

"Oh, I remember, Latimer. I remember."

"Get out of here, Frank, before I call Agent Manning back to bend your ear some more."

I got up and left. The sergeant at the checkout desk had my gun waiting for me. He made a lame joke about how I should just get a locker. I signed his sheet and headed for the street.

It was late by the time I stepped off the tram for the short walk back to my apartment. A kilometer and a half over my head the glow tubes on the giant spar that runs down the center of Star City had been turned down to provide the illusion of night. The only illumination was provided by the streetlights on the corners and the garish signs of those businesses still open. It is my favorite time of the day.

I thought of turning in at one of those signs and having a drink at the Blue Moon, but thought better of it. This time of night the place would be crowded and noisy, and I was in no mood for that. I realized I hadn't had anything to eat since the sandwich at the café. The diner on the corner was still open. I grabbed a stool at the counter and ordered a bowl of the stew and a cup of joe. Neither was that good, but both were hot, which for the moment was enough for me. I lingered over the slab of bread that had come with the stew, but the dirty looks of the counterman who wanted to close up convinced me to move on.

The Aldeberon Arms, the apartment building where I lived, is on the other side of street from the diner, just across from the Blue Moon, which is normally convenient. It's a holdover from a time when the neighborhood had seen better days, a time when New Minglewood was still envisioned as a park, rather than the slum inhabited by grifters, whores and two-bit punks that it became. It had been a nice place once, built in a style I believe they call Art Deco Nouveau or something. The apartments are large by Star City standards and the rents are cheap, being so close to New Minglewood. I call it home.

The security on the front door of the building is nonfunctional more often than not. It was in one of the nonfunctional modes. I opened the door and didn't even bother trying the elevator. The exercise keeps me fit. Or so I tell myself. I walked up the three flights of stairs to my floor.

The door to my apartment does have a good security system. I installed it myself. I make sure that it's in working order, too. That doesn't stop me from using a bit of low tech when I feel the need. I noticed that the piece of paper I had wedged in the door had dropped to the hallway floor. I pulled out the needle gun from its holster and checked that the dart clip was engaged and a dart was in the chamber. Then I opened the door with my left hand like I wasn't expecting visitors.

A light was on in the living room at the front of the apartment. That room looked out on the street and had a small balcony. The light was from the lamp next to the chair where I like to sit and put my feet up after a hard day of doing nothing. There was someone sitting in that chair. He was reading one of the books from the case along the wall.

He was dressed conservatively all in black except for a thin sliver of white at his neck just over the Adam's apple. He was of medium height, not overweight. His hair, which was cut short, was a silvery grey and his face showed the weight of years.

"Excuse me," I said, pointing the needle gun at his chest. "I seem to have mistaken this apartment for mine."

"You'll have to forgive me, Mr. Sladek. I took the liberty of letting myself in. I thought it would be less conspicuous." If he was worried about the needle gun aimed at him, he didn't show it. "Allow me to introduce myself. I'm Father Pagani."

"Father? Whose father? I'm pretty sure you're not mine, though mother was always a little vague on the subject."

"It's a religious title, Mr. Sladek. I'm a sort of clergyman. I'm here acting as an agent of the Curia of the Reconstituted Catholic Church."

"Very interesting—Father Pagani. Just what sort of agent would that be? I wasn't aware that the Catholic Church was so desperate for converts that they had taken to breaking and entering."

"Oh, you'll find I didn't break anything, Mr. Sladek. Though I will confess to the entering part, obviously. But to business. I am employed by the Church to restore its heritage."

"There seems to be a lot of that going around," I remarked.

"I take it you are referring to Mr. Manning, so called agent of E.A.R.T.H. I wouldn't trust that one, Mr. Sladek."

"I'll keep that in mind."

"But to the point. The Curia has commissioned me to recover certain items that are the property of the Holy Church, which have, for various reasons, gone missing over the years. As you may be aware, the Church has had a somewhat turbulent history over the last millennia, and much of its patrimony was dispersed during the worst of the episodes."

"I seem to remember hearing something about that," I said. The needle gun was still pointing at the father. I have to admit he was handling that very well.

"My particular mission at present is the recovery of a first edition of *The Divine Comedy*. I am aware that you are also interested in that item, though for a different employer."

"I don't have it, if that's what you're angling at."

"I am aware of that, as well, Mr. Sladek. You were too late for Mr. Quinley and Mr. Melbourg."

"I take it from your visit that you don't have the book, either?"

"You are unfortunately correct in that.   Neither does Manning.   It would seem there is another player in our little game, Mr. Sladek. You wouldn't have any idea of who he or they would be, would you?"

"Frankly, Father, until this afternoon, I wasn't aware of any other players besides my employer."

"That is regrettable. I was hoping you might enlighten me."

"Afraid not."

"The Lord moves in mysterious ways."

"If you say so, Father. Personally, I wouldn't know about such things. I hate to seem inhospitable, but it is getting late and I've had a trying day. If there is nothing else, I'll see you out."

"There is one thing, Mr. Sladek. You know that the book is rightfully the property of the Holy Church. The Church would look favorably on anyone responsible for its restoration and would show its gratitude, both in this world and the next."

"As to the next world, I wouldn't know about that, Father. Star City is the only world I've ever known. But in this world I make it a habit of only working for one client at a time, and as you know, I'm already engaged. A matter of professional ethics, you understand."

"I can appreciate your honesty, Mr. Sladek. It is an admirable quality. However, if circumstances should change your mind, I can be reached at the Rigel Royal. And with that, I will bid you adieu as they say."

He stood up carefully so as not to appear threatening and walked to the door.

"Good night, Father."

"Good night, Mr. Sladek. Peace be with you."

After he left I checked to makes sure that the door security was armed and then went to bed.

In the morning I received a call. It was Miss Hohenberg. "Mr. Sladek. I understand there have been developments. Would it be possible to meet to discuss them this morning?"

"That would be a pleasure, Miss Hohenberg. Would you like me to come up to the house?"

"I would prefer to meet elsewhere. Could I come to your office?"

"I don't actually have a physical office," I admitted. "It has always seemed like an unnecessary expense." Somehow, I couldn't see inviting her to the place I usually conducted business, the Blue Moon. "We could meet in a café somewhere, or you could come to my apartment."

"Your apartment might be preferable, Mr. Sladek. From the standpoint of privacy." I hadn't had many women put it that way.

"That would be fine by me. Would 1030 be acceptable? I live in the Aldeberon Arms. Fourth floor."

"I will see you then, Mr. Sladek," she said, then broke the connection.

I tend to keep the place fairly tidy. Not that I'm overly fussy. I just find it easier that way.

I was finishing my morning cup of joe on the balcony when I saw Miss Hohenberg walking up the street. She was dressed in a grey skirt and a black, high-necked sweater. Her movements, as she strode up the street were graceful but precise. It was 1029.

The door rang a minute later. I didn't need the door cam to know it was her. I opened the door and ushered her inside to the living room.

I could see her eyeing the place over. The place had come furnished in what could charitably be described as an eclectic style, though most people would call it junk. Over the years though, I've managed to replace most of the furniture with better pieces, some by judicious shopping in second hand stores, but mostly by picking through the discards of people moving away from the building. It's surprising what some people will throw away. The apartment had acquired a certain comfortable elegance.

"Can I offer you some refreshments, Miss Hohenberg?"

"Tea, if you have it."

"I think I can brew something up." My tastes don't normally run to tea, but I did have the makings, a remnant of a former lady friend.

"I must say, Mr. Sladek, this isn't quite what I expected." She was looking at the painting of an alien landscape that hung over my sofa.

From the kitchen area I said, "That was a gift from a friend."

"Your friend has good taste. That looks like an original Lucinda."

"Yes, she gave it to me before she left. There's another in the bedroom that I'm particularly fond of. The one in the entryway not so much." The later is one of the few paintings she'd done of a human figure. No one but Lucinda and I knows that it is entitled "Portrait of Frank Sladek." Our parting had been strained.

"Yes, I was wondering about that. It seemed so atypical."

Some things are better left undiscussed. I busied myself with the tea things. When I came out of the kitchen she was examining the bookcase against the far wall.

"Thank you," she said accepting the cup.

"I hope the tea is acceptable. I don't usually drink tea myself."

"I wouldn't have thought so," she replied with a smile. "I see you do read."

"There's a lot of down time in my line of work. I can't spend all of it drinking in some saloon." The fact was, one could, and I often did, but there are limits if one wants to keep working in my business, and keep alive.

"A couple of Marcus Fitzroy's and even a Jack Feldman. Interesting tastes, Mr. Sladek."

"Marcus is a friend of sorts. Feldman gave me his book when I helped him with a bit of trouble, but then I think he gives books away to anyone who will take them. Personally, I found it pretty awful."

She smiled at that. Fifteen years ago Feldman had written one book that was the talk of the galaxy for about a year, no one knows why. He came to Star City and never left, dominating what there was of the local art scene.

"If you didn't like it, why have you kept it?"

"You never know. Feldman might enter a black hole some day, and then it could be worth real money. Anyway, it would be rude to get rid of it after he gave it to me."

"Your sense of propriety surprises me," she said as she continued to look over the contents of the bookcase. "An interesting assortment in any case, Mr. Sladek."

"I pick up whatever I find interesting, Miss Hohenberg. Say, do we have to be so formal? It seems it could get in the way. My name is Frank."

She thought that over for a moment, as if the decision was a matter of life or death. Finally, she replied with one word, "Crysalis."

It was an unusual name, but then in Star City, where people come from all over what's called human space and even beyond, unusual names don't often warrant much notice.

"We should get down to business—Frank. Just what happened yesterday?"

"I used the tracker to run down the pair that took the book, two yokes named Quinley and Melbourg. Unfortunately, someone got there before I did. Quinley and Melbourg were dead, shot at close range. The book was gone."

"How did whoever killed them find them?" The fact that two men were dead over a book didn't seem to faze her.

"That's a good question, Crysalis. The guy that did it knew about the tracker. The disk had been removed from the book and dropped into the bottom of a flower vase. I'm not sure, but I think he got to them about four or five hours before I did. The cops might have a better idea."

"This is most distressing, Frank. Without the tracking disk, how will you find the book?"

"It makes it harder, I have to say. Still, he found out about Quinley and Melbourg somehow. There's a good chance he left some traces behind. That's the kind of thing I'm good at, finding traces."

"I hope you're right, Frank," she said thoughtfully.

"Whoever has the book still has to move it. Either sell it or get it off of Star City. That will make him vulnerable. Unless he stole it just to sit and read it on the john."

"I doubt that is the case, Frank. You keep saying 'he.' Are you sure it was a man?"

"No, I'm not sure. But the killer was a professional. Each of them was killed with a single laser pulse to the center of the forehead, just above the nose. That takes a lot of skill and a laser pistol with a short cycle time. Not your typical pocket-book weapon. I've known women who could shoot, but not like that. Besides, I can't see Quinley and Melbourg letting some strange woman into their apartment if you get what I mean."

I wasn't trying to sugar coat things. This book business was getting serious.

"You're probably right, Frank. I'll defer to your judgment."

"We've got another problem, though. Actually two. One is a guy calling himself Father Pagani who says he acting for the Curia of the New Vatican. He might actually be a priest, but I would swear he was carrying a laser pistol in a shoulder holster. Not your typical clergyman. He visited me last night offering me rewards both temporal and spiritual if I turned the book over to him."

"The Church forfeited any claim to the book long ago, Frank."

"That's not my call. Don't worry, though. Once someone hires me I don't change sides."

"You mentioned two problems, Frank."

"Yeah. While the police had me they let some guy named Jordan Manning talk to me. He claimed he was an agent for something called E.A.R.T.H."

"I've never heard of it," Crysalis said thoughtfully.

"Neither have I. The guy seemed too good to be true. He looked more like an actor playing the part than an actual agent ever would."

"Do you think he is an imposter?"

"Right now, if you asked me, I'd say there was an even chance he is a con-man trying to bluff his way to a big haul. Let's face it; it will take three weeks to get a message to Earth and back confirming his existence. He's not working through the local consulate, so they don't know whether he's the real thing or a phony anymore than anyone else does."

"Do you think he will cause trouble, Frank?"

"Right now, I'd be more worried about the padre. I'd lay odds he's killed before. Manning, I'm not so sure."

"Do you think this Father Pagani was the one who killed the two men and took the book?"

"No. Both the padre and Manning acted like they were as much in the dark as we are."

"What are you going to do now, Frank?"

"I'm going to do what detectives have been doing for the last thousand years—leg work. You can tell your employer not to worry. It may take me a day or two, but I'll find the book."

"That's reassuring, Frank. I have to get back and tell the Captain what's happened. Thank you for the tea. It was lovely."

"Any time, Crysalis. The pleasure was all mine."

She set her cup on the tray with the tea things and rose gracefully. At the door she said, "Keep in touch, Frank," before making her exit.

I knew she only wanted to hear about the book, but I seemed to read more into her tone. It was probably just my imagination.

Even on a place like Star City, where the double cross is the national sport, there are only so many gunmen who could be as clean and precise as the one that had shot Quinley and Melbourg. Sure, there were plenty of toughs willing to rough someone up for a few credits or terminate them for a few credits more, but most of them tended to the crude and sloppy. The real pros, the ones working for the syndicates behind the big casinos could show finesse when they wanted to, but mostly when they used violence, it was to leave a message. When they didn't want to leave a public message, they were more likely to stage an "accident" than go in for a hit.

So, starting with the two million or so on Star City, eliminate all the honest citizens, then eliminate the dishonest ones who didn't go in for violence, then discard the punks who couldn't place two shots within spitting distance of each other, and rule out the working pros, and what was I left with. I did the math in my mind. I came up with a big zero. It just didn't feel like local talent.

That pretty much meant that whoever had taken the book was from off Star City. Not surprising, really. The book would be impossible to fence on Star City. There just wasn't any local market. That argued for someone with connections to any one of the planets where there was enough money to make it worthwhile.

On the surface, that wouldn't seem to improve things much. Star City, by its very nature as the major transit hub of human space has, at any one time, upwards of a hundred thousand passengers in transit, lying over for periods ranging from hours to weeks while waiting to make their connection. But, again, most of those passengers were perfectly honest citizens going about their business without a gram of violence in their blood. All I had to do was eliminate all but the bad guys.

Fortunately, I had a friend, who for fifty dollars Crockett and the promise of dinner, would provide me access to the passenger manifests of incoming liners. Strictly illegal, of course, which was why my friend was such a valuable asset. I figured I could probably ignore anyone who had arrived much before the book had arrived on Star City, and anyone who had left before Quinley and Melbourg had been killed. That narrowed it down to a few hundred individuals. I had my friend zip me the transit records and passport info on them and spent the morning going through the list.

Most of the people on the list could be eliminated just because they didn't fit the profile, they were too well known, they came from the wrong planet, and so on. Remembering Crysalis's question about was it a man, I didn't automatically eliminate all the women on the list, but I was still convinced that the killer had been a man. After working through the list I had narrowed it down to five individuals. Manning and Father Pagani were among the five, but unless they were playing a really devious game, both of them were acting like they didn't have the book.

That left three. And of those three, one caught my eye. He had been on New Virginia and had arrived on the same starliner as had Crysalis. That, in itself, might have been a coincidence, at least a dozen passengers for that run were still on Star City. The manifest listed his name as James Miller. A perfect alias. Miller was a common enough name to actually be his true identity, or it could be a carefully chosen fake. His transit records and passport provided him with a plausible background, but most of it wouldn't be capable of verification in anything like a reasonable amount of time. He was more or less of average height and weight, brown hair and eyes, with no distinguishable features. Perfect attributes for someone who would want to blend into a crowd. I reflected that the description would fit me nearly as well.

There were two other names on the list, but neither of them had any connection to New Virginia or the book. I decided that I would concentrate on Miller for the time being. I could check the others later if Miller proved to be clean.

His transit file listed him as residing in a building that provided small residential suites available by the day or week for those passengers in transit that didn't want to stay in a hotel. Not fancy, but they offered limited kitchens, maid service, and other amenities for those willing to pay up front. With the constant turnover of occupants, a place like that would be perfect for someone trying not to attract attention. I decided to check it out.

The building was located up towards the passenger end of the city a few blocks down from the best hotels, casinos and other passenger diversions. I headed out, planning to catch a tram, but after a few blocks I noticed that I was being followed. It was Manning, and he wasn't doing a very good job. Even if his height and build hadn't made him stand out from the crowd, the aggressive checked pattern of his jacket would have flagged him as not a local.

I had plenty of time to waste, so I jumped a tram heading away from the passenger end. Manning had to hurry to catch the car. At the next stop, I waited until the tram was just getting ready to pull out and then jumped out, transferring to a circumferential tram. I played that game for about fifteen minutes, always taking care not to lose him, building up in him a false sense of confidence in his ability to tail me. After the tenth or so transfer, I timed it just right so that I grabbed an up tram leaving him panting at the stop. As I looked back, I waved. He saw me, and instinctively began to raise his hand in response before he caught himself.

I knew the tram schedule would give me a minute or two to disappear when I got off before the next tram would pass through that stop. I rode it one stop beyond where I should have gotten off, and then walked back towards Miller's building. It was the middle of the day, and I chose a street lined with shops, so there would be a crowd to hide in. I kept looking over my shoulder, but I didn't see any sign of Manning. Once I thought I saw a dark figure in a black hat, but when I looked to make sure, it was gone. Given the carefully controlled climate of Star City, hats of any shade are a rarity.

I zig-zagged for a couple of blocks, but didn't spot either Manning or Pagani. Satisfied that I had brushed off any tail I headed to Miller's building. I walked past it on the far side of the street, giving it a casual examination. There was nothing to distinguish it from a half dozen similar buildings on the street. There was a discrete entrance, book-ended between a noodle shop and one selling travel bags and other such accessories. Through the door I got a glimpse of a reception desk with a middle aged woman standing behind it.

At the end of the block, I turned the corner to see if there was a less public entrance. As was typical, there was an alley running behind the building to facilitate deliveries and trash hauling. I entered it, trying to estimate which of the rear facades matched up with Miller's building.

Maybe it was that that tripped me up.

"I was told to keep a look out for you, Sladek," a voice said, coming out of a dark recessed doorway on the other side of the alley. "From your reputation, I didn't think it would be this easy."

I turned slowly to take a look. It was Miller, holding a 50 Kilojoule laser. The face, which had looked so calm and innocent in his transit file, seemed hard and cold in the darkness of the alley.

"Keep your hands where I can see them."

I lifted my hands so they were level with my shoulders.

"Take the gun out of your holster and place it on top of the trash container there, Sladek. Do it carefully."

I did as he asked.

"I won't bother asking how you found me. It doesn't matter. This cover is obviously blown." I didn't bother to tell him I hadn't told anyone else about him.

"Look, Miller, or whatever your name is, I don't want any trouble. I'm just after the book."

"Aren't we all," Miller said. He was still partially concealed in the doorway, the light only illuminating half his face.

"The way I figure it, Miller, you may have the book, but you're going to have a hard time getting it off Star City. My employer might be willing to cut a deal. A suitable recovery fee in exchange for the book. No questions asked, and you can catch the next starliner out of here."

"Interesting, Sladek. You've got a point. Just how much are we talking about?" The voice seemed amused by the idea.

"I don't know. I'd have to ask my employer."

"Still, the book is worth millions to the right person."

"But getting it to them might not be easy. Think about it. I can see how much my employer is willing to pay. You can give me a call and see if it's worth your while. I'm in the directory."

"You seem to think I'm going to let you walk out of this alley, Sladek." The voice had turned cold again.

"Why not? I'm unarmed. I'm pretty sure you don't have the book on you, so there'd be no point in my trying to make a play."

"I have to say, you're taking the situation coolly, Sladek. Most men wouldn't."

"I've been around a bit, Miller. Panic doesn't get you anywhere."

"I'll keep your offer in mind—"

"Hold it!" This came from up the alley. I turned and looked. It was Manning. He was holding a very large and lethal looking laser pistol.

"You let yourself be followed, Sladek?" Miller asked. "I'm disappointed in you." His pistol was still trained on my heart.

"Where's the book?" Manning asked.

"As Sladek here observed, I don't have it on me."

"Drop the pistol," Manning ordered.

"I think perhaps you should be the one dropping his weapon." This came from the other end of the alley, from behind me. It was the voice of Father Pagani. I looked over my shoulder. His pistol was smaller, but every bit as lethal looking as the one Manning was holding. Interestingly, it was pointed at Manning, not Miller. When I looked back, Manning's laser had moved to cover the padre.

"We seem to have what I believe is called 'a Mexican standoff,'" Miller commented. He still had his weapon pointed at me.

"As an agent of E.A.R.T.H., I am declaring that I have the proper right of ownership to the book. Please turn it over to me. If you do so, I can promise leniency at your sentencing."

"Bah!" Pagani exclaimed. "I don't believe there even is such an agency as E.A.R.T.H. I've certainly never heard of it before. Have you Mr. Sladek? In any case, the book is the property of the Reconstituted Catholic Church."

The two men glared at each other, some twenty meters separating the tips of their pistols in the dark alley. I tried to edge out of the line of fire. As I did so, I noticed that something was missing from the little tableau. Miller had taken the opportunity to slip away.

I waited what seemed like several minutes but was probably only a few seconds before announcing, "Gentlemen. I believe Miller has made good his escape."

The two men turned to me, glaring.

"This is your fault, Sladek," Manning cried.

"Admit your own stupidity, Manning," Father Pagani, said quietly. "I admit mine. Where did he go, Mr. Sladek?"

"I don't know. I was watching you two. He probably left through that door." I pointed to the small door in back of the alcove where Miller had been hiding. I tried the handle, but it was locked. "It's a pretty sturdy looking door. I doubt that you'll be able to get it open."

"It's too late, anyway," the padre remarked. "You were the one that tracked him down to this place, Mr. Sladek. Why?" He still had the pistol in his hand. It wasn't exactly pointing at me, but it wasn't exactly not, either.

Manning's own weapon was wavering between the padre and myself. "What's the deal, Sladek?"

"Miller, at least that's the name he was using, has a suite in that building, there. I was casing it to see if he was home."

"Do you think the book is there?"

"It was. I doubt if it is anymore." I was hoping that Miller had had a chance to clear out with the book. That would avoid having to argue over its possession with the padre and Manning. "Of course we could go look."

The two stood there a moment with blank expressions on their faces before they realized the obvious.

"Do you mind if I recover my pistol?" I asked, turning to grab the weapon from where I had left it on top of the trash container.

When the back door proved to be locked, the three of us went in through the front. The receptionist gave Manning's credentials a dubious look, but allowed us to go up to Miller's room with a pass key. That proved unnecessary as Miller had left the door unlocked. He had also cleared out everything of his from the suite, including the book.

I left Manning and the padre in the empty apartment arguing about which one had ownership rights to the book. Neither one of them seemed to notice my leaving.

I felt that I should notify my client about this new development. I admit that part of my motivation was that I wanted to hear Crysalis' voice, but I also had a few questions for her, such as had she encountered Miller on the trip from New Virginia?

When I suggested that we meet to discuss things she said that she wasn't at the house and she didn't think that we should discuss matters over the comm. I couldn't argue with that.

"I'm on my way to a new exhibit at the Museum of Art. Would it be possible for you to meet me there?"

"That shouldn't be a problem," I replied.

"The Sumner Gallery then, in, say half an hour?"

"I'll be there."

"I'll be waiting for you." I knew that she was just stating a fact, but there was a hint of promise in that warm contralto voice. Or at least I chose to imagine that there was.

Passengers in transit through Star City often have to wait for hours, even days before making connections, and not all of them want to spend their layovers eating in over-priced hotel restaurants, shopping or gambling in one of the casinos. In an effort to offer something for everyone, the powers that ran Star City provided a number of high-brow cultural venues. The Museum of Art was one of them. It had a small, but respectable permanent collection, but its bread and butter were the various traveling exhibitions that occupied its galleries for periods ranging from weeks to months. As nearly everything that travels between star systems passes through Star City, stops at the museum were easy to arrange. For those so inclined, this provided opportunities to see a representative sampling of the best of human culture.

I wasn't a regular visitor, but I'd been there enough to know my way around the rather rambling collection of buildings just across the street from The Casino. A sign at the entrance to the Sumner Gallery proclaimed that an exhibit of early Terran printed material was currently being shown.

Every few decades some prognosticator makes a prediction about the demise of the printed word and the extinction of physical books. Yet with the inevitable incompatibilities of electronic data formats arising from never ending changes in technology and the realities of a human civilization that had spread across hundreds of planets, each in a different stage of economic development, somehow this has never come to pass. The printed format has proved to be the only one guaranteed to be readable on any planet over any time period. That, plus the simple pleasure of holding something in your hand, has ensured the survival of what many consider an anachronistic medium.

The Sumner Gallery was composed of a number of different halls of various sizes. It appeared that for the exhibition each hall had been dedicated to examples of the printers art of a particular type or era. I didn't immediately spot Crysalis, so I chose the expedient tactic of just wandering through the different rooms while keeping an eye open for her.

The first hall held a collection of what were described as "comic books," though to judge from the vivid illustrations there seemed to be nothing particularly humorous about the stories they portrayed. Instead, they seem to show what appeared to be an odd array of human mutants struggling against an equally improbable range of destructive obstacles. The exhibit was interesting, but somehow I didn't think that it would have much attraction for Miss Hohenberg.

I passed through into the next hall. This was dedicated to crime fiction from the Twentieth Century with a particular emphasis on the cover art. If anything, this was even more sensational than the art of the "comic books," with its depiction of a range of well endowed blonds in tight dresses facing various forms of jeopardy or mayhem supplemented with the occasional fedora wearing hero facing impossible odds with only his two fists or single gun to aid him. If one were to judge from only the evidence of these first two halls, it was amazing that anyone on Earth had survived the Twentieth Century to explore space. Not surprisingly, I didn't see Crysalis examining the items in that room either.

I passed on a room containing "science-fiction art" whatever that was and entered a hall containing examples from the 15th-17th centuries, as being more promising of holding Crysalis. I was rewarded with a glimpse of her gazing into a glass case containing what must have been an extremely early example of a printed book which was opened to a particularly beautifully engraved title page.

As I approached her, I noticed the complete look of concentration on her face as she was focused on studying the printed page before her. It wasn't just a look of appreciation, but bordered on obsession. For a moment I was afraid to disturb her, but only for a moment.

"Miss Hohenberg."

She remained still for a moment, blinked, and then turned to flash a smile that would melt an icicles heart. "Frank. I'm so glad you could make it," she said as if this were just a casual meeting.

"I wouldn't miss it for the world," I replied, not sure which world I meant. "An interesting collection, don't you think? I've been admiring some of the later works."

She laughed at that, with her warm contralto laugh. "There really are some treasures here, Frank. They have a page from a Gutenberg. It's incredible." She was almost breathless. Me, I like a good book, but I prefer ones I can read.

"But you wanted to talk," she said, suddenly serious. "Perhaps we should adjourn to the gardens for some privacy.

"Shall we," I said, offering her my arm. I was pleased and a little surprised when she took it, wrapping her long, graceful fingers around my arm. I escorted her through the French doors at the end of the hall out into one of the gardens on the museum grounds. We must have looked like two innocent lovers seeking a bit of privacy.

One outside, I led the way to a bench in the center of the garden courtyard. It would give us a clear view of our surroundings so we could be sure we weren't being overheard.

I gave her a brief description of the events with Miller earlier in the day. A look of concern flashed over her face, but only for an instant.

"This Miller guy arrived from New Virginia on the same liner that you did. Are you sure you didn't run into him?"

"Miller? I don't remember a Miller. Are you sure he was using that name?"

"That was the name on the passenger list when he disembarked. Starliners usually frown on passengers changing their names in flight." I showed her the picture from his file. It didn't do him justice. "Are you sure you don't remember him?"

She hesitated a moment as if concentrating. "No, I'm sure I don't remember anyone of that name. But it was a big ship with nearly a thousand passengers, and I spent much of the time in my stateroom."

"That's too bad. I was hoping to get some insight on him."

"You think he has the book?"

"I'm pretty sure. He knew who I was." I didn't mention that he had gotten the drop on me. "He was a cool customer, too. He didn't flinch when Manning and the padre showed up. Either he has the book, or is working for whoever does."

"So you think he might not be working alone?" There was a touch of panic in her voice. At the time I thought it was just concern for the book and the problems an ever enlarging cast of characters trying to gain possession of it might cause.

"It would be my guess that he was working for someone. He's good at what he does, but he's more muscle than anything. Someone is supplying the brains, and I don't think it's him. Someone who knew about the book and who has some idea of how to dispose of it. To realize anything close to what it's worth will require contacts."

"Yes, Frank. I can see you're right. What do you think we should do?"

"Well first, I think you should have the Captain contact the docking authorities to have them on alert for someone trying to get the book off of Star City. They should be on the alert for Miller, too."

"I'm not sure he will agree to that."

"It's our best chance. As long as the book doesn't leave Star City, Miller can't really get rid of it. No one but your boss has enough money or interest in it to buy it. If Miller realizes that, he might be willing to deal, to offer to ransom the book."

"Do you think so, Frank?"

"If he doesn't have any other choice. He might figure some cash and a chance to get away is better than nothing or getting caught."

"Yes, I can see that. And if he does turn over the book for a ransom, what then, Frank?"

"Well, that would be up to the Captain. If it was me, I'd let him go. Less publicity that way, and no questions of ownership from the Church or the Terran government."

"Yes. I can see that would be wise." She seemed relieved.

"You said that's what we should do first, Frank. What should we do next?"

"I'm glad you asked that, Crysalis. I think next you should skip the rest of the exhibition and let me buy you dinner. I know a nice little place not too far from here."

"You are incorrigible, Frank. But I should call the Captain, first, so he can contact the authorities."

I let her make the call while I stared at the gardenias. She spent some time explaining the situation, but in the end it appeared that he agreed. After she broke the connection she turned to me all smiles. "Shall we go to dinner, then?"

Now Star City has some of the best, and most expensive, restaurants in human space, but the reality is that they cater mostly to the VIP passenger trade and not us poor slobs who actually live here. They feature the choicest ingredients brought in on the great starliners from the planets of dozens of star systems, and no aspiring chef can consider his resume complete without a stint in the kitchens of one of the restaurants of the first tier hotels, those closest to the passenger docking ring.

Those of us who actually live here mostly make do with vat grown protein which comes in appetizing flavors like "meat," "fowl," or "fish," often referred to as "brown," "white," and "that other kind of white." Carbohydrates come from a different set of vats in much the same range of designer colors. Vegetables mostly come in the form of pastes in colors like green, red, or occasionally orange. Now don't get me wrong, I'm sure all of these contain the necessary balance of vitamins and minerals needed to insure a balanced diet, but flavors tend to be a low priority add on. Not that anyone starves to death or suffers malnutrition on Star City.

But there are, to those in the know and who have a level of disposable income that allows the occasional splurge, some fairly decent restaurants. Granted, their kitchens are mostly run by people not native to Star City, and they tend to be located in those neighborhoods where the rent is cheaper. Still, they are worth seeking out, particularly when one is trying to impress ones' dinner date.

It is to one of these, the Pomme d'Terre, that I escorted Crysalis. It was far enough that we took a tram, but close enough that we got off after only a few stops. It occupied the ground floor of a corner building in a space that had once been a women's clothing store. It was clean, well lit, with large windows facing both streets that allowed the patrons to view the passing scene. A handful of small tables were outside on the sidewalk, but we chose to dine inside where it was quieter and more private.

The cuisine could be considered eclectic, but in this day and age with mankind scattered across hundreds of planets, what isn't. More importantly, the restaurant had established connections guaranteeing fresh produce, and the meat, while it arrived frozen, had at least once been part of an actual animal.

Equally important, the chef, a large Montegan woman, knew what to do with what the pantry and cooler supplied.

The head waiter knew me slightly and had reason to see that as something positive, so we were seated at a quiet table towards the rear of the restaurant and away from the kitchen.

"I don't actually get many opportunities to eat out," Crysalis said after we had been seated and the waiter had brought a carafe of water and a basket of rolls.

"That's a shame. I would have thought a woman like you would enjoy dining," I replied.

"The Captain prefers that I usually dine with him. It's only due to the fact that there is a Kaminski-Jones liner docked that is captained by one of his cousins that I am free tonight. He's hosting a dinner for the officers and I was informed that my presence would be unnecessary."

"Their loss is my gain," I replied gallantly, though even to my ears it sounded like a lame cliché.

"Don't get me wrong, the Captain sets a fine table, much better than I could ever afford on my salary. But the Captain does tend to monopolize my life."

"Pardon my asking, and don't feel you have to answer, but do you and the Captain have some sort of arrangement?"

She smiled at that. "How old fashioned. No, there is nothing like that. The neurological damage the Captain suffered in the accident precludes anything of a sexual nature on his part. It's just that he tends to be possessive of those things he thinks of as his. In his mind, I'm just another employee owing complete obedience."

"Why do you stay, then?"

"Why? Because the pay is good, the living conditions are much better than I could ever hope to afford, and I have the opportunity to work with some incredible materials. Don't get me wrong, Frank, the Captain isn't a bad employer, it's just that he's—well, he's just very impersonal. But let's not dwell on the subject. Why don't we talk about you, instead? How does one become a private detective?"

I was saved from answering that by the waiter coming to take our order. I had a chicken dish prepared with tomatoes and peppers. Crysalis ordered a filet of some sort of fish I had never heard of. The waiter suggested a wine that would decimate my account with the bank. My knowledge of wine being limited, I agreed. When it came, it seemed the waiter knew his stuff. Crysalis did the thing of sticking her nose in the glass. She seemed to be nearly as enthralled as she had been when looking at the book in the museum.

Dinner went on for hours, neither of us seeming to be in a hurry. It was a slow night in the restaurant, so they didn't seem to mind, either. We talked of this and that, some of my more amusing cases, her trips searching out rare books for the Captain. Eventually I noticed that we were the last table left in the restaurant and my friend, the head waiter was standing at the kitchen door twiddling a napkin.

He seemed relieved when I motioned for the bill. Despite the fact that I could have eaten at the corner diner for a month on what the bill came to, I left a generous tip. It had been worth it.

Outside on the sidewalk I said, "It's getting late. I could escort you home if you'd like."

"You can be a gentleman, Frank," she said with that faint smile she had. "Actually, the Captain isn't expecting me back at the house tonight. These parties tend to run quite late. I was planning to get a hotel room for the night—but if you have a better idea, I'd be open to suggestions."

I can be a little slow on the uptake at times, but not that slow. We took the tram to the stop nearest my apartment. From there it was a short stroll through the Souk. There was a sidewalk café still open at that hour. We stopped for small cups of strong coffee, the real thing, not joe. I was giving her ample opportunities to change her mind. She didn't.

The next few days I played the waiting game. I'd put out feelers on Miller, but nothing turned up. Miller had definitely gone to ground. It seemed like my best bet was to hope that he'd decide he couldn't smuggle the book off of Star City and his only option was to ransom the book.

It was the middle of the afternoon, and I was sitting in the Blue Moon. I was leisurely sipping a glass of brown on the rocks, not really interested in getting drunk, but just to pass the time. My comm was sitting on the bar next to a stack of half credit coins the barkeep had given me in change. I was hoping that Miller would give me a call. That's actually a lie. I was really hoping that Crysalis would give me a call so we could arrange something for the evening.

I had to admit it to myself. I had it, and I had it bad. I was in love. I didn't know why and I didn't know how, but there was something about Crysalis that had grabbed me in a way that no other woman ever had. Maybe it was the way she had stared at a 17th century folio in the museum exhibit. Maybe it was her perfect diction or the way none of the hairs on her head ever seemed out of place. Maybe it was her long, slender legs, the subtle curves of her breasts, the graceful arch of her neck, the deep pools of her eyes. OK, there was a lot to be said about the latter. Crysalis had the complete package, but what I was feeling was more than physical.

I wasn't fooling myself. She was smart, educated, and classy and I was a two bit private dick scraping a living out by staying just inside of the law. I didn't see what she saw in me. I couldn't see it lasting. The worlds we came from were too different. But I didn't care.

I was musing on this, staring at the ice cubes floating in my glass of brown, when I noticed a shape sliding into the seat next to me. I looked up and recognized Latimer. Rossetti, his partner, wasn't with him. That was a good sign. Rossetti hates my guts. The feelings are mutual.

Latimer motioned to the barkeep, pointed at my drink and held up two fingers. If the barkeep was surprised by this pantomime he didn't show it. A moment later two glasses of brown on the rocks appeared before the detective. He slid one of them over to me. I looked up, trying to read the expression in the coppers face. Something was up. Latimer never bought drinks. At least not for me.

"Geez, Frank," Latimer said after he had downed a slug of his drink. "Why didn't you tell me that you were working for the Captain. It would have made things a lot easier for both of us. I'd have told that jerk Manning to beat it."

"It wasn't my call, Latimer. My employer wanted to keep his involvement quiet for reasons of his own. I saw no reason to argue. That changed when we found out who had the book, but it was still his decision. No offense intended, just business."

"You know, Frank, you should stop playing the hard-ass all the time."

"Yeah. I get that a lot. Guess it's just me being me." I smiled, picked up the glass he had slipped me and took a swig.

"So what is this thing, this book?"

"It's a book, pretty old." I gave him a physical description without letting on what it really was or what it was worth.

"I guess it must be pretty valuable, then?" Latimer said.

"To the right people. To anyone else it's just some yellowing paper slapped between two boards covered in animal hide."

"But it is worth enough that someone killed two people over it."

"Quinley and Melbourg were just two petty thieves who got caught with their hands in the till. They didn't mean anything to Miller. You know the type. He'd kill his own grandmother if the price was right."

"Tough cookie, huh?" Latimer asked.

"Don't underestimate Miller. He's a real pro. And not just a good shot. He's cold inside. He's not going to care about how high the body count gets."

"So how is this going to play out, Frank?" Latimer asked, looking me in the eyes.

"If your guys are doing your jobs, Miller is going to realize that he can't get off of Star City with the book, so he's going to try and cut a deal, offer the book to Kaminski-Jones in exchange for a bag of cash and a ticket out."

"Just like that?"

"Just like that."

"And what's your part, Frank?"

"Me? I figure I'll probably end up the bag man."

"You'll let us know?"

"I will if you promise to give me space to make the exchange."

"I don't like it, Frank. Things could go wrong."

"Things can always go wrong, Latimer. Miller will call, and we'll set up a meeting. Someplace quiet. I'll go in. You can form a perimeter after I go in if you like, as long as you don't come rushing in before I walk out with the book."

"But after you're in the clear, we can take Miller?" Latimer might take a little squeeze now and then, but at his heart he's an honest cop.

"Once I have the book in my hot little hands, you can nab Miller for Quinley and Melbourg if you like. It's no sweat to me. I'm not sure what Kaminski-Jones will say to that, but that's between you and the Captain, and not me, understand."

"Sure, Frank. I get it. Anything else?"

"Yeah. Keep Manning and Father Pagani out of it. Manning's a joke, but the padre might cause real trouble. Either one of them could mess things up."

"I'm not an idiot, Frank. I'll make sure they keep their distance. Any other players I don't know about?"

"Probably. But if there are, I don't have any better idea who they are than you do."

"What about this Hohenberg dame? Is she going to be part of it?"

"She's no dame, Latimer," I said defensively. "But, no, she's not going to have any part of the action when things go down."

"Getting to you, eh, Frank? No offense intended." There was a silly grin on Latimer's face as he downed the last of his drink. He stood up and said, "Let me know when you hear anything. Be seeing you."

"You'll be the first to know, Latimer. Thanks for the booze."

He waved a salute and walked out into the daylight. I went back to staring at ice cubes.

I was getting frustrated. Miller hadn't made a move, and it was starting to look like he might have found a way to slip the net. Hard to do, but not impossible, particularly if he had local help. But most of the frustration was due to the fact that Crysalis was finding it hard to slip away so that we could spend time together.

I know that I'm sounding like a lovesick schoolboy, but I'd fallen, fallen hard for a woman who by any rights shouldn't have given me the time of day. Maybe it was the fact that behind the prim façade she seemed such an innocent. Innocent dames were mostly outside my experience. Or maybe it was that she seemed to have some inner need and I was hoping that I was the guy that could fill it. But I had to face the fact that I was in love.

That's why it was almost a relief when the call finally came from Miller. It was brief and to the point. He'd trade the book for a "no strings" credit stick with a hundred grand in Crockett dollars and an irrevocable exit pass. The first would be easy enough if Kaminski-Jones was willing to cough up the money. Basically, an NSCS served the same purposes as bearer bonds had done in an earlier age. With no means of communications between star systems faster than a swift starliner available, credit sticks had become the universal means of exchange between planets. Encrypted with a theoretically unbreakable code, a stick could have any amount downloaded into it. Once that was done, the transaction couldn't be revoked, restricted or traced. All the possessor of such a stick needed to do was present it at any participating bank anywhere in human space and he could walk out the front door with the cash equivalent in any currency desired.

The exit pass posed more of a hurdle. Anyone boarding a ship leaving Star City needed such a pass. For most passengers it was not a big deal. All they needed to do was present their ticket at the gate and get on board. Provided, that is, they weren't on a hold list in the central database. An irrevocable pass sidestepped that requirement. Mostly, they were used by those with diplomatic credentials, which was why they were so hard to obtain. It would be interesting to see if the Captain had enough pull to obtain one. That is if he was agreeable to the whole deal.

Miller kept his call short. He said that he'd call back in six hours to make the arrangements for the swap. If Kaminski-Jones couldn't or wouldn't come up with the cash, he said he'd investigate alternate arrangements. By that, I assume he meant the padre. Neither one of us seemed to think Manning could come up with enough cash to make it worthwhile.

As soon as he broke the connection I called the Captain. I explained the deal, but he didn't seem to warm to the idea.

"Sladek, I'm paying you to find the book," he blustered. "What have you been doing the last week except entertain Miss Hohenberg?"

"You're paying me to recover the book, Captain. That's what I intend on doing."

"At the cost of a hundred thousand dollars Crockett!"

"You're only out the hundred Gs if Miller gets away with it," I pointed out calmly.

"What do you mean? He'll have the credit stick and an exit pass. What's to stop him?"

"He's still wanted by the authorities for the murder of Quinley and Melbourg. Once Miller's in custody the exit pass won't be worth the plastic it's printed on and the credit stick can be recovered. It might cost a few hundred to keep it off the record, but I figure that's cheap."

"You can arrange all this without messing it up, Mr. Sladek?"

"I've already talked to Latimer. He's the detective assigned to the case. He might be a cop, but he's no fool. I make the swap, he sets up a loose perimeter. Once I've got the book, he closes in. Miller gets frisked and the credit stick gets returned. All clean and simple."

I didn't really feel all that confident. There was a lot that could go wrong in a deal like this, but I wasn't going to let Kaminski-Jones think I wasn't in control of the situation.

"And what's to keep you and this Latimer from walking off with the book and the credit stick?"

"Where would I go, Captain? And let's face it, a hundred large is a lot of money, but it won't set someone up for life. Particularly when it's split two ways. Besides, Latimer is nearly as honest as I am. He's more interested in making lieutenant than going off somewhere."

"OK. But if this goes wrong, Sladek, I'll be holding you responsible."

"You can have the credit stick and the exit pass ready?"

"They'll be ready, Mr. Sladek. I'll have Crysalis bring them to you once the final arrangements are made. I'm sure you'll like that."

"I'll let you know as soon as Miller contacts me."

"I'll be waiting, Mr. Sladek."

Miller was right on time with his callback.

"Do we have a deal, Sladek?"

"It's a deal."

"You have the credit stick and the pass?"

"I'll have them for the meeting. When and where's it going to be?"

"Tonight. Midnight. You familiar with the lighting spar?"

He was referring to the beam that ran down the central axis of Star City. It carried the glow tubes that provided what passes for daylight. It carried a lot of other things, too, like the conduits that fed the sprinklers that provide the artificial rain that gets turned on once a week to wash down the dust and grime. The spar was really just a mess of pipes and conduits and power feeds and maintenance catwalks and who knew what else.

"Couldn't you have picked someplace more inaccessible, Miller?"

"What's a matter, Sladek? Afraid of heights?"

The inside cylinder of Star City is three kilometers in diameter. That's fifteen hundred meters from the spar to the street. That's a long way down. Most buildings on Star City are only four or five stories. Was I afraid of heights? I didn't know. I'd never been high enough for it to matter.

"The spar is access restricted, Miller. Maintenance personnel only."

"That's what makes it a good place for the exchange. From up there I can see if anybody is following you or if you've tried to cook up something to scam me."

"Would I do that?"

"In a minute if you thought you could get away with it," Miller said with a laugh. "Now listen close. There are four main maintenance catwalks up there. They're labeled with letters, A through D. The meet will be on A at a staging platform about a kilometer up from the down end of the station. You'll make your approach from that end. Understand?"

"I understand." That didn't mean I liked it.

"Get there right at midnight. Don't be early. If I see anyone else on the spar, the deal's off. Understand?"

"Yeah."

"We make the exchange, and then you stay there for a half hour while I make my escape. I'll be able to see you, so don't think you can pull something fast on me. And no guns and no cops."

"Sure. Whatever you say Miller. All I want is to get the book. How am I to be sure that it's the real deal?"

"That's your problem, Sladek. But don't worry. It'll be the real thing."

"I'll see you at midnight, Miller," but I was talking to dead air.

I called the house on the Hill. Kaminski-Jones said he had everything ready and would send Crysalis over with them a couple of hours before midnight. He didn't seem happy with the deal, but I sensed that he wanted the book badly enough not to screw things up with plans of his own.

My next call was to Latimer. He wasn't that thrilled either, when I told him about the meeting place.

"Could he have picked a worse place, Frank? From up there he can keep an eye on half of Star City if he's got a pair of binoculars."

"Think of it this way, Latimer. The spar can only be accessed from either end. Once I go up there, all you have to do is put men at the base of the maintenance elevators at each end and he can't get away. How else is he going to get down, fly?"

"I wouldn't put it past him."

"Don't be such a pessimist. Are we set then?"

"Yeah. I'll have my men in place. They'll be wearing maintenance uniforms and arrive in ones and twos, so they shouldn't attract attentions."

"Sounds good. Just make sure they keep out of sight until after midnight. Better add enough time after that for me to make the exchange. Got that?"

"Yeah, I've got that." I could tell that Latimer was chafing at having to take directions from me. I didn't really care.

"Frank," he said, "There's one more thing." I didn't like the note in his voice. It was that of concern. For me. This can't be good, I thought.

"What is it?"

"Just as part of the routine of investigation, we questioned all of the passengers that arrived on the same starliner as Miss Hohenberg and Miller, those that were still on Star City. There were about a dozen of them. Most of them didn't know a thing, and didn't recognize either one of them. But there was one, a little old lady who had been visiting her son on New Virginia. She recognized your girl friend right away. She recognized Miller, too. She said that she had seen the two of them together. A lot. The words she used were 'as thick as thieves.' I just thought you should know."

"It's probably nothing, Latimer. Maybe Miller was checking her out to see if she had the book with her. Maybe it is just a coincidence. Two people traveling on the same starliner for a week with nothing else to do. People form casual friendships all the time on those things."

"Yeah, you're right, Frank. It's probably just a coincidence." I could tell he didn't believe that for a minute. "Anyway, I just thought you should know."

"Thanks," I said, not meaning it for an instant. "Are we set then?"

"Yeah. We're set." We were back to being just a cop and a private dick. That was the way I wanted it. He broke the connection.

My stomach was churning. Was it possible that Crysalis was working with Miller? I didn't want to think so, but the part of me that was a private dick and professional hard case couldn't leave the idea alone. How had two low-rent characters like Quinley and Melbourg known that the book was arriving on that ship and was worth stealing? And how had Miller found out they had it? And that there was a tracking disk on it? It had all the hallmarks of an inside job, but there were only two people on the inside, Crysalis and the Captain. It was too easy to put two and two together and come up with four, no matter how much I wanted the answer to be five or three.

I didn't like the math, but what else could I do except go through with the exchange and hope I was wrong? I checked the time. It was six hours before midnight. Too much time to sit and brood. I poured myself a double shot of brown over ice and set the entertainment system to play some jive samba. I had another after that as the sensuous rhythms of the music washed over me. Great music to forget a girl by. I thought about a third drink, but decided against it. I needed to be sharp. No matter how things went down, Miller was a dangerous customer.

It was three hours before midnight. The glow tubes on the spar had dimmed for the night, and I was sitting in the dark, the room illuminated only by the glare from the sign on the Blue Moon across the street. I turned off the music and sat in the silence.

Crysalis showed up on my doorstep promptly at 2200. She was looking more casual than I had seen her before in a grey skirt and soft grey sweater. Her hair was hanging loose around her shoulders rather than pulled back and up as she normally wore it. If I had seen her like that before I had talked to Latimer—now, though, there was that shadow of doubt between us.

"Frank, what's wrong?" she said, seeing something in my expression.

"Wrong? It's nothing. I'm just a little tense."

"Is it going to be dangerous?"

"Who can say," I shrugged. "Miller killed two people for no good reason—"

"You will be careful, Frank, won't you?" she said, reaching out to me with her hand. There was something in her eye that said her concern was real, that she wasn't trying to pull a con on me.

"Don't worry," I said with a laugh, feeling that I hadn't misjudged her after all. "Do you have the stuff?"

"The credit stick and exit pass? They're right here." She fished around in her handbag and pulled out an envelope. When I looked inside I found the credit stick, a piece of titanium about the size of my thumb, and the exit pass, a laminated card of plastic with a hologram stripe along one side. I put them in my jacket pocket.

"Care for a drink?"

"Thanks, I could use one, Frank."

I went into the kitchen for some ice. When I came out, she had gone out onto the balcony where she was staring up. You can just see a portion of the spar from there, a dark line drawn in the sky against the lights of the far side of the cylinder that forms Star City.

I handed her the drink. Watched as she tilted back her head to take a sip, saw the long line of her neck silhouetted against the glare of the sign on the Blue Moon across the street. I wanted her. I wanted to believe that she wasn't playing me for a patsy; that she wasn't working with Miller.

I hadn't told her about Latimer and his men. At first it had just been an oversight. Then it had been because of the suspicions. Now I just didn't want to spoil things.

"You're not drinking, Frank?" she asked.

"No. I had enough earlier. I want to keep a clear head for heights."

"Have you ever been up there before?"

"No," I said, truthfully. "No good reason. There's not much up there except the glow tubes and plumbing."

"You will be careful, Frank?"

"Don't worry about me. I'm a big boy. I can take care of myself."

An awkward silence followed. I knew that she could sense that something was wrong, that something had come between us.

I looked at the clock on the wall. It was 2230.

"Look, I've got to get going. You can stay here if you want. I'll come back here after it's over."

"I'll be waiting, Frank." I couldn't tell if that was a lie. I wasn't sure she could.

I pulled out the needle gun from its holster, checked that it was loaded and ready. I'd done that earlier, of course, but you can never be too careful. As I stuffed it back in place under my left arm I glanced up and caught the look of concern on her face.

"There won't be trouble, will there?" I couldn't tell if she was worried about me or was afraid that she might be the one facing the barrel of my gun.

"No. This is just for contingencies," I joked.

I checked once more that the pass and the credit stick were in my pockets. At the door I said, "I should be back by one if everything goes right."

"And if it doesn't?"

I didn't answer that. I couldn't. I went through the door closing it behind me.

I made the short walk to the down city tram line. I was almost at the stop when I noticed Manning was following me. I didn't care. He didn't really matter anymore. I figured one of Latimer's men would pick him up if he got in the way.

The tram ride was a quick ten minutes. Not that much traffic, not many stops that hour of the night. There was only one other passenger in the tram car, a maintenance man on his way to work from his appearance. I half-way suspected that he was one of Latimer's.

I got off at the last stop on the line where the cars reverse and change over to the up city line for the return trip. There was a docking ring worker leaning against a post looking at his comm.

Another of Latimer's, or just some working stiff on his way home? Hard to tell.

A freight robot rolled past me in the street, towing a container off to some warehouse space. You don't find a lot of people hanging around the freight end of Star City. Most of the real work is done by machines. What you do find are crew men from the freighters coming back to their ship after drinking up their pay in one of the saloons that cater to them. There weren't any around that night.

The door to the elevator up to the spar was at the end of a long dark alley, an anonymous hatch with a cryptic label and the words "Authorized Personnel Only" printed in red at eye level. A card reader with a keypad sat just to one side. I inserted the ID card I had been given into the reader and entered a code. It must have been the right one, because the hatch swung open.

I went through into the cube of a small elevator car about two meters on a side. The walls of the car were metal painted grey. A single glow tube in a fixture in the center of the ceiling glared down on me. The control panel only had two buttons, up and down. There were no intermediate stops. I pressed the button with the up arrow.

The door shut and the car began to ascend. It was a slow trip. There was no reason to rush. A small readout in the control panel displayed the progress. At ten meters a second it would only take two and a half minutes to reach the spar.

There's a curious thing about Star City. There is no real gravity. What there is, is the illusion of gravity produced by the centrifugal force due to the twice a minute rotation of the giant cylinder about its axis. The strength of this force depends on your distance from the axis. The closer to the center you are, the less force you feel. There isn't much difference between the ground and the fifth floor, the height of the average Star City building, not enough for the average person to notice. But as you get closer to the spar, the force drops, until when you reach the level of the maintenance catwalks, the pseudo-gravity is less than a tenth of what it is at street level. One of the reasons that catwalks don't run down dead center of the axis is so that there will be at least some minimal force to hold one down.

I hadn't really noticed the change riding up in the elevator car. I hadn't been moving around. But when the car pulled to a stop my stomach gave a lurch. For a moment I thought I was going to lose that last glass of brown I had drunk three hours earlier and fifteen hundred meters below.

The door of the car popped open. No need for pass codes and access cards at this end of the shaft. I stepped out into the narrow space of the landing. To either side going up in a tight curve a catwalk ran to the other elevator shafts forming a ring some twenty five meters in diameter. Ahead of me trailing off into the darkness was another catwalk maybe two meters wide heading straight out as far as the eye could see until it converged to a point in the distance.

I hadn't known what to expect. There wasn't any wind to speak of. Not much in the way of noise, either. With the giant glow tubes dimmed for the night there wasn't that much light, either, just small safety lights that provided just enough illumination for you to find your way. Overhead was the spar itself, a mass of girders and struts, conduits and piping, the whole designed more for rigidity than strength. In principle, at least, strength wasn't needed, all the forces were supposed to balance out.

I checked the time on my comm. It was 2330. I had 30 minutes to walk a kilometer of catwalk. I had a feeling I was going to need it. I took the first step down the walkway. I almost fell over. I wasn't used to walking in what was less than a tenth of normal gravity. My stomach gave a lurch as I struggle to right myself. I found my best plan was to shuffle along, feet barely leaving the surface of the catwalk. Despite the low down force, it seemed to take twice the effort of normal walking.

I also discovered that I don't really have a head for heights. The catwalk itself was solid so I couldn't look straight down. There was nothing, however, to prevent me from seeing down on either side of that narrow band of metal. It was a long way down. Fifteen hundred meters doesn't really sound like much when it's on the level, but it's a long way down when there is nothing between you and the ground except air.

I found myself tightly clutching the hand-railing on either side of the catwalk. There was a metal rod running along the top of the railing held off by posts every ten meters or so. The idea was that the maintenance crews were supposed to wear a safety harness with a tether that clipped onto that rod to prevent them from falling in case of an accident. Needless to say I didn't have one.

Every hundred meters the catwalk was intersected by the ring of a cross walk that ran around to the other catwalks. I checked the time when I reached the first one. It had taken me five minutes to go the first hundred meters. I'd have to quicken my pace.

I made better time to the second, and by the time I passed the ninth intersection I was really moving along. I reached the meeting point and checked the time. It was midnight.

"I was afraid you weren't going to make it," came Miller's voice out of the dark. He had been hidden up one leg of the intersecting cross walk.

"I wasn't sure I was," I replied. "Couldn't you have picked a better place to meet?"

"Oh, I like this place just fine, Sladek."

"Well, it's your call," I said, trying to sound like it didn't matter.

"Do you have the money and the pass?"

"Do you have the book?"

"Right here," he said, showing a small parcel wrapped in paper.

"The pass and the credit stick are in my pocket." I made no move to pull them out. Neither one of us had displayed a weapon, but we both assumed the other was armed despite the instructions.

"Do we take each other on faith?" Miller said with a smile.

"I doubt it. Why don't you unwrap that package so I can take a look at it?"

"You're an expert on early Italian printing?"

"I've seen images of the item in question. I think I can figure out if you've faking it."

"Fair enough." He began to unwrap the package. Once unwrapped, he gingerly opened it to the title page and held it under the one overhead light so I could look at it. Like I said, I had seen several images that Crysalis had made. As far as I could tell it was the real deal.

"Satisfied?"

"Yeah. Mind if I reach into my pocket?"

"Go ahead," he said with a shrug.

"Here's the credit stick and the pass," I said, holding them up so he could see them.

"As far as I can tell, the stick might hold a Crockett nickel and the pass might be for the Hoboken trolley," Miller said.

"I'm not quite sure where Hoboken is. I assume you have a reader on you?"

"Yes. Of course."

"How about I pass you the pass so you can check it. If it's okay, you give it back and I give you the credit stick. If that checks out we swap the book and the pass and go our separate ways."

"Sounds like a workable plan. I take it you've done this before?"

"A couple of times," I replied with a shrug. I handed him the pass.

His comm had a reader function built in. He placed the pass on the screen for a moment, and then checked the readout. He seemed satisfied. He handed it back. I gave him the credit stick. He plugged the stick into the port on his comm. There was a low beep. Miller smiled as he read the screen.

"Seems you're playing by the rules, Sladek. What now?"

"I'll hand you the pass using my left hand, you do the same with the book. When I give the word, we both let go."

"Simple and direct. I like your style, Sladek. Ready?"

"Ready." I held out the pass. He did the same with the book. We each grabbed the item with our right hands.

"Now." Surprisingly, it worked. We both let go with our left hands and stepped back a pace, me holding the book, Miller holding the credit stick.

"You know that I know about the police waiting?" Miller said as he tucked the pass and stick away.

"I'm not surprised. You don't seem too concerned."

"Why did you think I wanted the exchange up here?" It didn't seem a rhetorical question.

"I admit, that's had me puzzled. I assume you've got an ace up your sleeve?"

"The problem with you and everyone inside this rock is that you've never been off this place. You can't envision life anywhere else but inside a giant tin can."

"True enough," I agreed.

"Ever hear of a para-sail?" Miller said as he walked a few steps up the cross walk that he had appeared from. He reached down and picked up some sort of back-back which he proceeded to strap on.

"Can't say I have."

"It's a lot like a parachute, except you can steer it. It's considered a great sport on many planets. You climb up some tall building or mountain and jump off. The para-sail lets you glide gently down to a safe landing."

"Sounds like a good way to break your neck," I commented.

"Or get past the cops coming up on the elevator."

"I see your point. I take it that dingus you're strapping on is one of these para-sails?"

"You aren't as dumb as you look, Sladek."

"I've been told that once or twice. Of course I've been told the opposite just as many times."

"You aren't going to try and stop me, then?"

"Not my job."

"Just as well. I'm beginning to like you, Sladek. Be a shame to have to kill you. Well, I think this is where I make my farewell."

He turned and was about to climb over the railing of the catwalk when a voice came out of the darkness. It was a voice I knew, and she was holding a laser pistol, a heavy Kunstler. She looked like she knew how to use it.

"Stop, James."

"Crysalis, baby," Miller said as he got off the railing and turned towards her with a stunned look of surprise on his face.

"Take off the para-sail, James."

"Look. I can explain. I knew that they had me pegged when Frank here found my hiding place. I knew that we wouldn't be able to get off Star City as planned. I figured they would be watching you, so I didn't want to contact you or do anything that might throw suspicion your way. I thought that if I could get away, we could meet up later. I was going to send for you once I was safe. You've got to believe me."

"Without the book and with only a hundred thousand to show for everything, James. That's not what I had in mind."

"I've learned to cut my losses, babe. There'll always be other scores to make."

"That's not what I want, James. That's not what you promised. Now unstrap the para-sail."

He started to comply, unbuckling the harness. With a shrug of his shoulders the pack slid off and he bent over to lower it to the catwalk. That was when it happened. With his body turned away from Crysalis, he reached inside his jacket and came up with a small Baretta laser pistol. He wasn't fast enough. Crysalis was. A dark spot appeared on his forehead and he slipped to the catwalk.

She turned to me. "I want you to remove that needle gun in your holster, Frank. Carefully. I really don't want to shoot you."

I did as she asked, using the thumb and forefinger of my left hand. I set the weapon on the catwalk and then straightened up. Using my foot I slid the gun out of reach.

Keeping her laser trained on me, she moved over to where Miller's body lay. Reaching in, she removed the pass and credit stick from his pocket. Then she began to strap on the para-sail.

"You know how to use that thing?"

"Sure, Frank. I learned while I was on New Virginia. James taught me."

"So it was all a con from the beginning? I mean everything?"

"Not everything, Frank."

She was having problems with the backpack straps. She had to take it off and readjust them for her smaller size.

"I mean that, Frank. I do like you. You can come with me. With the money on the credit stick and what we can get for the book, we'll be set for life, Frank."

"Is that why you're doing this? For the money?"

"Why else? All my life I've been around people with money. Other people. It was never my money. Do you have any idea what it is like being cooped up in that house with a man like Kaminski-Jones. He's not sane, Frank. That accident fried his brain. All he can think about is acquiring more things, things he can never use or enjoy. And I had to play along because he was the one with the money and he made the rules."

There was a note of hysteria in her voice as she struggled with the straps of the para-sail pack. Finally, she seemed satisfied.

"One last chance, Frank. Will you come with me?"

"I can't do that, Crysalis. I'm sorry, but I can't."

"Me too, Frank. Now give me the book."

"I can't do that. I made a deal with the Captain."

"You're a fool, Frank."

"Probably," I replied.

"I'll second that," came a voice from out of the gloom farther along the catwalk. It was Latimer and a pair of uniforms. Latimer had his laser out as did his men. "Now drop the weapon, Miss Hohenberg."

"No-o-o." She fired of a quick shot in their direction and then lunged at me trying to grab the book out of my hand. She reached for it, but my grip was too tight. Her momentum and the light gravity caused her to lose her footing, and she went over the railing. I rushed to the railing, but I was too late to grab her.

There's a funny thing about centrifugal force; the closer you are to the axis the smaller the acceleration away from the center is. Crysalis was falling, but in slow motion, picking up velocity slowly, not with gravity's ten meters per second squared but only at one meter at first.

For whatever reason, the para-sail never opened. I don't know whether she panicked, or there was a problem with the harness or what. She struggled for a moment, and then gave up.

It took a long time for her to fall; only slowly gaining velocity. For the longest time I could see her face clearly as she looked up at me. She seemed to say something as she fell, but I couldn't hear. I thought it might be "I love you, Frank," but I'm probably fooling myself about that.

Fifteen hundred meters is a long way to fall, but it wasn't the impact with the street that killed her. Some tech tried to explain it to me. Star City makes roughly two rotations every minute. At street level, a kilometer and a half from the axis that means a sideways velocity of something like thirteen hundred kilometers per hour. That's the speed with which the building hit her when she got close enough for it to matter. Death was instantaneous. But she had had long seconds to know that it was coming.

The Captain got his book. He got the money on the credit stick back, too, so he was happy. Manning disappeared and we never did find out if he was legit or not. Father Pagani lost interest when it became obvious that the Star City courts would never support the Reconstituted Catholic Churches claim. He took the next liner out in search of some other lost treasure.

Me, I got paid what the Captain promised. But as I sit here in the dark nursing a tumbler of brown on the rocks, with the glow from the sign out front of the Blue Moon coming in the front window, with some jive samba playing softly in the background, all I can think of is seeing Crysalis slowly drifting off on the long, slow drop to her doom.

Author's Afterword

I think it is a fair think to say that the stories in this collection owe more to the works of Raymond Chandler than to those of science fiction writers such as James A. Schmitz or Floyd Wallace. I'm sure one can also sense the influences of all the early TV series I watched in my youth, in particular Peter Gunn with all its 1960s 'cool' and hip jazz soundtrack.

I started *Ray Guns on Star City* because for some time I had been wanting to write a space opera. Most of what I had been writing recently had been the legal fantasy stories that ended up in *The Laws of Magic* and *Trial by Magic*, and *A Death at Station Alpha* which is detective novel set on Mars in the not too distant future. I was feeling the urge to write something that was not as bound by reality as those works, something more freewheeling and action oriented. I had also recently read the short stories of Raymond Chandler which made a big impression on me. *Star City Stories* is the result.

Frank Sladek, the central character in the stories is the archetype of the private eye, quick with a gun but quicker with a smart response, a man responsible to no one but himself. He's the last of a long line of hard-boiled detectives dating back to the pages of *Black Mask* in the 1920's. He bears more than a passing resemblance to Frank Slade in my novella *The Fictional Detective*. For some reason, probably because I watched too many old movies and too much TV growing up, I seem to be drawn to that type of character. For those readers familiar with Michael Moorcock's *Eternal Champion*, think of Sladek as an incarnation of the Eternal Detective.

Raymond Chandler's Los Angeles was as much an artificial construct as Star City, the setting of the stories in this book. With their semi-crooked cops, cheap hoods, fast money, loose women and the inevitable double-cross, there is more than a passing resemblance between the two. That one was rooted in 1930's California and the other circles a brown dwarf star some thousand years in the future and hundreds of light-years from

Earth is largely irrelevant, at least to the characters populating them. It all comes down to life and death, love and betrayal. I make no pretense of being anywhere near as good a writer as Chandler, but I do think that *Star City Stories* is some of my better work to date.

The first four stories, "Ray Guns," "The New Minglewood Blues," "The Sun Never Rises" and "The Fear of Falling," were written in the order in which they appear in the book. The first of these, "Ray Guns on Star City" is a homage to the stories of Raymond Chandler, especially "Guns at Cyrano's", though apart from the title they have little in common. It was one of those stories that almost wrote itself. I sat down at the keyboard and got up three thousand words later. The rest of it flowed out almost as easily, and I never found myself staring at a blank screen waiting for an idea of what to write next. The last time that had happened to me was when I wrote the first five thousand words of *The Fictional Detective* in a marathon session that started at ten in the evening and ended only when I realized I had to go to work in a few hours.

"The New Minglewood Blues", the second story, was meant to be a story of love and betrayal. The New Minglewood of the title is the slum area of Star City, an area of walk-up apartments where all the grifters and low-lifes live, preying mostly on each other. The New Minglewood Blues is also the title of an old blues song that the Grateful Dead covered on their first album. There is no obvious connection between the two. As I mentioned, the story was meant to be about love and betrayal, and it certainly ends up that way, though not, perhaps, in the way I had originally intended. That's half the fun of writing.

The third story, "The Sun Never Rises", was inspired oddly enough by an Anthony Bourdain travel show about Morocco. In that episode he talks about the expatriate community and William S. Burroughs. I found the idea of an artist's colony on Star City intriguing. I started with the character of Marcus Fitzroy, a writer modeled loosely on a young Hemingway before he became famous. After that, things kind of got away from me with additional characters dropping in for no apparent reason other than to lend color to the tale.

The last story, "Fear of Falling", is the only one in which science plays a significant part, and then only in the form of Newtonian mechanics. It started with the idea of the final, fatal scene which I then put a story around leading up to those last moments. The plot involving a first edition of Dante's Divine Comedy is merely something to keep the characters occupied until the end of the story.

"Lizardmen Always Carry Two Guns" and "The Second Shot" were something of an afterthought, written when the publication of Star City Stories was delayed. "The Sun Never Rises" and "Fear of Falling" had kind of gotten away from the original premise of a hard-boiled shoot-em-up. The title for "Lizardmen" occurred to me one day while I was walking my dogs and I just couldn't resist writing the story. "The Second Shot" was started before I finished "Lizardmen," and was meant to provide a sort of gritty interlude in the narrative. Over all, I think the addition of these two stories adds to the tone of the book.

A note about the jive samba, Frank Sladek's music genre of preference. The name comes from a Julian "Cannonball" Adderley composition. In my mind's ear I think of it as sort of late '50s-early '60s cool jazz, the kind of music that goes well late at night with the lights down low and a glass of scotch on the rocks, sort of mellow and soulful at the same time. Something like the albums Paul Desmond and Jim Hall did together, if you are familiar with them.

Star City Stories is science fiction mainly because it takes place on a failed planet circling a star that never made it some thousand years in the future. Sure, there are ray-guns and laser pistols, the occasional alien, faster than light starliners, and the down side of the Lorentz Contraction effect. But these stories might just as well have taken place in Los Angeles in the thirties or New York in 1960 or any of a dozen other times and places. Mostly they are about men and women, greed and betrayal, love and death.

These stories are best read late at night with the lights turned down and the cocktail of your choice at hand. Put some jive samba on your sound machine, or failing that Cannonball Adderley, cool Miles Davis, or Modern Jazz Quartet, and immerse yourself in a tiny world far, far away.

SPECIAL PREVIEW!

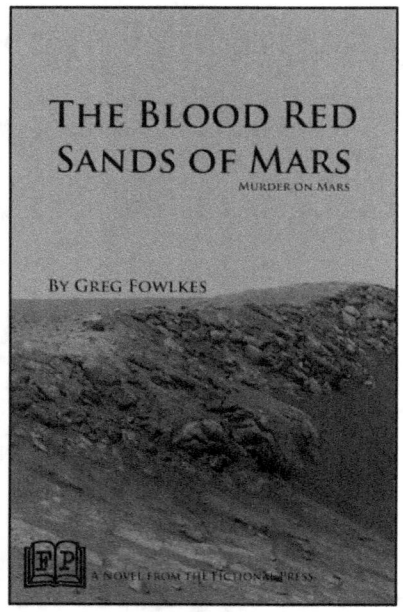

THE BLOOD RED
SANDS OF MARS
By Greg Fowlkes

Book One from the Murder on Mars Series

Now available from The Fictional Press
www.TheFictionalPress.com

THE BLOOD RED SANDS OF MARS

The wind was blowing again against the west wall of the hut. He could hear the grains of sand abrading the thin aluminum skin that protected him from the outside. Through the window, half frosted from the continuous onslaught of sand and dust, he could see clouds of dust obscuring the sky. The sky was a pastel pink, a color no sky had any right to be. The wind, despite its 120 kph. velocity, made only a thin howl as it blew over the half buried cylinder of the hut.

McKernan lay on his cot trying not to admit that he was awake. It was a losing battle. After a few minutes he surrendered and glanced over at the clock sitting on the crate next to his bed. The dim red digits of the LED display read 7:58. It was too early to get up, too late to go back to sleep. He rolled over, shivering at the cold. The temperature couldn't have been more than ten degrees Celsius inside the hut. For the twentieth time he thought to himself that he would have to fix the heater before winter—if he could get the parts. Either that, or put in more insulation—if he could find that. The cold finally forced the decision to get up.

Standing, he felt the cold plastic floor beneath his bare feet. With his foot he fished the worn and patched pants from beneath the cot and pulled them on. He dug underneath his pillow and came up with a switchblade knife that he stuck in his pocket before drawing on the turtleneck sweater that had lain next to his pants. The cold feel of the cloth did nothing to dispel the cold from his body. From the crate he picked up a shoulder holster with a small automatic pistol and put it on. McKernan drew the weapon, worked the slide once, and after examining it perfunctorily, placed it back in the holster. Satisfied, he pulled on a worn pair of leather boots and placed another knife in a sheathe between his skin and the boot top.

Dressed, he went over to the shelf that served as counter and table. He put a pan of beans onto the heating unit and got a soysteak from the small refrigerator that held up one end of the shelf. The steak went into the frying pan on the other heating element. An egg would have been nice, but at the current price of three dollars apiece it was an extravagance that he would have to put off for a while.

As the food cooked he drew a liter of water from the spigot in the corner of the hut and watered the plants in the garden under the window. The carrots and tomatoes were doing nicely. He smiled briefly because it would be good to have fresh vegetables for a change. The big, leafy oxygen plants were doing well, too. He would be able to cut down on his oxygen ration this month and save some money.

He took the beans off the heating element and replaced them with the coffee pot. The beans were still half cold, but he wasn't in the mood to hassle with them. He only had the two heating elements, and he didn't want to have to wait for his coffee. He forced down the beans and then wolfed down the steak. It almost tasted like real beef, but then maybe his memories were fading. As usual, the coffee tasted terrible and tepid, too. The air pressure in the hut was too low for water to boil properly.

He finished his meal and scraped the remnants of food into the pressure vessel that served as a compost heap. The gauge on its neighbor showed that he had almost half a tank of methane. He'd be able to sell that soon and use the money for something useful, like a still. Completing his rounds, the gauges on the life support systems showed that everything was still working at keeping him alive. He went back to the pots and scrubbed them clean with sand. That, at least, was plentiful and cheap.

He checked his watch against the clock. It was time to get going. Pulling on his jacket he went to the airlock at the corridor end of the hut. After checking the gauge to make sure that there was pressure on the other side, he undogged the latches and stepped through. Closing the door behind him, he repeated the process with the outer hatch, latching both doors behind him. The outer door he locked with a heavy padlock.

He had entered a low tubular corridor made of the same aluminum foil and plastic foam construction as the hut. The walls, however, were even thinner, and no pretense was made of heating it. He could see his breath condensing in front of him as he began to walk down its length. It was a hell of a way to live, he reflected, not for the first time. But then, it had been hell living in L.A. where he'd been born, with brown air, rats, a chronic shortage of water, and overcrowded tenements. He had made his choice, but sometimes it seemed as though life was a continual shiver.

The corridor was pierced at regular intervals by hatches identical to his own. The huts behind the hatches were identical, too, except for the modifications the owners had made to make them more livable. This part of the city was old, dating back a couple of decades to the first days of the settlement when it had been part of a scientific base. The scientists had departed, at least from that corridor, and been replaced by those who had the money to buy or rent the huts from the Trust Authority. Maintenance was pretty much left up to the residents.

Along the sides and overhead ran the pipes and conduits that pumped in the gases, liquids, and power necessary for sustaining life. The whole system looked as jury rigged and fragile as it actually was, though surprisingly few people died whenever the system failed. Martians were a cautious lot. One didn't talk much about injuries. Accidents on Mars didn't leave many.

A hundred meters down the tube he came to an airlock. Going through the same ritual that he had used on his front door, he went through to another length of corridor indistinguishable from the one he had just left. Continuing on, he passed through two more airlocks until he entered a corridor that sloped downward. The hatches were farther apart, and larger. Signs overhead indicated the businesses or functions that were carried out behind them. The air was warmer because the corridor was buried beneath the sand which provided insulation. At the end of the tunnel was a larger airlock set into a wall of fused silica bricks, the first substantial piece of construction he had met that morning.

Passing through the portal was like entering another world, which in a way he had. This was the public Mars, the planet seen by the corporation men and the officials of the Trust Authority. It was also the planet seen by tourists, the brave new colony, man's first outpost on another planet. The tourists didn't really care to see the hut town. They were part of the same world as the corporation men and the government types. It still took a great deal of money or power to reach Mars.

The difference was more than one of degree. For one thing, the temperature was a comfortable twenty. For another, the walls were flat and met the floors and ceilings at right angles, unlike the inflated skins of the huts and corridors. With a little imagination it could almost be an enclosed shopping mall on earth, though the presence of fused silica blocks was more prevalent than any architect would allow.

The most important difference, however, was the sight of people scurrying along. He hadn't met anyone in the outer corridors. People rarely lingered there because of the cold. Now, McKernan could see at least twenty people and it was still fairly early. No airlocks interrupted this corridor. Extending for two hundred meters in either direction, it was twenty meters wide and ten high, the largest enclosed volume on the planet. Arrayed along its length were the offices and store fronts of the corporations that owned Mars, as well as the more prosperous saloons and bordellos.

One day the Trust Authority promised that the whole city would be like that, with apartments and condominiums for the ordinary workers, but neither the Authority nor the corporations had yet come up with the money. For the moment all that existed was the one street of a few blocks.

McKernan headed towards the Authority's offices which dominated one end of the mall, but turned aside at the last moment when he noticed that a small, dark doorway was open. He knew that he should resist the temptation, but he was not in a very disciplined mood. He went through the doorway into the darkness beyond.

Finnegan's was the only real, honest bar on Mars. There were any number of saloons and even a cocktail lounge in the Mars Sheraton, but only one quiet, dark place where a man could drink in peace. McKernan felt the need for some of that peace at the moment.

He sat down on one of the stools before the only mahogany bar on Mars. Finnegan, himself, was behind the bar, though in fact he almost always was, no matter what the hour. The bartender looked up and greeted the newcomer, "Good morning, Constable. Beer or whiskey?"

"It's too early for beer. It's too early for whiskey, but give me a shot, anyway."

Finnegan poured out a shot glass of amber liquid and placed it before McKernan and then stood back polishing a glass while he studied the man opposite him.

McKernan knocked back half the glass before he spoke. When he did, there was a bitter edge to his voice. "Sometimes I wonder if it's worth it, Finnegan. I could be back on a planet fit for human life."

"Could you, now, Constable?" Finnegan said, putting down the glass and picking up another in equally gleaming condition. "If mother earth was such a bed of roses, why are you here?"

He breathed on the glass and examined it against the light for a moment, then looked at McKernan with the same intentness. "You're here because you're not the sort to live off the dole or to spend your life with another man being your boss. Instead you'll spend your life trying to make this planet a fit place to live and retire in twenty years with a nice pension. Now drink up and get to work, laddy."

"Yeah, sure. Sorry to burden you with my problems. Early morning depression, I guess. See you." He finished off the shot and left five dollars in Authority script on the bar.

The bite of the whiskey so early in the morning didn't really help his disposition, but it did give him enough courage to make it to the office. The morning ritual at Finnegan's was becoming too much of a habit. His three years on Mars were beginning to show.

The jail wasn't in the brick part of the Authority building, but in the complex of pneumatic architecture that sprawled behind it. The huts were old—older than his own—but dated back to the days when governments had not begrudged a few billions for exploration, back before space had to show a profit. For that reason, they were sound and well insulated, though a bit tacky looking.

The jail consisted of two huts joined together, one for offices, the other for the two makeshift cells and storage. Ferris was the only one there when he walked in, a young kid, younger than he had been himself when he had come to Mars. He was still impressed enough with his responsibilities and had not yet been worn down by the grim realities to take his job in any way but seriously.

Ferris greeted him with a solemn, "Good morning, sir," with a stress on the sir. As a three year veteran of Mars, Ferris looked on his boss with more than a touch of awe.

"Anything exciting happen overnight?" McKernan didn't really expect much. A few fights in the saloon district, a knifing maybe if things got out of hand. Petty thievery, or perhaps not so petty. He looked at Ferris and saw a flash of excitement in his eyes that the younger man was trying hard to suppress in order to match the hard bitten image he had of his superior.

"Yes, sir. We've got a murder on our hands."

"Another knifing down at Thelma's?" he asked, naming an infamous saloon and bordello that figured in a quarter of all the police reports.

"No. A prospector was found out on his claim yesterday, over on the far side of Olympus Mons. He was shot, Inspector."

That was bad, McKernan thought. People on Mars weren't supposed to have guns. With the thin skins of most buildings and a hostile atmosphere outside that would support life exactly as long as you could hold your breath, they were dangerous, and not just to the targets. The Authority had made them illegal and the corporations had been more than willing to agree. They weren't easy to get—not something that could be picked up casually or made, like a knife. Even without the details it sounded like the work of a real criminal and not just a squabble over a claim or a woman.

"Okay. Let me have the report. I'll take a look at it."

He took the folder from Ferris who looked a bit crestfallen. He probably expects me to go rush off to the outside and track down the murderer like an Indian scout, McKernan thought. He'd learn in time. Mars was a big planet and a dangerous one, but because of its nature there were also very few places that a man could run to and none where he could hide indefinitely.

He was leafing through the report when he came to his door. For the thousandth time he read, "Inspector Erik McKernan, Chief Constable." Mother would have been proud, he thought sardonically. She had hated the L.A. cops like all the other residents of the barrio. He went through the door into the little cubicle that was his real home. There, sitting at his desk, he began to read the report, sketchy though it was, to look for some explanations.

The Blood Red Sands of Mars is available now from The Fictional Press. Find it on TheFictionalPress.com, or buy it on Amazon.com!

BOOKS BY GREG FOWLKES

From the Wizard at Law Series:
The Laws of Magic
Trial by Magic

From the Murder on Mars Series:
Blood Red Sands of Mars
A Death at Station Alpha
A Corpse in Hut Town
Murder at the Mars Club

From the Fictional Detective Series:
The Fictional Detective
A Fictional Detective Trifecta

Star City Stories: Space Opera Noir Featuring Frank Sladek

The Uncorrupted Corpse

Tequila Visions

Cargo From Paradise

Ice Viking

FROM THE WIZARD AT LAW SERIES BY GREG FOWLKES

THE LAWS OF MAGIC

Egil Njalsson was an aspiring lawyer. A lawyer with a difference. Not only had he passed the bar, but he had an undergraduate degree from the most prestigious school of magic in the country, the California Institute of Thaumaturgy. Needless to say his caseload and clients tended to the unusual. Like witches; or vampires. And the opposition, well they were likely to be demons. But Egil Njalsson had sworn an oath to uphold the law of the land, and... *The Laws of Magic*!

TRIAL BY MAGIC

Egil Njalsson is just another practicing attorney. Except, that is, for the occasional unusual client. Such as the ghost who retained his services using e-mail. Or the wolf who has been cursed by an Indian shaman to turn into a human during the full moon. Or the Leprechaun who is facing the loss of his saloon. Even when the clients are human, they have unusual problems like the Creole chef accused of making a rival a zombie or the scientist accused of transmuting a man into a statue of silicon. Yet somehow, Egil manages to resolve all his client's problems whether legal or magical. Of course it helps that he is a wizard as well as a lawyer.

Trial by Magic includes five new tales from the same world as *The Laws of Magic*.

FROM THE MURDER ON MARS SERIES BY GREG FOWLKES

BLOOD REDS SANDS OF MARS

On Mars the wind was rising. The grains of sand could be heard abrading the thin aluminum skin that was the only protection against the outside. On the far side of Olympus Mons a prospector lies dead in the sand. Inspector Erik McKernan, head of the handful of men that make up the small Martian police force must find the killer while threading the maze of corporate and international politics that govern the planet, and he must do it while trying to survive . . .*The Blood Red Sands of Mars!*

A DEATH AT STATION ALPHA

Station Alpha, a remote Martian research facility isolated by a planet wide dust storm. When one of the scientists is found murdered, it falls to Inspector McKernan to determine which of the remaining twelve people at the station wielded the fatal weapon. But, as the crime was committed in a locked laboratory with no possible access and all the suspects would seem to have unbreakable alibis, it will take all his skills as a detective to solve the puzzle of *A Death at Station Alpha*. Thirty years in the making, the long awaited sequel to *The Blood Red Sands of Mars.*

A Corpse in Hut Town

Hut Town is the remnants of the original Martian settlement; a collection of inflatable buildings abandoned by the Trust Authority and the mining corporations and now occupied by those catering to the baser needs of miners and construction workers in for a spree. But when a corpse is found in one of the service tunnels, Chief Inspector McKernan is called in.

He has plenty of questions. Who's body is it? How did they die? How did they get to Mars in the first place, and why weren't they missed? And the most important one on the Inspector's mind— are there any more bodies down there?

Murder at the Mars Club

The Mars Club was the sanctuary of the rich and powerful on Mars, so when one of the members is found dead, Chief Inspector is called in to solve the case as discretely as possible. Will the solution of the case prove to be the one man he'd least like to implicate?

FROM THE FICTIONAL DETECTIVE SERIES BY GREG FOWLKES

THE FICTIONAL DETECTIVE

Mystery writer Ezekial O. Handler has been killed in a suspicious car crash. Private detective Frank Slade has been hired by Handler's beautiful girlfriend to investigate. Handler, seemingly with a premonition of his death, has left a trail of clues. Can Slade discover the murderer, or will he instead uncover a secret that will shake his existence to the core?

A FICTIONAL DETECTIVE TRIFECTA

The Fictional Detective has gotten out of the Private Investigator game. Instead, he's trying to write hard-boiled masterpieces such as *Death Buys a Condo*. But despite the fact that the door of his office now says WRITER, some of his clients haven't gotten the word. And a strange lot of clients they are. A man that only contacts him during séances because, well, he's dead; a female impersonator who has inherited a house that's just a little too haunted for the market, and a small time gambler who's trying to end an affair with Lady Luck.

Three All New Novellas featuring the Fictional Detective!

The Fictional Press
www.TheFictionalPress.com

The Fictional Press is a small, independent press specializing in the publication of fictional works by emerging authors. If you are interested in bringing your fictional works to life in print as well as electronically, contact us! We can help!

Find out more at www.thefictionalpress.com.